Krìsis

Deirdre Gould

For Aiden, Ian, and Laura, who I could never let go.

CHAPTER 1

The phone. It always started with the phone. Ruth tried to ignore the ringing. *Am I on call?* Something about the thought seemed off and she let it drift away into the dark. But the ringing went on. Over and over. *Is Mrs. Williams in labor?* She half shook her head. Mrs. Williams had given birth to her son Toby more than six years ago. That one wasn't even recent. The ringing began to jar. Ruth tried to focus. *It's not the clinic. Clinic's gone.* It had started this way though, with the phone.

She couldn't even remember who was first. It was a long, blurred streak from the first call until the end. She'd woken up like this, in the dark, and held the receiver to her ear. *Was it the brothers?* It didn't matter, not even as her brain tried to organize the memory, but she thought it was the brothers. One had bitten the other so hard he'd needed stitches. She rubbed her eyes and told them to go to the hospital. But it wasn't the stitches they'd been worried about. It was the kid that had done the biting. He couldn't stop. Wouldn't stop. Screaming and flailing and biting.

"You mean a tantrum?" Ruth asked, still drowsy.

"Listen, lady, I'm a competent adult," growled the father through the phone, "I know when my kid's having a tantrum. This is no tantrum. This is— is *madness*. It doesn't stop. He won't even slow down when he's out of breath. Cripes, he should have worn himself out by now, it's been hours."

"Some kids can go—"

"Dr. Socorro, I *know* my kid. This isn't

normal. Something's *wrong* damn it! I don't know who else to call."

"Okay," Ruth nodded sleepily, though the man couldn't see it, "I'll meet you at the hospital in half an hour."

She could remember stitching up the younger brother because the emergency room was strangely packed for the wee hours of a Wednesday. She'd admitted the biting brother with a sedative and called psychiatric services to follow up. She'd been unsure what else to do. The little boy had thrashed and snapped as the father strained to hold him. The boy growled or screamed when she'd tried to talk to him. It had just seemed like a ferocious tantrum to her and she wasn't trained for that. She'd gone from there straight to the clinic where her partners were already moving through a waiting line of patients, though it was too early to open. The waiting room was full, tired mothers flipping through colorful magazines meant for children. Most of the kids looked listless or slept. It was strangely silent for a pediatrician's office. No one running around, nobody scolding in hissed whispers. It ought to have unnerved her, but after the morning's loud start, she was relieved rather than nervous.

"Better get ready," said her nurse as Ruth picked up a file, "looks like a flu or something going around. We have almost thirty more we couldn't fit in today."

"Thirty? Didn't know we had that many patients."

"You're telling me. No serious symptoms yet though. Small fever, listlessness, a little bit of a scratchy throat, that's about it. I think it's mostly first-time parents calling. I've told most of them just to stay home and keep their kiddos hydrated. If it gets worse, give us another call."

Ruth glanced back into the waiting room. "Doesn't seem like they are listening," she said.

"Well, every clinic has it's nervous patients."

"Have we received any alerts?"

The nurse shook her head. "A fax from Sam, doesn't make much sense though. He sent me a bunch of clippings and some patient reports from down his way. A huge collision in France, a riot in New Delhi and it looks like a mild strep epidemic in Venezuela. I don't know what he's trying to get at. And you know his handwriting—"

"Let me see, I always typed his notes for him in school, I'll decipher it," said Ruth. The nurse handed her the packet of papers with a shrug.

"That's why you get the big bucks. I'll give you a few minutes and send the first patient through. Sarah Parvey, mom says she's really out of it, stumbling, listless, slurring like she's been drinking. No recent falls or bumps to the head that mom can remember ..." the nurse's voice trailed off as Ruth frowned over the fax. She nodded and wandered toward her office still untangling the letters on the page. There were over a dozen names on the front page, most she knew from school or conventions, but some she didn't. How many people did he send it to? The articles still had ragged, torn edges on their fax pages. That must have been why he hadn't emailed.

No time, hospital slammed. Very important. For elevated temps with accompanying violence test for strep. Note the strain and contact New Delhi. Fax number enclosed. Also CDC?

That's all it said. *Violence?* She thought, and focused immediately on the little boy from that morning. She shook her head. Sam was a long way away. Besides, the CDC would have said something. She picked up the phone anyway and ordered a strep test on the brother she'd admitted. She didn't have time to read the articles so she flung them onto her desk for later and walked into the little patient room with Sarah Parvey and her mom.

Ruth watched as Sarah swayed and stumbled trying to walk the straight, bright line taped onto the carpet. She checked the girl's eyes, but they seemed to be focusing correctly. Her ears were clear and the girl said she didn't feel dizzy when asked. Ruth gently tapped Sarah's knee to check her reflexes but glanced up as the mother said sharply, "Stop that!" and grabbed her daughter's hand.

"I'm sorry," blushed the mother, "she won't stop biting her nails. She never did this before. But in the past few days, she's gnawed down to the quick. Oh! There— now you're bleeding."

The girl grabbed her hand back and began sucking on her bleeding finger.

"Sarah, I have a bandaid for that," said Ruth calmly. She pulled open a nearby drawer and grabbed a piece of gauze and a bandage. "Here, let me see. I used to bite my nails too. It got so bad, my mom used to put hot sauce on them so I'd remember." She laughed lightly and held her hand out to take the little girl's.

But Sarah shook her head and kept sucking on the finger.

"It won't hurt, I promise, just a bandaid," said Ruth, but Sarah shook her head again. The mother became flustered and turned red.

"Sarah, give her your hand, let her help you," she said, half under her breath as if Ruth weren't standing right there.

The girl pushed herself back on the table, the paper crinkling and bunching behind her. She growled as her mother reached for her hand.

"It's okay," said Ruth quickly.

"I'm sorry, doctor, but it's not. She's being rude and I don't allow that—" She reached for Sarah's hand and pulled it out of the girl's mouth. The girl drooled a long string of blood and a deep roar burst from her open mouth. Ruth gasped as the little hand flashed in front of her, the skin from the upper end of the finger was gone, the light pink muscle tissue pulsing scarlet with flowing blood. And then the hand was gone, wrapped around Sarah's mother's shoulder as the child leapt up on the table and launched herself toward her mother. The mother caught her out of pure instinct, wrapped her in her arms before the girl could hit the floor. Sarah didn't hesitate, lunging forward and biting down on her mother's soft cheek. The woman screamed and Ruth pulled at the edges of Sarah's mouth to make her let go. But the girl was locked on, dark blood bubbling down the places where their faces met. *Like nursing,* thought Ruth perversely, but it made her realize what to do. She pushed the girl's nose closed. Sarah choked and released the bite. She turned toward Ruth as her mother fell into a chair, moaning. Ruth slammed the emergency intercom button and turned quickly out of Sarah's path. The kid's reflexes were still slow, and Ruth was behind her before Sarah even realized she had missed. Ruth held the small arms behind her back forcing her to remain facing away. The nurses began streaming in to help. It took another half hour to sedate Sarah and treat her mother before sending them both to the hospital. Almost as an afterthought, Ruth ordered the strep test. She hadn't even checked Sarah's temperature yet.

There hadn't been any more like that, not that day. Other kids who were listless and clumsy, but no biters. She had been nervous for a while, but began to relax as the day wore on. Every time she came out of the patient rooms, though, she could hear the phone ringing. It never seemed to stop. Not that day, or in the week to follow, not even when the authorities came in white plastic suits and shut the place down. It still rang. At work. At home. She'd wake up just to tell people there was nothing she could do. It kept ringing over and over. Until the power went out. She'd go to her grave believing the sound of the phone was what made Charlie finally snap. Even though she knew better, in her heart it was that hellish ringing that had pushed her son over the edge.

Like now. How was it ringing now? It was months since the lines went down. She opened her eyes at last. It was the tiny wind up alarm clock. It brought her back into herself. She switched it off. It meant the test was done. Time to check the lab. She scrubbed her face with her hands and slowly sat up. Bill turned over as she moved and fell back asleep. *How can he sleep through that?* She thought. But she knew how. If he could sleep through Charlie's screams, then it wasn't surprising that he could sleep through the little alarm. She got dressed in the half light of the window and headed downstairs.

Ruth flipped the light switch, but nothing happened. *Shit,* she thought, *I hope the incubator finished, or I'll have to run it again.* She closed the basement door and threaded her way through the dark living room toward the mudroom. She hissed through her teeth as she slammed a hip into the side table in the hall. But there was no answering shriek. She hadn't woken Charlie or Bill. Ruth let out a shaky sigh and moved on.

She found the shin guards by feel and strapped them on. The rifampin, especially, had been hard to find. It would be hard enough to get the correct dosage with the small stockpile she had. If the test had to be run again, they might have to go even further to find more. She adjusted the velcro on the lacrosse pad around her arm. She tried not to remind herself that this was the *last* test. The pull of knowing was terrible. Half of her hoped the generator failure would mean she had to run it again, just so she could pretend for one more day. The other half was wild to find a cure for Charlie. She pulled the umpire mask down and wriggled a little against the tight chest plate. She reached down, her fingers crawling over discarded boots and Bill's set of armor until they found one of the gas cans. There were only two left. They'd have to go down to the station again today or tomorrow.

Ruth hated that chore, but there was no choice. The lab wouldn't run without electricity, and Charlie wouldn't get better without the lab. *One crisis at a time,* she told herself, and carried the gas can to the door.

Lifting the edge of the cardboard that hung over the glass, she peered out into the bright street. It was quiet this morning, at least in front of the house. No fresh bodies, for which Ruth was grateful. She hated having to identify her neighbors, and the cremation pile always attracted more. It had snowed overnight, hiding the rusting tangle of cars and the more recent bloodstains. It would mean a more difficult trip for gas, but for now, she was thankful for the illusion of peace. The gas was getting heavy and she strained to see the sidewalk to the left and right as she always did. The door's overhang was too deep, just as it always was. With a sigh, Ruth opened the front door just wide enough for her and the gas can to slide through. She leaned out of the overhang and darted a look in both directions. Nothing moved, not even the loose top snow. She shut the door and scuttled down the steps in her protective gear. Ducking into the lean-to that ate up her tiny grass lot, Ruth fumbled with the generator's gas cap. She hated doing this, especially alone. Bill usually got the damn thing started again, while Ruth kept watch. It had just evolved that way. Probably because Bill would use weapons on the Infected, and Ruth preferred to just push them backward with an armored arm when she could. She didn't like hurting them. It wasn't their fault, it was the Plague. Bill was more practical.

"It's them or us, babe," he'd said, "I won't hurt anyone if I can help it, but I have to protect us. It's not like they just want to steal your purse."

"But they're sick. Just sick people, Bill," she'd argued.

"So was David Berkowitz. But I wouldn't gently shoo him away either."

"Someday soon, they will start getting better. Or someone will come up with a cure. You don't want to be remembered as the neighbor who beat sick people, do you?"

He hadn't said anything, just shook his head. That had been almost eight months ago. Ruth tipped the gas can up, listening to the gurgle and slosh. The sharp smell burned the rim of her nostrils in the clean, cold air. She hadn't realized it then, but she realized now, with a kind of slow dragging depression, what he hadn't said. He never believed there'd be a cure, not even then. He hadn't believed that anyone would come back. Not even Charlie.

Swiping at her nose with the back of a gloved hand, she recapped the generator. *It's because he doesn't love Charlie the way that I do. This whole Plague is another reminder that he isn't our biological child,* she thought. The December Plague had swept through the giant metropolis in a matter of weeks. Almost everyone had succumbed, and many of those who didn't become infected with the plague couldn't survive the aftermath anyway. It was extremely rare to have immunity, but you had a better chance if a parent was also immune. Ruth knew of only a handful of healthy survivors, and most of them had fled. None of them were lucky enough to have a spouse that was also immune. None of them but Bill and Ruth. *If we'd been able to have our own child, maybe things would be different.* She pushed the thought away. She had thought it almost every day in the past year. She pulled on the generator's choke and then yanked the cord. It roared to life again, but not before her mind whispered again, *things would be **better**.* She scrambled out of the lean-to and jumped up the steps, expecting dozens of Infected to come pouring down the street at the sound, but nothing came. She wondered sadly, whether there had been many freezing deaths the night before. The ones she'd seen recently had been thin, fighting with each other. She thought of Charlie being out there like that and the agony that hit her heart convinced her, once again, that it made no difference that he had been adopted. She went inside and locked the door behind her.

The armor tumbled off her piece by piece. She picked it up and piled it neatly next to the empty gas can in front of the door. It would remind her to plan a supply trip. They were almost out of peanut butter, too. Charlie's favorite. She thought she remembered seeing some at the Third Street market the week before. Bill would raise his eyebrows at that. It was one thing to make a hike that long for rifampin, but for peanut butter? She added it to the list anyway. He couldn't accuse her of spoiling Charlie anymore. The peanut butter was more to make her feel better. After she'd added a half dozen small items to the list and puttered around cleaning the kitchen for half an hour, the pull of the petri dishes became too strong.

The basement light was on when she opened the door. She thought she'd flipped it off, but shook her head and descended into the impromptu lab. Bill was sitting at the table, waiting for her. The harsh fluorescent light added a decade to his face. Ruth smiled uncertainly. "Hi," she said.

He smiled back, but it was a habitual smile. "Hi, hon."

"What's up?"

He slid a pile of bloody bandages across the table toward her. "Charlie bit through the wrappings again."

"Dammit," swore Ruth, "His hands were almost healed. All right, let me just check up on today's test and I'll go rebandage him."

"Ruth," he reached for her hand as she turned to toss the old bandages into the trash barrel for burning. "How long are we going to put him through this?"

She whirled back to face him. "What are you talking about? I have to bandage his hands, we can't just leave them, he'll get a secondary infection —"

"I'm not just talking about his *hands* Ruth, you know that."

Ruth was silent for a moment, stunned. "You agreed to give me time, to let me research. To give his body time to fight the Plague," she felt her chest start to squeeze in.

"It's been over a year. He's not getting better. He's not even fighting it. Nobody is. You said it yourself, his body isn't even recognizing it as a threat. There's no cure, Ruth. It's time to talk about alternatives." He held out a hand to her. She didn't want to take it, thinking it would be like agreeing with him. But what they were discussing was so distressing that she *needed* him. She slid a hand into his warm one and let him run a thumb across the skin on the back of her hand.

"I have one more test Bill, this could be the one."

He nodded. "But it won't be. And then what? You move on to herbal remedies? Raid university chem labs to find forgotten research?"

Ruth's lips thinned into a bloodless slash, but she didn't say anything.

"In the meantime, Charlie just gets worse. His hands are torn apart. If he's awake, he's furious and starving, even right after we've fed him. I know you don't want to hear this sweetheart, but he's in pain *all the time.* He hasn't had any rest in a long, long time. Neither have you. Neither have I."

"What is it that you want me to do? Let him go? Let him wander out into the street to attack someone or be attacked by another Infected or shot by a stranger?"

"No, I don't want him to die alone on the street. He's still my little boy."

Ruth took a stuttering breath and squinted her eyes against the sharp tears that sprang upon her. "But we *are* talking about him dying?"

"If there were some improvement— if there were even periods of calm or moments when I could glimpse the real Charlie, I wouldn't be discussing it."

"This isn't terminal. He's healthy except for his mind. I know he can beat it, we just have to find the right treatment to help him. He's still in there, Bill, our Charlie is still inside."

Bill shook his head and his eyes became red. "I hope to God you're wrong, Ruth. I hope there's nothing left of him at all. He would be so confused and frightened and suffering. You think he understands why his mom and dad don't hug him anymore? Or why he isn't able to play outside of his room? Christ! Ruth, we shackled him. His own parents. The restraints make sores on his skin. We only touch him to change bandages or clean him or fix the straitjacket. I hope he's not in there at all. He wouldn't understand."

Ruth sobbed. "We're only *protecting* him."

"I know," said Bill, rubbing the back of her hand, "But it's become torture. For all of us."

"I'll find another restraint system. We'll make a safe, padded room for him. I can't just abandon him—"

Bill began shouting. "But that's what we are doing, one way or another." He took a deep breath and lowered his voice. "Let's say we continue this way, and let's say we are *very* lucky in this bad new world we live in, and we manage to survive for forty more years. So will Charlie. You said he's a healthy kid other than the brain damage. And his hands. Let's say we can continue to keep him healthy. We'll find antibiotics for when he bites himself and prevent him from dying in agony from sepsis. We'll start tying him to a telephone pole in the street on sunny afternoons so that he can run and exercise. That way he won't develop seeping bed sores or atrophied muscles when his room gets too small. We'll sedate him every night and brush his teeth and scrub him and change his diapers so he doesn't wallow in his own filth. Day after day for forty years—"

"Stop!" cried Ruth, "Stop it! I would do it all for him. Every day. I knew what I signed up for when we adopted him."

A wail of rage tumbled down the basement steps. Charlie had heard them and was awake. Bill swiped the back of his hand across his eyes as the scream renewed itself.

"I know you would Ruth. I would too. But we became parents in another world. We could do all those things and more, but it will never take away even a fraction of his misery. Listen to that. That is his *entire* existence. How can you bear to see him in such anguish every day? Even if you could stand it, what would happen to him when we die? There isn't any institution to take him to when we get too old to care for him. There're no other relatives to take over. He'll starve to death. Alone, chained up, his brain still a lost little boy's. He'll suffer for days and days before he finally dies. Is that what you want?"

Ruth just sobbed, clutching his hand.

"I worry about it every time we leave him," Bill continued, "every time we go out to get supplies or medicine, I think, will this be the trip that kills us? Will my little boy be here abandoned and starving or freezing when the generator dies? Will someone break in and hurt him or— or *eat* him? I can't do it anymore," Bill's voice broke and he dropped his head into his hands.

After a moment, Ruth said, "You're asking me to murder my child."

"I'm asking you to help me stop his suffering."

"There could still be a cure out there."

Bill let go of her hand. She crossed to the incubator and pulled out the plate. She didn't even need the microscope. The bacteria had swarmed over the filter disks in milky gray clumps. The medication didn't even slow them down. Bill could already see the despair in her face. He stood up and walked over to her. He took the agar plate from her hand and put it on the counter. "We've done everything that we can do. There's nothing else to try. It's time to let him go," he said.

"Maybe I just need to try a larger dosage."

"The dosages you tried were already too large for a child."

"Then I must have contaminated the samples," she cried, and picked up the plastic plate again. "It's this house! I can't keep the lab sterile. Everything just seeps in here, no matter what I do." She flung the bacteria into the trash barrel. She picked up a glass beaker and flung it too. Bill grabbed her arms and wrapped her in a hug.

"It's over Ruth, *there is no cure*. There's nothing else to try. We can't go on this way. It's time to let him go."

"Not today. Not yet," she cried.

He pulled back from her for a moment. "The longer we wait, the more dreadful this will all become."

"Please, I just need a little more time. To get things ready. To do it right."

Bill shook his head, his bristly beard scraping through the hair on the top of her head.

"We'll just keep putting it off."

"I can't Bill. He's our baby. I can't."

Bill was silent and the distant shrieks from Charlie poured into the lab, filled the quiet with misery. At last Bill sighed and gently pushed Ruth away. "It took me a long time to understand how much Charlie is suffering. But you've been distracted by your work and the hope you had of curing him. Your tests are done. Take some time. Spend some time with him. You'll see he isn't the little boy you remember. Eventually you'll see that the alternative is kinder. I'll wait." He didn't wait for her to answer, just climbed the stairs to the kitchen.

CHAPTER 2

In February, Charlie and Bill got sick from something they'd eaten. Before it would have meant a day home from school and work. A few slices of toast, flat gingerale and a marathon of cartoons. Ruth's mind listed all the things it could be now: cholera, dysentery, killer flu. Her thoughts rolled over and over, jagged stones that banged in her head. She went out, looking for something, anything to help them. Toward evening she panicked, slogging through the snow to each store she could remember, but they were all ransacked and even the generic, over-the-counter drugs were gone. She'd been looking all day, trudging from broken glass door to broken glass door in freezing rain and fresh snow.

Exhausted and wet, she thought of going home. But Bill had begged her to find Charlie a sedative instead of stomach medicine. Enough to stop his misery. Ruth didn't tell him she'd already set it aside. It was locked in the cabinet in her lab, where Bill never went. Charlie's screams had died into whimpers and toneless sobbing after two days of near constant vomit. She hadn't thought any of them could be more exhausted than they already were, but she'd been wrong.

Charlie's weak cries had fooled her into believing he was the boy she'd known a year ago. He had barely even fought when she cleaned him up, she wasn't even sure he needed the restraints. He'd lain on the floor where she put him when she was finished, dozing and starting, his dark hair sticking to his forehead with sweat, his cheeks bright with fever. She wanted to curl up next to him, to rake her hand through his hair to get it off his skin, to fan cool breezes onto his face and kiss him. She knew that she couldn't, but it didn't stop her aching for it. The pain they were all in almost made her agree to do it, right then. But she'd escaped instead, with a made up mission to find medicine that wouldn't do much anyway. If she went back now, she might give in. Then there would be no Charlie, not even the mindless version that had replaced her funny, handsome little boy. Ruth couldn't go much farther without risking getting lost in the blizzard, though, and she would freeze if she didn't get back to the house soon. A bookstore was all that was left, but she went in anyway, to delay going home for a few more minutes.

She was surprised to see that the store was almost as badly ransacked as all the others. She realized that most of the books were being burnt to stay warm, because a few of the wooden shelves were broken into splintered slabs and piled in a corner near the door. She looked around at the few remaining books and eventually found one on natural cures. In other days, it might have made her roll her eyes in private. There was nothing, in Ruth's mind, better than modern medicine. Sure, people had used natural remedies for thousands of years, but the life expectancy of those people was decades shorter before medicine and technology made giant leaps forward. But now— now it wasn't just a way to stall for time. Now it was an entire book full of things Ruth might have overlooked. A handbook for a city girl after the city was gone. It was armor against Bill and his despair. It was a way to find a cure, maybe. Or for now, at least to ease an upset stomach. But where was she going to get these plants in the middle of winter? Even in the spring she could go weeks without getting a glimpse of grass between the pavement. She shrugged off her doubt. For now, the book was enough.

She returned home, ready to face the misery that waited for her.

By the time the storm had cleared, Bill and Charlie had recovered. But something had changed. She didn't know if it were her own resolve that had weakened or if Bill was more depressed than before, but both of them knew that they couldn't go on as they were for much longer. Neither one brought it up.

Ruth began going to the botanic gardens, though the usual early thaw didn't arrive and the streets were a treacherous mix of icy crust and decaying metal cars. She saw few of the Infected, anymore. Most often they would surprise her by stumbling out of an alley or snarling at a feral dog. It wasn't hard to escape them. Even though they could run as fast as she could, they were weak and clumsy, and Ruth simply threaded in between car wreckage until they lost interest. Most of the Infected that were on the street simply had the bad luck of wandering out into freezing conditions. Some made it long enough to begin to starve, but most were dead within a day or two.

The greenhouses at the botanic gardens were almost as cold as the rest of the city, but the glass was intact and the wind couldn't whip through them the way it did outside. The sun was only a pale cold coin and the condensation had turned to frost on the waxy leaves of the dead plants. Ruth regretted that the tropical plants were dead, there would be no replacing those, but she combed through what was left for anything she could salvage or recognize before spring. The walkways were a tan, sodden slush of old leaves that hadn't been swept since the Plague, probably. In just a year, the beds had become tangled and overrun.

She picked through the dead stems holding leaf after leaf up to the pale light to study its shape, one hand on the open herb book, completely forgetting the cold. She was hovering over the agrimony on her hands and knees, picking up the burrs and sealing them in a plastic container when she heard someone clear their throat behind her. Ruth's muscles froze with a painful jolt.

"I don't much care if you're desperate or stupid," said a woman's voice, "but the vegetables are needed for others. You'd better put them back and go, while I'm still willing to let you."

Ruth's heartbeat was so fast, that she began to feel dizzy. She slowly raised her hands to show they were empty. "I didn't come for vegetables or any food. I have plenty." There was only silence behind her and she began to panic. *Offer her something,* she thought, *Offer anything. Just get out of here.* "I'll share with you if you like, just think about what you are doing first," she pleaded.

"What did you come for then?"

Ruth's thoughts were sizzling and leaping. She caught one thought a self defense class had taught her years before: *Make it hard to kill you. Make yourself more human.* "I've got a little boy at home, and a husband. They are sick. I can't find any medicine anywhere, so I came here to make some if I can. See?" she said, holding up the book. She felt the woman take the book from her. "Is it okay for me to turn around?" Ruth turned as she asked so that the woman wouldn't refuse. If she could see her face, maybe she had a chance.

She was Ruth's age, softer around the middle maybe, in a jumper and wool tights. She looked like she'd walked here from her second grade classroom. Ruth didn't know if the woman's normalcy made her feel better or more frightened. "Are you a gardener?" the woman asked.

Ruth brushed the soil from her hands. "Ruth Socorro. I'm a— I *was* a pediatrician." She held out a shaky hand to the woman. The woman grinned and closed Ruth's hand in both of hers. Ruth almost sighed with relief.

"You're a doctor?"

Ruth held up her other hand to stop her. "I *was* a doctor. Now I'm just someone who knows how to apply a bandaid. If I can find one, that is."

"Oh no, you're *much* more than that. You're the only sane, living doctor I've met in the past year. I desperately need your help."

"I don't know—" began Ruth, pulling her hand back.

"I'm not after your stockpile of drugs. I just need a little of your time. There are people you can really help, people in pain."

Ruth stared at her for a long moment. She wanted to believe the woman, but she knew Bill would tell her she was crazy, that people were only looking out for themselves these days.

"Look, if you won't do it out of the goodness of your heart—" the woman began, but Ruth waved at her to stop.

"Of course," she said, "Of course I'll come and help them. But I haven't got much in the way of medicine."

The woman nodded and bit her bottom lip. "Maybe we can trade secrets. You teach me a little bit of first aid, and I'll teach you a little botany. I can't tell you how to make medicine out of them, of course, but if you find the name of a plant you can use, I can probably help you find it. I know almost every plant in the conservatory and more than half of what's in the outer garden. I've been coming here to take care of them since— since the power failed anyway. My name's Juliana. I was a Home Economics teacher."

Ruth agreed to meet her at the greenhouse the next day, after she had gone home to Bill and Charlie. She hurried back through the icy streets feeling lighter, purposeful. Better than she had in weeks. Maybe she just needed other people. Maybe help would convince Bill they could do this, if Juliana's community was a good one.

But Ruth got a nasty shock when she returned home. Bill was slumped on the top step, holding a bloody towel to his side and watching the front door shudder in its frame as a series of loud thuds exploded behind it.

"What happened?" Ruth ran up the steps to help him.

"Charlie got loose. He must have chewed through the straps or something." He drew in a hissing breath as Ruth lifted the cloth from his wound to inspect it. "I went into his room to give him lunch, and he leapt at me. I tried to push him back and shut the door, but it was too late. He bit me and he wouldn't let go. I tried everything. It hurt like hell and he wouldn't stop. I had to hit him."

Ruth drew back a little to look at Bill's face. He shook his head. "I didn't want to. I slapped him. I slapped Charlie. But it didn't do any good. He started whipping his head back and forth, like a puppy with a toy. Like he wanted to take a chunk out of my skin. So I hit him in the head with that vase thing in the hall. You know, the one he made at that day camp, that's squashed on one side?" Bill was crying, wiping his face with a sleeve. "The pain was so intense, I couldn't think of anything but getting him to let go. And Charlie's vase was in reach. I'm sorry. I'm so *sorry*." He sobbed. "I'm sorry, Charlie," he yelled toward the door.

She wanted to tell him that it was okay, that everything would be fine. That he'd only done what he had to. But instead she thought secretly, *I would have found another way. I wouldn't have hit him. I love him more.* The wrongness of it overwhelmed her. So the rational, doctor side of her stepped in to save them all.

"Come on," she said, "We have to get you out of the cold." She wished she'd said something more loving, something to make him feel better, but she didn't know what.

Bill shook his head. "Charlie's still loose. I can't go back in there and risk doing something even worse."

"We can't stay out here. You need stitches

and it's so cold. And what would happen to Charlie?"

Bill was silent, still crying. Ruth knelt down and squeezed his hand in her own. "Okay, I'll get Charlie to his room. Don't fall asleep out here, I'll only be a few minutes." She took off her heavy coat and wrapped it around him. Charlie was still banging on the door and Ruth decided to use his distraction. She went into the yard and climbed carefully onto the rickety generator shed. She tried to ease open the living room window without making too much noise. She could see Charlie now, flinging his little body at the door. His head was caked with drying blood. Ruth wasn't sure she could forgive her husband for that, despite realizing that he had done only what was necessary to survive. The window wiggled and Ruth pushed it up inch by inch, holding her breath. It was a long drop, but there wasn't anything she could use as a step. She jumped down as softly as she could, the thud lost in Charlie's own pounding. Ruth scanned the room for anything she could use to restrain him. Most of the furniture had been pushed back to make space for the wood they'd scrounged to burn in the fireplace. Otherwise, the room was empty. The restraints in Charlie's room were broken. She had to keep him still long enough to fix his wound and get him safely back where he couldn't harm anyone. There wasn't really any choice. She slid the window closed and held her breath as she crept behind Charlie to the kitchen. The lab door squeaked and Ruth winced but a glance back at Charlie told her he wasn't noticing anything but his own rage. She closed the door behind her and went down to open the cabinet. The tray of small glass bottles glittered like something sharp and hot. She pulled one out. It rolled in her hand, smooth and heavy. She unwrapped a syringe and looked at it. *I could finish it now*, she thought, *just a little extra and all this misery would be over for him. For Bill too. But not for me. It'll never be over for me.* She pulled the right dosage into the needle and stopped. *Not today. Not on a bad day, I'll wait for a good one, when we aren't all trying to hurt one another.* Bill would have told her that there *were* no more good days, but he wasn't there to argue, so she went back into the kitchen and found an old tablecloth.

She moved quickly, more concerned with getting it done than making noise. Throwing the tablecloth over Charlie's head, she wrapped one arm around the boy and pinned his arms. He stumbled and struggled against the cloth, but Ruth just held him tightly. She pressed gently on the back of his knees with her foot. He collapsed into a kneeling position and Ruth held him there. She pulled one thin arm out of the cloth and patiently waited for his struggling to pause. She was ready when he stopped to catch a breath through the thick cloth. He struggled so hard and he was so warm from the pounding and screaming, his veins weren't hard to find. Ruth injected the sedative and then carefully pulled the cloth down from his face. He tried to snap at her, but she was ready. Ruth rocked back and forth on the floor with the shrieking boy tight in her arms. The back of his head pressed hard into her chest and she could feel the wet warmth of sweat and blood seeping into her shirt. "I'm sorry Charlie," she said and closed her eyes while they sat there.

"I remember the first time I got to hold you," she said, though she knew he couldn't hear her. "You smelled like soap and talcum powder and the social worker pretended like she had the most normal job in the world. Like it was just another night at work for her. But it was actually the best night in all of human existence. And your daddy wanted to hold you, but I didn't want to let you go. It was so hard to let you go when you were so warm and soft. I thought it was the hardest thing I ever had to do. Until now. I can't let you go Charlie. I'm sorry. I'm so sorry, but I can't do it."

The boy's ragged breathing slowed into a smooth wave and his shoulders drooped. His head rolled slightly to the side and his cries became a sad, shrill, keening that made Ruth cry. She called for Bill, and he stumbled in through the door and collapsed beside them. He ran a gentle hand over Charlie's sleeping face and kissed his head. They sat that way a few more moments until Ruth picked up her son, who was sleeping deeply now, and started down to the lab.

"I'll come back and get you in a few minutes," she said over her shoulder, "I just want to get him cleaned up and safe first."

Bill got up with a groan and followed her. "I can walk," he said.

Ruth laid Charlie on the gurney she'd scavenged from the clinic and began finding her tools. Bill stood in front of the open cabinet, staring at the vials of sedative.

"You lied to me? Why didn't you tell me you

had it?"

Ruth shrugged and moved to another drawer, not wanting to discuss it.

"How long have you had it?"

"Only a day or two," she lied.

"Why do you keep putting this off? You know what we have to do. This is cruel, keeping him this way. You know that." Bill's face began to get red and she could see his fist holding the cloth tighter and tighter against his side.

"What you are asking me to do is unnatural. It goes against every better judgment—"

"The whole *world* is unnatural Ruth!" Bill shouted. Ruth blinked hard and began tweezing shards of pottery out of Charlie's hair.

"I couldn't live knowing I'd killed my own child."

"Then don't," said Bill softly. Ruth looked up from Charlie's head and gaped at her husband. He was crying. He swiped his free hand over his face and continued, "None of us should have survived. Things are shit and they are only going to get worse. You have enough. We'll do it together. No more suffering for any of us."

"It's *wrong*."

"So give me something to do that's right. Because what we're already doing sure isn't it."

"Do you really want today to be your very last day? The day you had to injure your child?" Ruth asked, gently washing the gash in Charlie's head.

"Every extra day that I'm alive I'll only relive it and know terrible guilt. And every extra day is another where I may have to hurt him again to save you or someone else. This is as good as life is going to get now. But things are starting to run out. Soon, whoever is left will be killing each other for the scraps. We're already out of most useful medicine and if we are around next winter, we'll freeze because there is nothing left to burn. That's saying nothing of food. Whatever gas is left is turning into turpentine so the generator and any running vehicles will be useless soon. The world's not going to go back the way it was, Ruth. There's nothing better coming." He watched her for a long minute as if expecting an answer. Ruth nodded and wiped her eyes.

"Tomorrow," she said, wrapping a soft bandage around Charlie's head, "I promised to do something tonight."

"Ruth—"

"I swear, I'm not stalling. I promised to help a group of people who are ill tonight. I'll bandage you both up and get Charlie to his room first."

"After what just happened? You're leaving to help some stranger? The world is over and you're still putting work before us? At the moment we need you most—"

"Please, Bill, let's not argue more. I'll make sure you're okay before I go. Let me do this one last thing. We've stolen food and supplies that other people, people who will be alive for years, could have used. We've killed neighbors to stay alive for this long. I just had to restrain and drug my own child because I'm too selfish to let him rest. Let me do one selfless act, let me make up for the time we stole from everybody else. It will help with— it will help me tomorrow."

Bill's face was still hardened into a scowl. "It's almost dark."

"I know. I'll be back in the morning."

"But you could get lost. You'll freeze to death out there."

"Considering what we're discussing," said Ruth, "does it really make much difference?"

Bill shrugged and for a second, Ruth truly hated him for it.

CHAPTER 3

By the time Ruth left the house, the sun had set and her flashlight's thin beam was all she had to travel by. She hoped Juliana hadn't given up on her and left the conservatory. Despite what she'd said to Bill, Ruth didn't want to freeze in the street. She wanted to hold her boy one more time before... the thought was so overwhelming that she struggled to breathe.

She tried to stop thinking about it. She concentrated on stepping in her own footprints from that morning so she didn't have to risk breaking a new path in the dark. The conservatory was dimly glowing from solar stakes scattered along the paths. It had been so long since Ruth had seen a light other than the one she or Bill made, it frightened her. She was hesitant to approach the greenhouse. What if the light drew others? But hers were the only prints in the snow. Juliana must come in another way. Ruth switched off the flashlight and stumbled through the doors. "Juliana, are you here?" she whispered. Something rustled in the brittle plants a few beds off.

"I'm here," Juliana's voice floated gently through the dark air between them.

"Sorry I'm late," said Ruth slowly. Juliana laughed as she appeared on the path.

"I don't think there is such a thing as 'late' any more."

"I don't have much in the way of medicine, I'm sorry. Most of it is gone now, and I didn't keep very much at my own clinic, just formula and the common vaccinations. I don't know how much help I'll be."

"You don't need to worry, these people will be grateful— *I'll* be grateful if you just tell me what I need to do to keep them healthy and what is likely to happen when they do get sick." Juliana clicked on a light and swung a backpack over her shoulder. "It's not far and it's warmer than here anyway."

"Where is the rest of your group? You don't come out here at night alone do you?" Ruth glanced around expecting more people to appear on the dim path.

"Why not? You did. No one will be out tonight. It's too cold for the looters. And the Infected— I'm afraid any that were out there must have frozen to death."

Juliana led her back out into the snow and Ruth felt a sudden jolt of panic. She didn't know this woman, had no idea if what she was saying was true. She tried to reason with herself. In a few more hours, nothing that happened now would matter much anymore. But deep down she knew she wasn't ready to die. It was like an appointment penciled in that she never meant to keep. She knew that what Bill said was true: the world and Charlie were only going to get worse. But something in her still rejected suicide.

Juliana led her down alleys that she'd never recognize, even in daylight, though she'd lived nearby for years. The unplowed drifts of snow squeezed in and choked the narrow side streets. No one on this side of town was taking care of bodies either. Ruth shrieked as the gray beam of her flashlight strobed over a corpse lying on the side of the alley. Juliana stopped and turned around.

"Oh, I'm so sorry. I try to keep up with them, but I already have so much to do. I just cleared this street before the last storm. Poor man. It must have been one of the sick ones. Lots of them seem to be wandering up from the subway stations. They're flooding, you know."

Ruth shuddered and moved her flashlight as if she were averting her eyes. "It's okay. It's not like I've never seen a dead body before. It just surprised me."

"We're almost to the hospital. Do you need a minute?"

Ruth shook her head. "The hospital? We're nowhere near the hospital."

"Sorry, I meant the psychiatric hospital. It's where we've set up."

"I thought that place was falling down. Why'd you choose there?"

"Most of it is intact. Our wing is fine. And there is a wood burning furnace that heats the whole place and the kitchen is original, so it has a hand pump for the well."

"How many of you are there?"

Juliana was silent for a few minutes and Ruth began to be nervous that she'd asked the wrong question or that Juliana was trying to think up a plausible lie. They came out of the alley onto a large street that dead-ended in a massive lawn punctuated by a sprawling concrete building. The windows were bright but the light was broken into barred slats that stretched over the snow.

"Look," said Juliana, "I haven't been completely honest with you about— about my group."

Ruth froze and tensed, her eyes darted back toward the alleyway.

"It's not what you think," said Juliana quickly, "I didn't bring you out here to rob and kill you. I meant it when I said I needed a doctor's help. But the people I'm with— I'm the only healthy one. The rest of them have the December Plague. I found them. Some here, some on the road, some were brought to me by relatives who couldn't care for them anymore. I take care of them. Well, I *try* to. I'm sorry I didn't tell you before, I thought you'd think I was crazy or refuse to come."

Ruth shook her head. "I wish I could help you, I truly do. I've looked for a year for a cure. I've tested every drug I could still find. Nothing works. There's no cure. My own son has it."

"I know the Plague can't be cured. I need help with everything else. One of them had a broken arm when I found him, another one has bed sores because her mother strapped her to the bed not knowing what to do. One of the others has some kind of flu or something. That's what I need help with."

Ruth nodded and they head toward the large building.

"I'm sorry about your son," Juliana continued, "but I'm grateful that I don't have to explain to you why I care for them. Other people ask why I don't just let them die or put them out of their misery, but you understand."

"I'd like to hear what you tell them though," said Ruth, trying to keep her voice casual.

"I tell them that we don't know what the Infected are feeling or thinking. Maybe they are asking for our help. Maybe they feel terrible about what their bodies force them to do. They are human beings just like us. I've heard some people call them zombies or undead. Can you imagine? They're just sick. We don't let people starve or freeze because they caught the flu do we? Why should this be any different? The human body is an amazing thing. Some of them may fight it off and recover. But only if they live to do so. What if they remember what we did to them? Some days it seems like all the kindness is gone from the world."

Ruth's eyes blurred and her voice was unsteady. "What if it's kinder to let them die?"

"What do you mean?"

"Have you heard them? They are constantly in pain. They never stop screaming and scrabbling — and if they ever do get better and remember, like you said, what about the things that *they* did to their loved ones? Do you think they'll want to remember that? What if, by keeping them alive all this time, instead of letting nature take its course and the population of Infected die out due to exposure or starvation or combat, what if *we* are the ones being cruel?"

Juliana shook her head. "If you really believed that, your son would already be gone." She put her hand on a thick iron bar that lay across the door. "I have to believe that their lives have some value, that their personalities or souls or whatever are still in there, hoping to wake up. Millions of people are dead, just in this city alone. A handful of us survived, including the Infected that have been cared for. Am I supposed to believe we're only here because of dumb luck? There must be a reason we're still here. *All* of us." She lifted the bar slowly upright until it clanked into place.

A chorus of howls and shrieks cascaded from the rooms near the entrance and traveled like a wave down the building until the whole place echoed with torment. Ruth thought she might be walking into hell itself. Juliana didn't even seem to notice. "They're all in separate rooms, you don't need to worry. And I do have their movements restricted, so you'll be safe. They're just hungry, it's past dinner time."

Feeding time, Ruth thought and then was ashamed. Juliana led her through the large entry that was dimly lit with gas lamps. The building was very old and Juliana seemed to be using all of its pre-electric advantages. But she would run out of gas soon, Ruth knew. *And then what?* They passed at least twenty rooms and Ruth wondered how on earth she was finding food to feed them all. Or water to bathe them. Or if she really was. Maybe Juliana was the world's new version of an animal hoarder. Maybe she thought she was helping but was really just starving them slower. Something scraped against a metal door next to Ruth, making her shudder. She couldn't be certain, but she imagined it was somebody's teeth. "How many do you have Juliana?" she had to shout to be heard, even though the walls and doors were thick and muffled a good deal of the noise.

"A few dozen right now," said Juliana, "but people bring me more from time to time." They passed most of the occupied rooms and left the growls and wails behind them. Juliana pushed through some swinging doors at the end of the hall and passed into a large stone floored kitchen. A large woodstove sat in the center, and Ruth had the feeling of stepping into some older, better time.

"I need to start dinner. You can join me or you can start inspecting the patients if you like. You will be safe, but I'd also like to learn what to do, you know, in case you can't be here."

Ruth looked around the empty kitchen. "How do you feed them all?" she asked, thinking of all the days she and Charlie and Bill had gone hungry when she couldn't find any cans to scavenge.

"The first winter was something of a trick," said Juliana moving toward another set of doors, "but there were only three of us then, so I managed. I won't lie, some days we were all hungry. But in the spring I remembered the botanic gardens had a victory garden patch and I—well, I'm not proud of it, but I stole some vegetables and some seeds. Next year I'll replant some things and expand it a little, but I needed those things to feed these people. I found a tiller there too and a little gas. I was measuring a plot when I found you this morning. Next year will be harder, but I'll get someone with a horse to come and rig up the tiller. Mostly since then, people have donated things. Food, time, medicine. I pretty much run this place, but when I take someone in, I ask for help. Most people are happy to give it. They come visit their loved one and spend some time weeding the garden or bathing the Infected or just drop off scavenged goods. They are relieved that they aren't having to do it every day anymore. Or maybe they just feel guilty. Either way, I need the help."

She opened the doors and they stepped into a

pantry with more canned food than Ruth had seen in over a year. What before would have simply seemed like an average stocked kitchen to Ruth, now seemed mythic. She touched the paper labels on some soup cans. "Those apples, for example, came from the Park. One of the families brought me those this fall. Who knew apple trees grew in all this concrete?" Ruth glanced over where Juliana had waved her hand. There were bins of fresh potatoes and apples and carrots. Ruth's mouth started to water. Suddenly, a thought occurred to her. She shook her head and turned to leave the pantry.

"No way. This is a death trap. I'm leaving right now." Her legs shook underneath her.

"What? What are you talking about? This isn't a trap. Have I done anything to threaten you?" Juliana held out her hands to stop Ruth.

"No, this is some kind of sick joke. Nobody has this stuff. Fresh fruit? Are you crazy? What's the deal? Do you bring people here, show them the huge bounty of food they could have and then trap them and let the Infected get them? That's how you feed them, isn't it? You just throw innocent people to them as if they were wolves. You're *sick*." Ruth pushed Juliana aside.

"I told you how I got these things. I'm about to cook dinner right now, and it isn't you. Look," she said, pulling an industrial sized can of tomato sauce down from the shelf, "it's spaghetti, okay? Quick and easy to throw together and the carbohydrates will calm them down. I'm a— I *was* a Home Ec teacher, remember? Part of that is nutrition. That's why I asked people for fresh stuff, it's why I grew it in the garden. Even if growing fresh food wasn't the best thing for us, the cans are running out. We have to start producing our own stuff if we're going to survive. That's not a miracle sitting in those bins over there, that's several months of sweat and toil."

"If that's true, then you shouldn't be showing it off to every stranger who wanders in here. It makes this place look like it houses the crown jewels."

Juliana laughed and pointed to a huge case of pasta. "Grab that for me," she picked up another can of spaghetti sauce and walked back into the kitchen. "Nobody just 'wanders in' to a mental institution Ruth. Not even after everything is gone. Besides, this place was abandoned for years before I got here. And I told *you* about it, because you had the opportunity to steal what's left in the garden this morning and you didn't. You didn't even try to find out where the vegetables were. I'm prepared to defend this place and the food if I have to, but I'm not bloodthirsty. Or sick. Not the way you mean anyway. You've been in this city too long, it's made you paranoid."

Ruth shook her head. "If what you're saying is true, and you got these things the way you said, then how can you possibly think all the kindness has gone out of the world? There's enough food there to feed an army for months. Most of the time, my family is lucky if we eat a meal each day. And this place is warm. Not just above freezing, actually warm. You must go through a ton of wood. I doubt you had time to cut it yourself."

"No, another helper brought us several cords

this fall. He said after the gas goes bad, we'll have to make do with less because he won't be able to use the chainsaw, but I've had several more folks volunteer to help him. I guess you're right. I should be very grateful for the people who are helping this place out. They aren't getting much in return, just a bed and care for one of their loved ones and they bring far more than feeds and clothes just that one person." She plunked the cans down on the thick wooden counter and cranked away at them with a large can opener. Ruth slid the case of pasta in next to her. "So, are you staying?" asked Juliana.

"For now," said Ruth, and sat down to watch how Juliana served something as messy as spaghetti to restrained people. Half an hour later, a cart full of mellamine bowls was rolling down the hallway while the inmates shrieked and scratched. Juliana stopped at the first door, opened it, placed the bowl on the floor and slid it in with the handle of an old broom. Then she shut the door again. She did it so fast, that Ruth didn't even see the person inside. They continued down the hall, sliding bowls into tiny cells and Ruth occasionally caught a glimpse of wild hair or an outflung arm or the flash of teeth or eyes. When they got to the last room, the hall was silent and Ruth thought she'd never heard anything more beautiful. She wondered how Juliana slept through the night after they started again.

"Okay," said Juliana, turning the cart around, "clean up time. And a chance for you to inspect them." She rolled the cart back to the first room. She pulled out a bucket of soapy water and some rags. She handed Ruth a tray of labeled toothbrushes. "Here, can you put some toothpaste on each?"

"How do you brush their teeth? I have to wait until Charlie passes out from exhaustion to do it."

Juliana held up a teething ring. "With this, you'll see. Are you ready?" Ruth nodded, dolloping small squeezes of toothpaste down each brush. Juliana opened the door. The spaghetti sauce gave the man on the floor a ghastly ring around his mouth. His hair was patchy, some of it long, some torn away leaving ugly scabs, some stubble in other spots, like a forest trying to recover after a fire. He was full now and quiet but he still growled and stood up to pace as far as the restraints would let him move in the small room.

"As long as we keep our voices soft and we move slowly, they don't get too agitated after eating," said Juliana in a sickly sweet voice. She slid the bowl out of the room with her foot, her eyes never leaving the man's face. "Loud noises or people getting too close will make them angry and want to fight."

"Aren't we cleaning them?" asked Ruth.

"Yes," said Juliana, "but I never said this was going to be easy. We have teething toys to distract them from biting us. I've found that they don't really know what they are biting, just that they need to bite *something*. They'll go after other humans first, but if they aren't hungry, they seem just to be driven to bite and don't appear to care what they bite, including themselves. We still have to be careful, even with the teething rings. And it's a completely different story if you ever have to—

ever have to *handle* them when they are hungry. Let me go first." She searched the tray and found a toothbrush that was labeled "Owen" with a permanent marker. The ink was rubbing off and the bristles flared like they had been scrubbing a floor. They were probably hard to replace.

"Is his name really Owen?" Ruth asked.

Juliana shrugged. "Maybe? Some of them I know because their families brought them. But some of them, like Owen, I found wandering and starving. I have to call him something. He looked like an 'Owen' to me."

Ruth's scalp prickled with discomfort. It was like naming a rescued dog. She wondered if anyone missed this man anymore. If anybody left would have recognized him and known his real name. Juliana entered the room and held the large teething ring in front of her. Owen scrambled toward her, his arms stretched toward her, fingers trying to grab her clothes, her hair, anything. The restraints stopped him halfway across the room.

Juliana cautiously slid the ring between his teeth. Owen clamped down around the tough plastic and Juliana let go of the far side as he jerked it away. Ruth was fascinated, despite herself. It made her think of the circus her father had taken her to when she was little. The lion tamer had frightened her and she'd watched the whole act through the cracks between her fingers. Owen chewed on the ring with one side of his mouth, a splatter of drool dripping onto the floor every few seconds. Juliana adjusted the arm restraints so that he couldn't grab.

"It's okay, you can come in now," she said.

Ruth picked up the soapy water and the rags, tucking her own kit under her elbow. She stood beside Juliana as she wiggled the toothbrush between Owen's teeth on the side that wasn't clamped down on the ring. "I do my best," she said without looking around, "but some of them are developing bed sores or getting sick anyway. There must be something I'm missing."

Ruth worked at gently cleaning the scrapes on his head and holding him steady for Juliana. Owen growled and tried to snap when Ruth hit tender spots, but the the teething ring kept him from biting. "I'm not sure what to tell you. I don't want to add to what is already a huge amount of work," said Ruth.

She wondered if she ought to be helping Juliana at all. The whole thing was insane. *Still,* her inner voice whispered, *if you weren't around, you'd hope Charlie ended up somewhere like here instead of shot or starved or freezing.* The least she could do is make sure that their existence wasn't one of physical suffering if she could help it. "You might want to shave their heads and find those heavy work gloves for their hands. They are pulling out their hair, see?" Ruth pointed to the large sores in Owen's scalp and Juliana glanced up. "They are also biting their hands because it's all they can reach. Charlie— my son, does it too. We keep his hands bandaged because those big gloves would just slide off his little fingers." She watched as Juliana's face became grim and then pitying. Ruth turned away for her scissors and gently cut the remaining tufts of hair around Owen's scabs. Then she checked the rest of him while Juliana continued washing him. The whole thing only took a few minutes, but the women didn't look at each other again. And then it was time for the next room.

It went on for nearly five hours, but it felt more normal to Ruth than most of the rest of her life. For a while she could pretend she was making rounds at the hospital and that she would go home through the bustling, brightly lit city to Bill and a sleeping Charlie at the end. That she'd wake Charlie up for school in the morning and Bill would make her eggs and coffee. That everything would be back the way it was. But the restraints, the missing supplies, the silence without the whir of hundreds of machines in the background, all broke the illusion and bore down bit by bit.

By the time they were nearing the end, Ruth was exhausted and even Juliana was flagging. The people they were treating had fallen asleep though, which made it easier and faster to get through. "You do this how many times?" asked Ruth.

"Once a day most of the time. Sometimes baths are every other day if I need to spend extra time on someone's bandages or something, but teeth get done every night and I try to at least wipe their faces."

"What about diapers?" asked Ruth.

Juliana cringed. "Don't think ill of me. I just have trouble fitting it around everything else. If I had help, maybe I could do it more often. Right now it's twice a day for each. I know I should check more often, but I need to grow the food to feed them and prepare it and get them medicine when they need and—"

Ruth put a hand on her arm to stop her. "Listen, I'm the last person to criticize. You're doing your best for people that no one else cares for, dozens of them. I can barely muster my best for my only child every day. There should be a fleet of nurses for these people, not just one person. Who's taking care of *you*? When are you sleeping?"

Juliana shook her head and waved Ruth off. "Never mind that, I get by. We just have one left and then we'll be able to clean up and go to bed. He's been coughing a lot and hasn't eaten much. I found him on the road about a week ago. He was already sick, but I thought warm food and being out of the cold might fix it. He's just gotten worse." She opened the door and Ruth knelt down beside the sleeping man. He was damp with sweat, though the room was not hot. She could hear his breath catching in his chest and she touched the back of his neck. It was so hot that it hurt her fingertips. "Get out, Juliana," she whispered.

"What?" hissed Juliana, " he's passed out."

"Get out, and shut the door. I'll be out in a moment. Don't come back in here and go bleach or burn everything that has touched this man."

Juliana backed out slowly as she pushed a battery powered lantern toward Ruth with her foot, then shut the door behind her. Ruth pulled the stethoscope from her kit, already knowing what she would hear. The question was how to prevent it from spreading to the rest of them. She pressed the diaphragm against the man's heaving back. The crackling she heard didn't surprise her. She halfheartedly tapped a finger over his chest, almost ignoring the flat thuds through the stethoscope.

She had no antibiotics. Even if she could find some, they'd probably be no good now. She didn't even know if it was bacterial anyway. The man was lost. All she could do would be to reduce his fever and try to keep him hydrated. If Juliana did it, she risked catching it herself and spreading it to the others. But if Ruth stayed to care for him, she risked taking it back to Charlie and Bill. It wouldn't matter much, she guessed. They would never even know they were sick.

Her eyes filled with tears. She was exhausted and running on anxiety alone. She sat in the harsh light of the lantern and cried for a few minutes. Juliana knocked gently at the door and the man beside her started. Ruth scrabbled away from him, expecting him to launch himself at her. He opened his eyes and stared at her, but didn't move. She opened the door and backed out.

"You have to stay away Juliana. From this room, from that man and from anything he touches."

"Why? And how can I? He'll die."

"He's got pneumonia. He's going to die anyway. It's very contagious. Better for someone that was already dying to do it alone rather than take twenty-five healthy people with him."

"But you can help him. What do you need? I'll find the plants—"

Ruth shook her head. "I can't help him. I don't even know if I could have helped him in the old days, because I can't tell if it's viral or bacterial. Even if it's bacterial, the antibiotics he needs take time to grow. At least a week if we didn't want to kill him with a corrupt batch, if we had the right materials."

"I'll start it tonight. What do we need?"

"He's not going to make it a week, Juliana. He's at the crisis point right now or has already passed it. He'll either get worse and die in the next several hours, or his fever will break once his body is successfully fighting off the infection on its own. All I can do is try to make him comfortable and keep him hydrated and breathing. I have almost everything I need, except the IV stuff. I need you to go to my house. My husband, Bill, will know what you need. Wait until morning. I'm not sure that the man will last that long, and it would make the trip pointless." Ruth paused with a hand on the door. "I need you to tell Bill why I'm not coming home in the morning. He won't believe you, but try. I need you to make him promise to wait for me."

"Wait for you to do what?"

"He'll know. Don't leave that house until he promises to wait for me, you understand?"

Juliana nodded.

"Come back when it's light and knock on the door. I'll tell you how to get there. But don't open the door to that room again until I say so. Do you have any alcohol?"

"You mean like disinfectant?"

"Yes. If you have some, put a small bottle outside the door with some rags that can be burned. I'll disinfect myself when I come out."

Juliana shook her head and blew out a small sigh. "Forgive me," she said, "this just all seems so — I don't know, old-fashioned, like something out of an 1800s book where the kid dies of scarlet fever or something."

"Modern medicine is over, Juliana. This place is evidence of how terribly it's failed. At least I know what to do for pneumonia." She quietly opened the door and shut herself inside with the dying man. She pulled a mask from her bag and fitted it over her face, but she knew her chances of avoiding infection weren't great. She rolled the man onto his back and pressed an ambu bag from her kit over his face. His eyes fluttered and his upper lip curled back in a snarl, but he didn't wake up enough to become agitated. Ruth knelt beside him and began squeezing air into his lungs in short bursts. It would relieve his body's struggle for oxygen, and it was the most she could do.

If he fights it off, he'll just wake up to more misery and pain, she thought. She stopped squeezing and watched the mist from his warm exhale cloud up the mouthpiece. She could end it for him. He was sleeping deeply, even in the depth of illness. He was probably more at ease than he had been since the succumbing to the Plague. He need never wake up to the shrieking and the hunger and the fury that he had known for the past year. He would die either way. Whether it was in a few months when Juliana's garden failed and she couldn't feed them or couldn't find wood to heat the place, or now from the pneumonia. No one ever need know it was her. He took a long shuddery breath. She pulled the ambu bag from his face. It was a sallow, exhausted face. The circles under his eyes made his skin look shrunken to the bones in the lantern light. It already looked dead and his chest rose and fell so slowly that she began to wonder if she even needed to do anything but sit by. But the wheezing came louder, became a soft scream of air through the thin space left in his lungs. Every time he inhaled, she felt the raw burn in her own throat and tasted the metallic, coppery slickness of blood. She couldn't listen to it any longer. She pulled a towel from her kit and folded it up.

She placed it over his mouth and nose, feeling the withering, humid heat of his breath soak through. "Sorry, whoever you are. I wish I'd gotten here sooner. I wish I'd done this for my own son. I'd want someone to do this for me." She pressed down. The towel dragged inward, away from her hand and he coughed. It was wet and sharp against the cloth. His eyes snapped open and he thrashed. He whipped his head to the side and Ruth wasn't ready, the towel slipped across his face and he took a stuttering breath.

"NO!" he cried. His head snapped back to look at her and Ruth scooted backwards in surprise. A low roar began in his throat but it was interrupted by a splashy cough. The man struggled to sit up, pausing every few seconds as his chest seized in a hacking cramp. Ruth stood up and backed toward the door. The man finally raised himself onto his knees. He looked up at her and held out his hands. "Help," he croaked.

"You can talk?" asked Ruth, "You weren't infected? Why is Julianna keeping you here? Are you a prisoner?"

The man stared at her, through her. "Help," he said again.

Ruth fumbled with a container of water. She crouched in front of the man and held the bottle up to his lips. He gulped and then choked. Ruth waited until his coughing subsided and then helped him lie down. "I'm going to help you breathe," she said, holding up the ambu bag, "Just relax and let the pump do the work for you, okay?"

But the man's eyes had already fluttered closed.

CHAPTER 4

Ruth pressed the mask into his face and began squeezing again. Every inch of her felt shaky and weak. What had she almost done? And what was Juliana doing, keeping a sane person in this cell? Maybe she didn't know. Maybe he *looked* infected. Ruth leaned closer to his face. Whatever scars he might have were not on his head. He was certainly drawn, but everyone Ruth had met in the past several months was starting to look thin. She shook his shoulder. His eyes popped open and focused on hers again.

"What's your name?" Ruth asked. The man made a sound like clearing his throat. Ruth thought he couldn't talk through the thick phlegm of the pneumonia. She leaned closer to hear better, turning her face so her cheek just brushed the rubber bulb of the ambu bag and her ear was closer to his mouth.

Suddenly there was a painful pull at the back of her head and she tried to sit up. But the man had a grip on her hair. She let the ambu bag go and it tumbled down between them as she reached back to pull his hand away. He snarled and roared, sitting straight up and pulling her almost underneath him by her hair. The restraints stopped his other hand and a fit of coughing overwhelmed him. Saliva and snot dripped onto Ruth's facemask as he hovered over her and she shut her eyes as she struggled to slide away from him. Ruth rolled free, a clump of hair ripping from her head and staying in his hand. She backed up against the door and pulled her kit over toward her with one foot while the man recovered his breath.

She inched her way out of the door and closed it. Ripping the mask from her face, she doused the rags Juliana had left for her with the alcohol next to it. It smelled almost like turpentine and it burned against Ruth's skin, but she didn't care. She swiped her face and hands and then slid down to sit in front of the door.

Behind her, she could still hear the man roaring and hacking, like some great blockage had been suddenly released. She could see now, why Juliana had thought he was infected with the Plague. Ruth wasn't entirely sure that he wasn't. But she'd never seen an Infected talk before, never had one ask for help. If that man could do it, why couldn't Charlie?

She picked herself up and went over to the window. The sky was bleaching to a dull gray over the city. It would be morning soon, Juliana would be back soon. Ruth couldn't risk exposing her, but she had to get a message to Bill and she had to find out who the man in the room was. Her head throbbed where the hair had been ripped out and her heart was still racing. She didn't want to return to the cramped cell, but she knew he'd need her help to breathe before long. The man's cries had subsided into a dull pattern of moans and rattling coughs. She listened at the door until the moans died off into a wheezing gurgle. Then she carefully slid into the room. The man was lying on his back, unconscious, his breath carving a pothole in his chest while he struggled, even in his sleep. The ambu bag was hurled against a far wall but was unbroken. Ruth carefully stepped over him to retrieve it. The towel she had tried to use was a tattered ribbon near his mouth. It gleamed like a dirty bone. She kicked it away and knelt by the man, careful not to let her guard down this time. She pulled a clean mask onto her own face and then pressed the plastic mouthpiece of the ambubag against his. He didn't wake up, and she felt sweat slide down her neck as she began pumping the bulb again.

Ruth watched the gray light well up in the cell's tiny barred window. Her mind played a litany every time she pumped. *One breath for him, one less breath for Charlie.* She knew she was close to panic. Bill wouldn't do it without her. He couldn't. Especially when Juliana delivered her message. Maybe he'd come see the man, and realize she just needed some time to figure out what made him different. He'd see there could be a cure for Charlie. But as the morning took on a sparkling radiance as the sun splashed onto the snow, Ruth only felt more dread.

At last, Juliana knocked softly at the door. Ruth leaned into it and called through. "I'm passing through the directions and a list of what I need. You have to tell Bill to wait, no matter what. Just wait for me. Understand?"

"I'll tell him, I promise," came the muffled reply.

"And tell him this man talked to me last night."

There was a long silence. "What?"

"This man, he talked to me, I need you to tell Bill— for our son."

"Ruth that's impossible. The Infected don't speak. At least, not in words. I think you are too tired. Maybe we should switch so you can rest." The doorknob began to turn.

"No! No Juliana, you can't come in here. I wasn't hallucinating. Please, just tell Bill. Make him promise to wait." Ruth slid the wrinkled bit of paper from her prescription pad through the crack. It disappeared as Juliana pulled it the rest of the way.

"Okay," said Juliana, hesitation making her speak slowly, "I'll be back as soon as I can. In time for breakfast anyway. Don't worry if the others get — loud. I'll be back soon and they are safe in their rooms."

She knew it would take about an hour to walk there, but it didn't make the time crawl by any faster. Her arms ached from pumping and the man's breath didn't sound much better. What had been just an attempt, a nod toward duty, was now dire need. Only a few hours earlier, she had tried to help him die. Now her son and husband's life was hinging on his survival. Though her arms felt as if they were on fire, she kept pumping air into his lungs and praying that they wouldn't collapse. Adrenaline could only sustain her so long, and she felt her body go slack and her breath slow in the warm sunlight poking through the thick window. She struggled to stay awake, splashing herself with the bottle of water and slapping her cheeks for the few seconds between pumps. At last, even the fear that he'd wake and rip her to pieces if she slept wasn't working any longer.

She wasn't sure if she'd dozed only for a few seconds or for hours, but she woke to a rap on the door. The man was still asleep and still gurgling and choking. Ruth quickly pumped more air into his mouth.

"Ruth, are you there?" asked Juliana. She sounded different. Wrong somehow. Ruth was too groggy to ask why.

"I'm still here."

"I'm leaving the supplies outside the door. I have to make the morning meal. I'll be back in a little while."

It took Ruth a second to realize she meant the IV supplies. "Did you make Bill promise to wait?" she called, but Juliana had already walked away. Ruth shrugged. Of course she had. Juliana had given her word that she wouldn't leave until he promised. And he wouldn't do it without her. She'd told him herself that she'd be back today. Charlie was safe. He had to be. She opened the door and pulled a large shopping bag full of supplies into the room. She frowned. There were IV bags and tubing packets just flung in haphazardly. At least the catheters were in their usual hard case. Bill wasn't normally this messy. It must have been a very bad day with Charlie. Or his wound was really bothering him. She hurried to get the IV set up, transferring some of her anxious energy into action, though it wouldn't help her get home any faster.

There was a clunk outside the door a little while later as Juliana set breakfast bowls beside the door. She hurried away again without speaking. Ruth watched her patient. The color was returning to his face as the IV fluids slowly dripped into him. She let the ambu bag go for a few minutes. His breath was crackling with phlegm, but he was sleeping easily now. Ruth decided to clean herself up and eat. She opened the door and wiped herself down with the alcohol and rags again. She ate the oatmeal that had cooled into a thick sludgy lump outside the door. With her stomach full, the sun shining through the broad hallway windows, and her own breath constricted from the face mask she kept on, Ruth dozed off. Not even the shrieks of the Infected as they cried for more food woke her. Juliana shook her awake as the sun was staining the glass in the window to a golden red. Ruth sat up startled.

"Is he okay now?" Juliana asked.

"I think so, let me check on his progress." Ruth got up and slid into the room. The man stared at her as she entered. The IV bag was almost empty. Ruth switched it out, glancing at her patient, but waiting for him to speak. He didn't.

"Are you— can you talk?" Ruth asked, without getting closer. The man wrinkled his brow and looked at her intensely, but nothing happened. "I need to check your breathing. Do you understand?" Ruth held up the stethoscope so he could see. She was shocked when he nodded. She slowly knelt near him. He didn't move as she touched the stethoscope to his chest and then walked behind him to check his back. She could tell the fluid in his lungs was subsiding. His body was fighting off the pneumonia. Was it also fighting off the December Plague? Ruth felt a jolt of excitement. There wasn't any more to do for him, he'd fight it off himself now. She'd tell Juliana and then go home. Go home and tell Bill.

"I'm— I'm going to get Juliana. She won't be

able to come in, because you are still contagious. But I'll be back later and she'll bring you food. If you show us that we can trust you, we'll take off those restraints. I'm sure this is very confusing. I wish I could explain, and I will, but first I think we need to concentrate on getting you well." The man just stared at her. Ruth offered him an awkward doctor smile and then bolted from the room. Juliana was waiting for her just outside.

"Is he okay?" she asked.

"He's fighting off the pneumonia. It'll take some time, but he should recover very well. No only that, but I think his body is also conquering the Plague." The mask crinkled around her cheeks as she grinned.

"Is that possible? Will they all start to recover now?"

"I don't know, it's still too early to tell if the bacteria has run its course or if it's been defeated by something in his immune system. But it means there's hope for the rest of them and for Charlie. What do you know about him? Did his family bring him? I'd like to talk to them."

Juliana shook her head. "Someone found him on the road, too sick to be a threat. He didn't have a wallet or anything, just rags of black clothes. And a bell was tied to his neck."

Ruth frowned. "A bell? Like a cow bell?"

"No— a hand bell. Like a teacher used to use a long time ago. The only other place I've seen them is in church. It was heavy. I thought that might be why he was having trouble breathing. That's all that he came here with."

Ruth shrugged and then disinfected her

hands again and rummaged around in her kit. There'd be time to find it out from the man himself. She pulled out a few more face masks. "Look, he's stable for now. I'll be back by this evening, but I need to go home and tell Bill. This changes everything—"

"Ruth," said Juliana, her smile fading.

"Look, it'll be fine. Just wear the mask and make sure to wash your hands before—"

"Ruth, I have to tell you something."

"I won't be gone long. You don't even have to go in, just slide his bowl to him from the doorway. I'm telling you, he's almost sane."

"Ruth!" Juliana raised her voice a little and Ruth stopped and looked at her. "When I went to your house, I looked for your husband everywhere. I called and called, but nobody came to the door." Ruth felt an oily wave of nausea begin in her gut. Juliana put a hand on Ruth's shoulder as she continued. "I knew you needed those IV supplies, so I went into your house. I kept calling for your husband, but there was no answer."

"Did you hear anything? Did you hear Charlie?"

"The house was quiet. I found your lab in the basement and grabbed what I could find from your list. I'm sorry, Ruth."

"Maybe they are out. Maybe Bill needed something. He's been really reluctant to leave Charlie in the house alone when we make supply runs. Maybe he found a way to take him."

Juliana shook her head. "I promised you I'd give him your message before I left. I thought if I couldn't find him, I'd leave him a written note at the very least. It seemed so important to you. I couldn't find any paper in your living room or kitchen. I should have gone back down to the lab. I'm sorry Ruth, I don't know why I didn't look in the lab instead."

Ruth's heart was pounding so loudly in her ears that Juliana's voice was almost lost in the rush of her own blood. She didn't want to hear the rest, but Juliana's hand on her shoulder felt like an anchor keeping her frozen in place. "I went upstairs to find some paper and saw a whole notebook lying in front of the bedroom door. They were in there."

"They?" asked Ruth.

Juliana nodded and she began to cry. "I'm so sorry," she sobbed, and tried to hug Ruth. But medicine had been a way of life for so long, that Ruth stopped her out of habit.

"I could be contagious," she said, her face a blank. Juliana just wiped her eyes and hugged herself, still crying. Ruth was confused. She thought she should be crying too, but she didn't really know why. Her mind, usually so busy and rapid, was like a cold, empty room. It had all stopped. "Okay," she said at last, "I'll go home and tell Bill. I'll go see him upstairs."

Juliana shook her head but didn't try to stop her. Ruth picked up her kit and walked back down the long gray hallway toward the entrance. She took off her mask and crumpled it into a ball in her hand. The city was a lavender shadow as she walked home. The thaw had finally started and Ruth fell through the dissolving crust into deep snow several times. It was slow going and she was soaked and freezing before she got halfway. Her brain kept trying to jumpstart, like she was being shaken partly awake. *Today was the day,* she'd think, but then the thought would shut off. *The day for what?* It was like poking a bruise. She tried not to ask too hard or too often.

She passed a corner market that she didn't remember scavenging before and decided to go inside. It was an Asian grocery. Ruth wandered around in the dark aisles looking for Charlie's favorite brand of peanut butter before realizing the shelves were almost completely empty except for a few marinade bottles and a some packets of freeze dried seaweed snacks. Even the tea was scattered and spoiled. She absentmindedly grabbed a box of rice candy that the mice and scavengers hadn't gotten to, some subconscious part of her knowing that it didn't matter anyway.

She stopped at the end of her street. The house was dark. *Bill must have let the generator run out of gas,* she thought. *I hope he's started a fire in the fireplace. Charlie will get cold.* Her brain took a sideslip again. *I can't remember if it's a school night. With all this snow they'll have to cancel. Maybe Charlie will play cards with me and Bill in front of the fireplace until the power comes back on.* She shook herself and looked around, realizing the thought was wrong, but not why it was wrong. She shrugged and trudged up to the house.

She went inside to get the last can of gas and powered up the generator. She frowned as she noticed the footprints on the little shed above it, forgetting they were hers from the day before. *I have to tell Charlie not to play on the shed. He could get hurt if it collapsed.* The generator roared on; out of habit, she glanced up and down the street, but nothing came. She went into the house and began shucking her wet clothes. The fireplace was dark and the house was as cold as the street had been.

"Bill?" she called. *Oh, that's right, they're upstairs,* she thought and put a hand on the banister. Something inside fought with her though, not wanting her to go up. Not wanting her to see what she already knew. She tried to remember why she'd rushed home. She had something to tell Bill. Maybe seeing him would make her remember. She started up the stairs to the bedrooms. She opened the door to her own first. Bill wasn't in there. She got dressed in dry clothing and then headed down the hallway to Charlie's room. She tripped over the notebook Juliana had mentioned and picked it up. Taped to the paper was a thin plastic syringe, it's cap on tight and a tiny silver bubble floating in the center. Below it were just a few lines in Bill's handwriting.

Ruth-

It had to be today. I'm sorry. We couldn't wait any longer. We'll see you soon.

She placed the notebook carefully on the accent table nearby. The syringe flashed in the yellow electric light. She opened the door to Charlie's room.

They were slumped on the floor, Charlie lying with his head on Bill's chest, just the way he had when he was small. The room was terribly silent. Ruth watched Charlie's stomach for a few long minutes willing it to bubble out with an inhale. She used to stand by his crib and watch the same way. She'd been so scared that he would just — just stop. Every night. She knew it was a compulsion, but she'd checked every night, for years. Always the same few agonizing seconds between breaths and then the relief of his rising chest and she'd blow out her own breath and realize she'd been holding it. But now his belly was still. She knelt down beside them, touched Charlie's cheek, hoping to feel warm skin. But his face was cold and stiff like canvas. She looked up at Bill. His eyes were closed and his arms were around their son. She had imagined they would look peaceful or eased afterward, but Bill just looked blank. Like a mannequin, expressionless, almost unrecognizable. She didn't have to check his pulse to know he was gone. She sat back on her haunches.

"But I had good news," she said, "why couldn't you wait? What was one more night? I could have saved us." She curled up next to them, the cold from their skin radiating into hers. She wanted to cry. She needed to cry. But she couldn't. A dull ache spread from her chest to the rest of her body. Shock, and pain and exhaustion overtook her.

Juliana found her asleep next to the corpses of her son and husband the next morning.

CHAPTER 5

Seven Years Later

It had seemed like such an obvious place to look. People had always gravitated toward water, why was it any different now? But she and Frank had covered hundreds of miles of coastline looking for survivors, new little towns springing up or just small bands of wandering scavengers. Almost a decade after the December Plague hit, Nella had expected hundreds, thousands of people even, to be clustered near the ocean, building new lives. The ocean was full of food; the fish population had thrived, and it was a quick escape if a village were threatened. It's why her home city sat where it did. But after the first few days, as they reached the edge of their existing trade network, they'd seen almost no one.

Once, they'd seen a few small boats on the horizon that Nella hoped were fishermen. And they'd found a lighthouse keeper who had been alone since the Plague hit, who kept the lamp lit anyway. Its beacon had saved their small sailboat, but Nella had the eerie feeling that he'd kept it going for someone else, for hundreds of ghost ships that would never arrive.

Then she and Frank had wasted almost a week scrambling through the burnt rubble of the capitol city. It was the first place they had planned to go, it had made sense. They had both given up on any kind of government rescue years before, on any kind of government existing, save their own military governor. But others wouldn't have given up. They would have flocked to the capitol looking for aid, to rebuild, to find other survivors. They had even avoided the port, hiding the boat miles away in case the people didn't turn out to be friendly.

They should have known almost immediately, though, that the capitol had been abandoned. It hadn't struck Nella as odd that nobody met them on the little back roads, that was why they had chosen the little hotel dock on the edge of farmland. A few days later, they reached a four-lane highway, and still met no one.

The highway was breaking up, saplings shooting up through the edges of the tar, charred rings dotted the roadway where refugees had lit campfires along the way. Stray cars had been moved into the median, sprouting grass in the cracks of the hoods and trunks, puffing angry balls of mosquitos from the wells of the flat tires. All the signs of people were there, but nobody moved along the road. There were no new signs or markets along the way, something common on the roads leading to Frank and Nella's city. Frank was just ahead of her, his body a cool blade of shadow against the hazy setting sun. He whistled as he crested a slight hill and turned back toward her.

"You've got to see this, it's incredible."

She hurried up the hill and looked down into a low plain. It was obviously marsh most of the year, the thick odor of decaying leaves still strong in the dry heat of the early summer. A herd of deer jostled and crowded each other, their brown backs like a heat shimmer over the long grass. More than a hundred of them wandering over eight crumbling lanes where thousands of cars had zipped through just a decade before.

"I haven't seen a deer in years," said Nella, "I thought they were all eaten. I thought the Infected got them."

Frank shaded his eyes with one hand. "It's the capitol, maybe the Infected were better contained here. I heard on the radio in the shelter that the President issued an executive order to shoot on sight. They would have protected the capitol before everything else."

Nella tore her gaze from the animals and scanned the horizon, looking for some sign of the large buildings of the capitol, buildings that should have been visible by then. "What about survivors? What are they eating? Wouldn't they hunt any game in the area?"

She saw a frown flash over his face, but he glanced at her and quickly exchanged it for a grin. "C'mon Nella, when have you ever heard of a politician performing actual manual labor?"

She smiled back, but when she took his hand, he squeezed it a little too tightly. *Joking aside, what about the refugees?* People who had camped on the road before them had almost certainly been hungry and used to providing for themselves. A herd of deer like this would feed hundreds of people. Unease began to rumble through her. She tried to shake it off. "Do you think we should go around them?"

He shook his head. "No, we can go through, they'll probably scatter when we get closer."

They walked down the slope, heavy hiking boots clumping against the road, the boxes of Cure darts jingling in Nella's pack. A few of the deer looked up at them, chewing lazily. None of them moved. Frank waved his long arms at them, but the few that had looked up went back to grazing and ignored him.

They were within reach of the outskirts of the herd. For a moment Nella forgot her worry in the thrill of touching a sleek, furry pelt in front of her. The doe she touched looked up at her and snuffled Nella's outstretched hand.

"Maybe they were petting zoo deer," offered Frank quietly. The doe's ears twitched but it didn't bolt.

"Or maybe they've never seen a human before," Nella responded.

Frank frowned. "That's impossible. The capitol is huge, there must be people that pass by here every day, even after the Plague."

Nella bent over and ripped up a bundle of grass. She offered it to the doe. The animal pulled it gently from her grip. "We haven't seen anyone."

"Maybe they blocked off this side for some reason."

"Maybe."

Frank began gently pushing his way through the herd. "Careful," said Nella softly, "if they get spooked we might be trampled." She followed him through the warm, shifting mass of beasts. "Are we going to make it before nightfall?"

Once they made it up the next hill and had left the deer behind, he pulled out a battered road atlas from his pack and spread it open on the warm tar, crouching beside it. "We only have about a mile left. We should start seeing lights soon anyway, even if my measurement is off. Want to keep going or are you nervous about getting there in the dark?"

Nella knelt beside him, her hand fiddling with the handle of a heavy folded knife. "I was nervous about bands of looters or desperate refugees. I was even nervous about what a new government might be like when we reached the city. But now I'm scared that there won't be *anyone*. We should have seen rooftops by now. Monuments, spires, something. We should have seen new farms to feed the people in the capitol out here."

Frank reached around her shoulder and pulled her into a hug. "The trees are taller now, maybe they're just blocking the view a little farther than they used to. Maybe they've turned their parks into farms like we did. There are a lot more parks here than there are behind our Barrier."

Nella nodded. "I hope so. I think I'm more afraid of finding nothing than I am of finding hostile people."

Frank shook his head. "There were millions of people living here. Probably thousands more that must have come here over the past few years looking for help. There must be somebody. Or messages for another safe place, or something. We'll find someone."

He folded up the atlas and tucked it back into his pack. They turned onto the freeway exit and walked toward the dark line of toll booths. Squat and whistling where the breeze blew through the broken glass, they reminded Nella of gargoyles. Glass and coins flashed in the low light. She gripped the knife, scanning each booth quickly. It was a perfect ambush point. But they were here to *find* people, not avoid them. She took a deep breath and Frank slowed down to walk beside her. They passed between two booths and nothing happened. Frank glanced back as they walked away from the splintered remains of the gate-arm, but nothing was there.

The exit ramp dumped them into a bedroom community just a few miles outside the northern edge of the capitol. Walking in twilight through overgrown lawns in front of brick colonial buildings, the flash of early fireflies disoriented Nella. She looked for steadier sources of light, but there were none. The large houses pressed together, shrinking the grass between them, and at last fell behind them as shopping centers and gas stations took over. It was very dark now, no street lights, no glow from any window or fire. Nella strained to hear any sound, any voice, but only her own footsteps echoing Frank's met her ear.

"I can barely see my hand in front of my face, Frank."

Frank sighed heavily. He rubbed his hand over his head, and Nella patted his arm. "We'll find someone," she reassured him. "There must be someone. Maybe there's no water on this side of town. Or maybe there was a barricade and nobody has bothered to dismantle it and expand this way yet. Remember, they don't have thousands of Cured to make room for. Even with thousands of refugees there is probably still far more space than people. But we can't do anything in the dark."

Frank looked relieved. "You're right," he said, "I had it in my head that there would be all these people, just like home, but of course there couldn't be. The whole point was to bring them the Cure. And moving resources like water and fuel is difficult now." He squinted into the dark and then pointed across the street. "There's a pawn shop over there, the security gate is halfway up but I bet we can secure it."

They found the door unlocked. "Hello?" Nella called as Frank rolled the gate down behind them. Nobody answered. Nella pulled the camping lantern from her pack and set it near the gate. It didn't give off much more than a dull glow. Frank looked at the lock and shook his head.

"It's broken. But I don't have the key anyway. We can lock the glass door and sleep in the back where there aren't any windows." He picked up the lantern and closed the door. "I think it's almost out of batteries Nella."

"Maybe we can find some here," she said feeling her way toward the interior. They slept on a pile of fur coats that had been hanging on the back wall.

Nella woke to a grid of gray light struggling through the security gate. She pushed the gate up and let the bright summer sun shine into the shop. It seemed intact. Nothing had been looted. It made sense, she guessed, what would anyone want old jewelry and electronics for now? She checked behind the counter for batteries. A few old ones rolled around the bottom of the cash drawer. She pocketed them but figured they were probably no good now. A large flashlight was tucked under the jewelry counter and Nella tried flipping it on. No good. She unscrewed the back, but the batteries had corroded the inside to a foamy white mess.

Frank emerged from the back holding a ragged sheet of newspaper. It was printed only on one side and the letters were muddy, like an old mimeograph.

"What is it?" asked Nella

"Well, there was someone here after the Plague. Someone organized enough to print and distribute notices anyway." He held it up so she could read it.

Any persons with electrical skills, medical knowledge, or ham radio operators needed. Please report to 6900 Georgia Ave on Monday, February 3rd. Food dispensation will double this week in case of severe storms. Please plan accordingly.

Residents are warned about killing protected trees for firewood. Trees in park areas belong to the community. Violators will be shot on sight.

Nella began folding the paper, uninterested in the rest of the announcements. She stopped when she glanced at the date. "Frank, this paper is over three years old now."

"Maybe this place was abandoned. There's nothing terribly useful here. Or maybe they forgot to change the date, or ran out of numbers or something. Dates don't seem to matter too much any more."

"I guess we need to go to Georgia Avenue to find out. What was there?"

Frank put his pack on the counter and fished out the atlas. "A medical museum. Or an army hospital? I think both."

"How long will it take us to get there?"

"A few hours if we cut through the subway. We have one more battery for the lantern, that should get us there."

Nella shuddered at the thought of the blank dark of the tunnels.

"I'm sorry, I forgot." said Frank, "We don't have to go into the subway. We can go through the streets if you'd rather, but we'll have to camp again."

Nella shook her head. "No, I can do it. Every hour we are away from the boat I worry that someone else has found it."

"I'll be with you."

Nella smiled. "I know," she said and kissed him.

CHAPTER 6

The thick glass door flung open and Ruth heard Father Preston's ragged flock hurling screams at the man who entered. She leaned forward in her seat and closed her paperback book around her thumb. She tried to peer through the filthy reception window, but she couldn't make out who it was until he came closer.

"Nick," she sighed. He pushed two rolls of toilet paper and a jar of cooking oil into the transaction drawer. "We talked about this. No kids."

The man fumbled in his pocket. He pulled out a coppery bit of metal. His hands shook as he placed the bullet on the bottom of the transaction drawer. Both Ruth and the man stared at it, dulled from years of rolling between the man's fingers. He shoved the transaction drawer closed and it popped open on Ruth's side of the window with a bang. She looked up again at the man. His nose slid sideways from a recent break. A filthy band-aid curled up from the stubble on his cheek and flapped with every ragged breath. His eyes were two reverse suns, weariness radiating from the creases in his skin.

"I don't do kids, Nick. Why do we have to go through this every week?"

"It's Emma's birthday today," said Nick and his lips split into a slow smile of relief, "she's eighteen today."

"I don't believe you," said Ruth pushing the transaction drawer closed. It opened with a squeal on his side of the window. Nick's face flooded with color and the creases in his skin deepened as a flash of rage passed over him. But then the slow smile came back and he reached into his back pocket. Ruth's stomach felt as if it were being sucked up by toilet plunger. Nick pulled out a dogeared, yellowing envelope. He threw it into the transaction drawer.

"I thought you might say that," he said, and closed the drawer again. Ruth picked up the envelope. "Emma Jean Fowler" was penciled lightly across the front, the marks so faded that she was almost reading the indents instead. Inside was a birth certificate. She put it back in the drawer.

"Are you sure?" she asked, "What about taking her to Juliana's hospital?"

Nick raised a fist and banged once on the glass. He leaned his face into his arm and looked at her through the smears. "Every week. I've come here every week since I heard about you six years ago, Ruth. I've begged and begged. You've turned me away every week. You tell me you won't do it for a child, but does she suffer any less than an adult? You think she doesn't feel as bad as the others? Or worse? She's confused. Scared maybe. All this time—"

"I won't do children because I *can't,* Nick. I've tried. I know, as well as you, how bad it is for them. I just can't."

Nick nodded against his arm. "I know," he sighed, "I'm not angry. I know why. But she isn't a child any more. And I can't watch her— *consume* herself any more. She screams, God, the screams! I haven't slept in eight *years*. I've given her the best care I could. The very best. Emma's wrists have permanent scars from the straps. I remove the straps every day. I clean them. I clean her. I replace the padding. Sometimes I can't bear to tighten them again when I put them back on, and she gets loose. She bites me, or claws me," Nick gestured to the loose band-aid on his cheek, "someday, she'll get loose and kill someone. I hope it's me and not someone else's baby. Nothing helps. She's still in pain. I take care of her mess, every hour or two. I put her in clean clothes every day. Wash the old ones in water I drag from the hydrant down the block. Wash her diapers, too. Brush her teeth and her hair, even though she tries to chew my hand off. Who else is going to do that for her? Juliana may be a good woman, but people say she's got more than a hundred of 'em penned up in there. Just her and that Father Preston, who yells at me every week when I walk through these doors. You think he's going to change my girl's diapers? He's not got a speck of mercy in him. And Juliana— it's a miracle she can get enough out of that little garden to feed them every day. She doesn't have time to bandage Emma's arms or untangle her hair. No one's going to give her what I have," a tear slithered down through the stubble on his cheek. "But it doesn't matter. It never gets better. She's in pain now, and she'd be in more pain at the hospital. I can't think of her like that." He stood up straight and cleared his throat. He jammed one hand in his pocket and pointed at Ruth with the other. "So you're going to give us her birthday present."

Ruth hesitated and the flush came back to Nick's skin. "What?" he cried, "Is this not enough? It's all I could scrape together. I'd hoped to get enough for you to do both of us—"

"I don't do healthy people either."

"I know. I can handle myself. But I need to know Emma's seen to first. I'll get more somehow. What do you want? Matches? Baby formula? Batteries? I'll find them, I swear. Just— just don't make us wait anymore."

Ruth shook her head. "I don't need more. I just needed to be sure that you were ready. I wasn't, when it came to it." She picked up the bullet.

Nick's eyes widened. "But I thought that you did this because of your own."

"I do. Nobody should have to kill their own child."

"Who did it for you?"

Ruth stacked the toilet paper and cooking oil in the empty supply cabinet and locked the door. She pocketed the bullet. "My husband," she said, "but he couldn't live with it either."

"I'm sorry," said Nick.

Ruth ignored him and walked out of the reception room, locking the door behind her. He looked even worse without the glass between them.

"Now?" he asked.

She put a hand on his shoulder. "If you want to take some time, say goodbye or— or get her dressed in something special, I can come tomorrow."

Nick shook his head. "No, now. No more waiting. Not another second of pain."

Ruth walk.ed toward the glass door. "Should I— should I wait here?" he called after her.

She turned around. "If you are comfortable here, it's as good a place as any."

He nodded.

"Don't come home before sunset," she said, "that's when the crazy priest leaves." She opened the door. The asphalt panted with heat. Father Preston's filthy black shirt clung to his chest and sweat matted his dark hair. His face hooked into a snarl as Ruth emerged from the police department. He looked almost as vicious as he had when he was Infected. She still felt the ache of her arms from compressing the ambubag every time she saw him. And all for what? So he and his rabid Congregation could hound her every time she tried to help someone?

"Murderess!" he shrieked, "Faithless, craven monster! Is she all nice and tied up for you? Waiting to be sacrificed on the altar you built for yourself? How many children, Ruth?" He smacked the community board behind him with the back of his hand. Ruth's eyes snapped to the photos.

"Don't you touch those," she hissed, "those are not for you."

The priest looked surprised and turned toward the board. Behind the plastic shield, dozens of faces smiled out. He turned back toward her. "Don't want me to ruin your trophies? You're sick. You were a *doctor*. How can you do this? You have to be stopped," he raised his arms toward the small group of people around him, "She's going to murder another innocent victim of the Plague. To bathe in the blood of a child whose only crime was falling ill. She was a mother too, she killed her own child and now she murders others. Heartless, unnatural, wicked harlot! Will no one stop her? Will no one be a warrior for God?"

Ruth just kept walking. She'd made the mistake of retorting before. One of the men took a step toward her, but stopped as the afternoon light sparked from the metal edge of the pistol hanging at her waist. An elderly woman farther up the street shuffled toward her with a broad smile. The gray braid that circled her head was fuzzy with fly-aways that caught the sunlight and made a white-hot halo around her. She held a great black bible in her thin arms and stretched it out toward Ruth. She hadn't been with the protesters before, she was new. Ruth sighed and slowed down.

"This isn't something I enjoy," Ruth offered, "The girl is in terrible pain. It never ends. And it never will—"

Father Preston began shouting over her. "Through suffering we are cleansed! If the girl and her father repent and pray, she will be cured. Nothing is beyond God! I was cured—"

Ruth whirled around to look at him. "You stupid, arrogant man. What makes you think you are better or holier than all the people who have succumbed to this? You think you're more guiltless than children? Than *my* child?" She was so angry she didn't notice the massive bible raised over the smiling old woman's head until the leather cracked with a loud thud into her back. Ruth stumbled forward a step and watched the other protesters begin closing in around her. She swung around and knocked the book out of the old woman's hand. It skidded across the baking tar and the thin leaves fluttered, their words floating on the translucent paper. Ruth fumbled with her holster and pulled out the gun.

"Back up!" she shouted, swinging in an arc, "All of you back up."

"You see?" yelled Father Preston pointing a crooked finger at her, "The monster shows her true nature."

The others looked uncertain as Ruth changed focus between each of them. She didn't waste her breath arguing. She backed out of the circle of people.

"I wouldn't waste the blood of the faithful on someone like you, Ruth," sneered the priest.

Ruth turned her back on them and walked into the silent city, passing into the cool shadow of the rusting buildings. After a block, she put the gun back in its holster and began the long walk to Emma's house.

The heat was muted between intersections, the sun had given up the battle and partially fallen behind the tall buildings, still blasting through the empty lots occasionally. The flooded subways made it worse, steam curling up from the stairwells, still carrying a foul human odor even after almost a decade. Swarms of mosquitoes hovered around the openings, breeding in the still water. Ruth wondered what they ate. Dogs maybe. There were still lots of them. Or maybe they fed on infected people who still managed to cling to life by attacking rats or pigeons or the occasional person that still wandered the street. She wondered if it was the lack of people or luck that had prevented a malaria outbreak. There were so many things to worry about now.

She'd thought it would stop after losing Charlie and Bill, that she wouldn't care any more.

And a part of her didn't. But Ruth didn't like the idea of suffering. Especially alone. At first, she'd just been trying to avoid the most brutal methods of dying. There were so many now. The sick people had roamed the streets for the first few years, attacking and killing anything they found. But winter, starvation, battles with others and secondary diseases had killed off a good portion of them.

Just after Bill had killed himself, bands of scavenging survivors had swept through most of the city, the last wave of people fleeing. They had taken what they wanted, when they wanted it. There were too many weapons just lying around. Everyone was armed. Ruth had hidden until the city was silent again. But the loneliness was deadly. A bad fall while scavenging, allowing a door to close and lock behind her, even letting a fire go out in the winter, death waited in the simplest things now. And that wasn't even counting the microbial threats. Ruth knew too much about those. Most diseases simply didn't have a method of transmission now that everyone was gone, even the corpses. But even a rusty nail could be the start of a terrible, unstoppable infection now.

The fear of a painful death had made her seek out the stragglers, the people that stayed. There were hundreds, maybe even a few thousand. But they were scattered all over the large metropolis. Ruth only knew a handful. But many, many of them knew who *she* was.

She'd come to Emma's address. Just another row house in the middle of a long string of others. Nothing special. Just like the day. *Just like Emma,*

Ruth told herself. But it was a lie. They were *all* special, all different. She'd done this dozens of times, kept expecting them to blur, meld, become one nameless face in her memory. But they remained stubbornly unique.

She stood on the top cement step and leaned in toward the front window. The summer sun was too bright and bounced off the glass. Ruth pulled her gun from its holster. She expected that Nick would have told her if Emma was loose, but she had been surprised before. The knob rattled loosely as she opened the door. Emma heard it and began banging somewhere overhead. Ruth put away the gun, satisfied that the girl was restrained. As she closed the door, the growling from Emma's room bubbled over into a shriek of rage. It was like raw, searing pain spilling into the air. Ruth couldn't stand that shriek, not since Charlie. She pulled a pair of headphones from her pocket and shoved one into each ear. A second later, Dvorak washed away the screams. But it couldn't mask the world around her.

The living room was barren, except for a few long clotheslines strung across it. Strips of torn cloth hung from them, the sepia ghost of old, washed blood staining them. Ruth touched one, realizing it was a homemade bandage. There had still been real ones for Charlie. She had thought their lives were so difficult that first year. But they had medicine and gas and food then. It had been almost six years since she'd seen a sterile gauze pad. Ruth ducked beneath the streamers of cloth. The back of the room was also bare, except for a pile of broken furniture and an axe sitting in front of a large old fireplace. It was nothing unfamiliar. They all did it.

Ruth and Bill had raided the hardware stores first, but that didn't last long, almost everyone else had the same idea. After Bill and Charlie died, Ruth raided the empty neighboring homes for anything wooden. But wood was getting scarce in the city. The stairs were just beyond the fireplace. Ruth climbed them slowly, examining each picture that hung beside them in the gloomy half-light. She pulled Emma's fourth grade school picture from its frame. One of Emma's front baby teeth was missing, its replacement half in and giving her smile a slightly crooked look. There was a star barrette pinning her hair back. Her white shirt was startling against the fake leaf background.

Ruth put the photo into her pocket, sliding it carefully under the slim MP3 player so that it wouldn't bend. She reached the top of the stairs. The hallway was narrow but surprisingly bright, one side studded with large, dusty windows. Three doors sunk into the opposite wall. There was a blue five gallon bucket in front of the middle one, and a heavy hydrant wrench lay beside it, its red paint flaking in spots.

Ruth pushed the bucket and wrench back to the top of the stairs, and opened the middle door, to see a small bathroom. The window was cracked and stuffed with rags to keep the breeze out. Wax ends of candles slumped over the edges of the sink and puddled in disks on the floor. Ruth picked two that were still large pillars and lit them. The wallpapered walls were dented in half a dozen places where they had been struck. The paper hung in thin, horizontal strips. where someone's nails had dragged down the wall. The mirror over the sink was long gone, leaving behind a lighter mark and a shallow, naked cabinet.

Ruth ignored the obvious signs of struggle and turned to the bathtub. She found the drain plug and squeezed it into place. Leather mittens hung from long straps that were bolted into the tile and a grey plastic hockey mask hung from the shower head, its inside dark with flakes of dried blood. Ruth quickly looked away.

Bill had always held Charlie while Ruth bathed him. She'd never had to strap him into anything. But she'd also had sedatives. Every time she did this, she became more convinced that Bill had been right. Charlie was better off this way. Ruth was better off. It didn't stop her from aching for both of them though. Ruth pushed back from the tub and left the room with the candles still burning.

The door to the left shuddered. Ruth ignored it, turning her music up. She opened the far door. A large mattress remained in the center of the room, but the rest was bare, the carpet still dented with the footprints of heavy chairs. A small pile of clothes sat where a dresser ought to go. The doors to the closet were also gone, burned some winter before. Ruth could see dresses still hanging inside and a thin pile of blankets and sheets stacked beneath. It occurred to her to wonder where Emma's mother was. She'd never asked. It was easy to assume Nick had done for her what he could not bring himself to do for Emma. It disturbed Ruth that it was far easier to imagine someone killing their spouse than their child— as if one life were less worthy than the other. She slowly flipped through the dresses and remembered how angry she'd been at Bill.

If he'd just waited until she got back— even if he hadn't believed her, even if it were just to let her say goodbye. Instead, twelve years of laughing together, fighting and loving all gone in one cold little line on a slumping notebook in front of Charlie's door. Why didn't she join them? Why seven more years doing the same penance over and over? Because that's what she was doing here, and all the other times before. Penance. Doing what she had failed to do for Charlie. She didn't have an answer for herself.

She pulled out a light summer dress, one that should have floated down the boardwalk at the beach. Ruth knelt down and found an untorn white sheet. Smacking the dust out of the cloth, she brought both into the bathroom. Then she picked up the bucket and hydrant wrench and headed back downstairs.

She stopped the music as she reached the front door. Emma still pounded on the floor above, and her cries had become plaintive. She sounded more like a small child who wanted her mother than a raging young woman. It deepened the ache in Ruth's chest, but she couldn't risk going into the street without being able to hear. She ground her teeth and stepped outside. The day was softening, leaking away. The cement world gave its heat back to the sky and Ruth knew she only had an hour before Nick returned. She opened the hydrant and let the sluggish water tumble into the bucket. She left the music off as she carried the water to the bathroom. It was time now anyway. The water sloshed into the dusty tub, but it took two more trips to get a decent amount. Then she pulled the picture from her pocket, reminding herself one last time what the little girl had been like, the face that *should* be remembered, not whatever paced behind the first door. She slid the photograph into the edge of the doorframe so she could focus on the girl smiling out at her as Ruth checked the bullet in her gun. Her eyes blurred, just as they always did at this point. She sniffled and blinked hard. She took a deep breath and raised the gun with one arm. Her free hand turned the door handle.

The door sank away into the room. For a second the dust hung sparkling gold in the afternoon light from the windows. Ruth exhaled and the dust bounced and spiraled in the tiny breeze. Then there was a low gurgling growl from the far corner. The light pad of bare feet on wood and Emma's face sprang up just beyond the barrel of Ruth's gun. The girl was grown up now, grown old. All the round softness chipped away from her face. Her sleepless eyes sunken and darting, looking for something. They never focused, never were still. Emma's hair hung in strings, caked with food and dirt, sweat and old blood. Her clothes were soiled though Ruth knew that Nick changed her every day. Her hands and arms were bandaged to the elbows, but Ruth could smell an infected wound. The secondary infection would kill her even if Ruth didn't.

Emma strained against the thick canvas

ropes around her wrists and ankles. The muscles in her neck and shoulders jumped and pulled as she snarled. She turned red with the strain and her teeth snapped shut over and over with a nauseating click.

"It's okay," said Ruth, "Your daddy sent me. It's all done. No more crying. You can rest now, Emma." She took a step forward as she was speaking, the gun barrel brushing lightly against Emma's forehead as she struggled to bite. Ruth pulled the trigger and Emma fell to the floor like a marionette whose strings had suddenly snapped. She put the gun away and wiped her hands quickly down the front of her shirt without even thinking about it. She pulled the picture from the doorframe and slid it back into her pocket. Then she picked up the bony girl, her arms and chin resting on Ruth's shoulders, the way a sleeping toddler would.

Ruth tried not to look at her, fighting to keep the image from the photograph in the front of her mind. Emma seemed even lighter than Charlie had, though he had been just nine when Ruth had carried him down the stairs to the gaping hollow in her tiny lawn.

She placed Emma on the cool tile in the bathroom and removed her soiled clothes. Then she lowered the girl into the water and did her best to erase the damage of the past eight years. Now that the snarling rage had gone out of Emma's face, she looked younger and pensive. But the rest of her body betrayed her. The scars on her hands where she had bitten them, the wound on her arm, the bruises from the restraints all shattered the peace in her face. Ruth drained the tub and gently dried the body before sliding the airy summer dress over it. She wrapped it in the dusty sheet and then looked around her. The light from the window seeped russet around the rag. Almost time. She blew out the candles and carried the stiff gray bundle back to Emma's room.

There was no bed to lay it on; Emma had torn it to shreds years ago. Ruth laid the body on the floor, then she looked around for a moment at the wreckage of the room. The furniture was gone. The carpet long ripped away, leaving the bones of subfloor beneath. The dry wall was mostly pounded into dust in the semicircle that Emma had been able to reach in her restraints. The studs stood like matchsticks gleaming in the wall. She thought how close to Charlie's room it must once have been and then tried to push the thought away. She wiped away a few slow tears and left the room, closing the door quietly behind her. She fled the silent house as the sun disappeared below the far end of the street.

CHAPTER 7

Juliana was up to her knees in the pond outside the conservatory. A thick film of algae clung to her jeans at the water line and to the outside of the buckets she filled. Ruth picked up two more empty buckets and kicked off her hot shoes before wading in behind her.

"This heat is killing everything but the tropicals you revived," said Juliana without turning around.

"Too cold in the winter and too hot in the summer. We've got to get out of this city. It's the asphalt that does it," said Ruth, pouring a bucket full of scummy green water over her head.

Juliana slogged out of the pond and set the full buckets onto the concrete, breathing hard. She sat on the warm walkway, her face lost in the twilight. "How can I leave?"

Ruth picked up her own buckets. "We could find a bus. One with restraints, like a prison bus—"

"Even if we could get one started, there hasn't been usable gasoline in this city for years."

"Sedatives then."

Juliana shook her head. "Too risky. Besides, there's a hundred of them and two of us. Can you imagine us trying to get them down the road before the sedative wore off?"

Ruth sat down beside her and was silent for a long moment. "No one could blame you if you just walked away tomorrow, you know. They survived for eight more years because of you. They aren't even yours. You don't owe anyone anything."

"If I leave, I'll have to either let them all go or leave them to starve. That's monstrous. I can't do it."

"There's another alternative, Juliana," said Ruth quietly.

"You mean we could kill them."

"It could be quick and quiet. The dried poppies we already have should be almost enough. Another month and this year's will be ready. They're in pain, Juliana. And you are wearing your life away to keep them that way. We can't stay here, Julie. The city is dying. Another winter and there'll be no food and nothing to burn. How many times have you chased looters from the vegetable garden already this year? And it's not even enough to support the people that you already care for. Relatives don't stop by to help anymore. They don't have anything left to bring you. Things are going to get violent again, just like when the looters swept through six years ago. Are you going to risk being killed for a cucumber? Or starving with the Infected? Why? They're just dying in slow motion. It can be over in one night, no more hunger, no more rage, no more agony. It should have happened years ago. Every day is just prolonging their misery and yours."

Juliana scowled. "That's the trouble with you Ruth Socorro. You think there's no value in suffering. That we ought to spend all our lives without pain or fear or sorrow. I don't remember hearing that an easy life was the only one worth living. We aren't entitled to a painless existence," she snapped. "Now come on, or all the plants will die of thirst and we'll *all* begin to know real suffering." She picked up her buckets and started into the steamy conservatory. Ruth followed after, wondering what had *really* caused her friend's sudden fury.

The heat made it a struggle to breathe, so they splashed the neat rows of herbs, but didn't talk. Every once in a while Ruth would stop to pull a stray weed, watching Juliana out of the corner of her eye. The conservatory was already filled with shadows and the solar garden stakes glowed dimly.

"Do the bandages on the red headed boy need to be changed?" Ruth asked, to break the thick silence.

"I can do it," said Juliana, but her tone had softened. "Who was it today?" she asked, swinging an empty bucket toward the smear of dark blood on Ruth's jean leg. Ruth blushed, ashamed that she had missed it when she cleaned herself up.

"You really want to know?" asked Ruth.

Juliana was silent, but didn't move.

"Nick Fowler's daughter. It was her birthday today," sighed Ruth. She splashed another clump of plants so she wouldn't have to look at the other woman. "I tried to persuade him to give her to you, but..."

"But he didn't want to leave her behind when he killed himself, that about it?"

"Yeah, that's about it." Ruth turned around. "Look, I don't need a lecture. We've been over and over this. We agreed to disagree—" She stopped, surprised to see Juliana sitting on a nearby stone bench, the soft glow of the solar lights making her face ten years older. "What is it? What's happened?" Ruth asked.

"I consider you a friend, Ruth. My best friend. The truth is, I think you'd be my best friend even if the world weren't as empty as it is. You know, if we'd met Before."

Ruth set the half full bucket down and sat down on the bench. She could feel the heat radiating off the other woman even a few feet away.

"What would you do if I asked you to help me at the hospital?" asked Juliana.

"Then I would help you. I'm not a murderer, despite what you may think."

Juliana sighed. "That's not how I think of you. If anyone left in the world understands you, it's me. I work with them every day. I know why you think you're helping. But you overstep. You take something that isn't yours to take." She shook her head. "That isn't what I wanted to say. I've been very tired these past few weeks. There isn't anyone else to ask. Father Preston is busy with his Congregation—"

"Father Preston," Ruth scowled as if she'd tasted something dry and bitter. Juliana ignored her.

"I just need a little help, in the mornings maybe. Simple things, laundry or meals or just reading to them."

"Then I'll be there tomorrow morning." Ruth looked around at the dim conservatory. "We should both go home now, before the scavengers come out for the night." She glanced at Juliana who looked more tired than Ruth remembered ever seeing her. "Why don't I walk you back to the hospital? I'll bring the bundle and make dinner."

But Juliana shook her head. "Go home. I'll see you in the morning." She got slowly up and carried the empty buckets to the doorway and then disappeared into the warm, concrete night. Ruth stared after her for a moment. Then she left the conservatory by the opposite door, heading back to the silent police station. A sliver of moon broke the edge of the jagged line of dark buildings but it didn't shine bright enough to change much. Ruth didn't care, she knew the way back by feel now. All the breaks and dips in the asphalt, every recessed doorway, all the tiny alleys that she had never dared to walk alone in Before, now they were home. In the past eight years, she'd used them to hide from the Infected, scavengers, and packs of feral dogs. She'd outlasted almost all of them.

The police station was as silent as the rest of the world. She stopped and slid the photograph of Emma behind the plexiglass of the bulletin board, knowing which spots were bare without looking. She tripped over Nick as she entered the station. For an instant she feared he had killed himself right there. Then he rolled himself up with a groan. "Sorry Nick," she whispered, "Want a cot to crash on?"

He grabbed her wrist. "Is it done?" he hissed.

"It's done."

He let her go. "I'm going home."

"Do you want me to walk you there? It's very dark."

"Is it? It doesn't matter. I know the way." He swayed as he rose to his feet and Ruth held out an arm to steady him. He turned toward her and she could smell the sour despair on his breath as he spoke. "Eighteen years ago, there wasn't a five foot stretch of darkness between here and my house.

The traffic was bumper to bumper because it was a Friday. Even the sidewalk was crowded with people. I took my wife to the hospital on the subway because I didn't think we'd make it in time if I drove. It was so hot, just like now. I thought Sarah would faint, but she made it to the emergency room. And the air conditioning slapped into us and the nurses scurrying back and forth—*so many* people. But they were just background noise." His voice broke and he gripped Ruth's arm. "The whole world was just background noise. There was just Sarah and me. And then, in a few hours, just Sarah and Emma and me. Alone in that electric, noisy world. And that was all right. It was all right. I know I'm supposed to say that I miss them. All those other people. That I'm sorry they died and left this stillness that covers everything. But I never missed them. I never had time to. After Sarah turned, I didn't even notice the rest of the world. The ones that were left were just in the way. Just taking medicine that I thought might help my wife and daughter. Just eating food I needed for them or burning fuel that could keep them warm. I killed my neighbors after they turned. And I burned their furniture, and all the files in their desks. Birth certificates, taxes, photo albums. Didn't matter. Hoarded their food for us, turned away healthy people who could have used it. I didn't care. There was only us."

"Why are you telling me this?" asked Ruth.

"So you know what Emma meant. So she's not just a spent bullet in the world when I'm not here to remember her. When the house burns down and every scrap of her is gone, someone should remember. I can't even make a stone marker for her. But you'll remember. That's why you keep the photographs, right? Because you think you'll forget. Because you think you've already forgotten what your son looked like. But you didn't. Not really. You know how much every one of them meant. Better than I do. You know how much people really loved them. You gave Emma the only thing that I couldn't. You gave all of them what they needed most, whatever that crazy priest thinks. He says I'll go to hell for turning to you. He thinks that scares me. The truth is, if that's the price it costs to give Emma and Sarah some peace, then I accept it."

"I'll get there before you will," mumbled Ruth.

"Then at least I'll have a friend," said Nick. "Goodbye, Ruth." He let her go and pushed open the heavy glass door.

"Goodbye, Nick," she answered. He was a shadow against the warm night. She thought she saw him raise a hand to her, and then he was gone, part of the stillness of the dead city. At last she turned and locked herself in the tiny reception area of the police station. She plugged the music player into her tiny solar charger, unbelted the heavy gun and lay down fully clothed on the cot, heartsick.

CHAPTER 8

Nella stood on the edge of the station platform. Frank held a hand up to her. She took a deep breath and hopped down with his help.

"Only four stops, okay? Then it's just a few streets over." He smiled and handed her the lantern. She flipped it on as they reached the steep hill that plunged out of the daylight and into the cool, damp throat of the city. She tried to concentrate on just her feet, watching one foot settle after another. She knew her fear of the dark had been irrational once, that she would have treated a patient with the same phobia by doing exactly what she was doing now. Exposure therapy. But it wasn't irrational any more. It was a survival instinct, some sense that had lasted through modern life until it became useful again. She didn't know that she *wanted* to treat it. She tried not to hear the scuttling noises of rats around them. Frank seemed completely at ease.

"Aren't you nervous?" she whispered.

"Not really. It's an empty tunnel. But I can understand why you are."

"Are you sure it's empty?"

"What would be down here? There's no food for wild animals— well maybe at the stations, but I doubt it. Nobody has been here in eight years. There's no litter or trash for them."

Nella tried to let the thought comfort her. "What do you think is down here?" Frank asked a moment later. Nella blushed.

"I don't know. I guess maybe I expected Infected or some sort of underworld gang."

"I doubt there're any Infected left. What

would they eat? I kind of felt like this whole mission was more of a goodwill thing from the governor, not really a rescue operation. I doubt we'll find more than an odd handful of Infected left in the whole world. And if we hadn't been through all that empty space yesterday, I might believe a gang would use the subway, but as it is, why lurk around down here when all those vacant buildings are just sitting, still full even, out there? There's no one down here but us. We'll be okay, but we can take it slowly. Do you want to get out at the next station and get a breather?"

Nella shook her head. "It's only four stops. Let's get it over with."

It was colder than Nella remembered a subway being. No lights at the station, no train exhaust, no hot water pipes overhead. She could hear the wind blowing down the staircases before they reached each station, like listening to the emptiness of a long-dead seashell, but the summer air didn't reach the track. It was a long time to be in dread and even Nella's adrenaline wore off long before the third station. The tunnels had been empty, an occasional rodent nest or some long-discarded trash, but nothing new. No food wrappers or empty cans, no water bottles or used up batteries. Nothing to show the tunnels had been used at all since the Plague.

Until they reached the third station.

Frank tripped over a loose sand bag, and Nella caught him before he could slam into the cement floor. She lifted the lantern higher to look around them. The tunnel should have opened into the smooth dome of the station, but the tunnel had been blocked with sandbags and trash barrels stacked above.

"Do you think it was to protect the city from the Infected?" asked Frank.

"I don't know. Did they really think they could quarantine the city? It had already spread through the population before people started showing symptoms. What good would a barricade do?"

"We have a barricade."

Nella nodded. "Yeah, we do. But we also have people manning it to let refugees in. It wasn't meant to keep everyone out, just to keep the Infected from overrunning us."

Frank shrugged and grinned. "Hello?" he yelled. There was a shuffling around them, but it was too slight to be human. "We've brought help! A cure. A chance to trade."

Nella winced at his lack of caution, but no one answered anyway.

"Well, it was worth a shot," sighed Frank. He started tugging on the debris blocking the tunnel, testing it for weakness.

"I don't know if you should announce what we have to the first stranger we meet. They may not all be friendly."

"I know you're probably right, but I've been thinking about what we've come all this way to do. The farther we go without seeing anyone, the more I think that when we *do* find someone, we might be the very first person they've seen since the Plague. I was hoping— *am* hoping— that we'll find a working government here. A massive crowd of healthy, sane people. That someone is putting the world back together."

Nella placed the lantern carefully on the ground and began pushing on the trashcans near the top of the tunnel. "If that was happening, wouldn't we have heard about it? Wouldn't there be missions sent to look for people? For us?"

"That's what I mean. In the back of my head, I guess I just assumed that somebody out there knew what was going on. That somewhere, the rule of law meant something, that civilization was creeping back from the edge. Even after all this time. I expected— I don't know, maybe not rescue, but some kind of organization or something to come along. But now— Nella, whatever is behind this wall, it isn't going to be like home. I know that. It probably seems pretty stupid to walk in waving a white flag and announcing ourselves. But what if *we're* it? Maybe you and I are the very first people to reach out to help anyone outside their tiny bands of survivors? What if everyone out here is waiting for *us*? If we want to rebuild a modern society, we have to act like we're already part of one. We have to be confident, pretend that we have so much extra that the thought of being robbed or attacked never occurred to us. Then the people we meet will trust us. They'll think we have an army behind us, a government. That someone, somewhere, cares if we disappear or are harmed. It'll make good people feel more secure and bad people hesitate. That's what I was thinking anyway."

Nella grunted and shoved against the trashcan, moving it a few more inches. "Whatever happened to sailing away to a deserted tropical island?" she asked with a half smile.

Frank leaned into the same trashcan. "Not quite ready to retire yet. Besides, I'm starting to get a little lonely as it is, aren't you?"

Nella stopped pushing and turned to her husband. She put a warm hand on his cheek and smiled when he looked at her. "We'll find someone Frank. There were hundreds of survivors around us. It's a big world. Bigger than it's been in a few centuries. We can't be the only ones. We'll find them."

He hugged her before turning back to the barrier. He pushed the trashcan the rest of the way through and it popped into the farther room with a hollow clang. Nella held up the lantern and Frank peered in.

"Well, I don't think we're going to find them here, at any rate." He let Nella take his place at the opening. She squinted trying to make anything out. The lantern fell on a gleaming red canister that lay on its side on the tracks.

"Is that an extinguisher?" she asked.

"I don't know," said Frank, pushing a sandbag out of the way to make more room, "but there're no lights and no people. If it were really important to protect this tunnel, you'd think they'd have left a guard."

They made a hole large enough to climb through. Frank slid through first, his feet puffing clouds of gray dust up when he landed on the other side. Nella handed him the lantern and climbed through. Everything was covered with thick colorless clumps of ash. Frank was looking at a tangle of shapes on the station platform. They looked as if they had been blanketed with dirty snow.

"Are those people?" Nella asked.

Frank leaned forward and gently brushed the ash from a small lump. Skin crackled like cellophane and fell away from a thin white bone. Frank shuddered and wiped his hand on his shirt. He held up the lantern again.

"So many. Why did they stay? Why did they block themselves in?" he asked. Nella carefully climbed onto a clean section of the platform and Frank followed. The far tunnel was blocked with more bags and the benches from the station. They picked their way through the tangle of people toward the stairs. Gold summery sunlight filtered down onto the staircase, glinting in the flying soot that Nella and Frank disturbed with each step. A strange, thick puddle of blackened glass lay at the base of the stairs. Nella stared at it as Frank climbed up before her.

"Why did this glass melt but the bones from the people are still here?"

Frank shook his head. "I think that was more sand, not glass."

"What?"

"Come and see," he called grimly. She shut off the lantern and climbed slowly up the stairs. Even before she reached the top she could tell that the light was all wrong. Overexposed, uninterrupted. As if the station emerged into an empty field instead of dense city landscape. Frank was shading his eyes with one hand and she couldn't see his face. The top of the stairs sunk from her line of vision as she climbed. A ring of sea green bubbles surrounded the stairwell, almost a foot high. Nella reached out and touched it. Cool and hard. More glass. She looked around her. The roads were obscenely exposed instead of tucked behind buildings. There were no buildings. A few square empty sockets, a few walls leaning here and there, a sea of broken concrete at their feet. And everything swirled with ash and grit that caught in her nostrils and the corners of her eyes. She wiped her face and spun around to look behind her. Far behind, she could make out the edges of buildings in the direction they had come from. They were like islands in a fog though, indistinct, wavering. Less real than the rubble she stood on.

"Everyone?" she asked.

Frank nodded. "Must be. It's miles of this."

She spun around, looking back the way they had come. The moving ash made a haze, but she thought she could just make out a line of buildings breaking the horizon. She tried to picture the capitol as it had been, tried to remember which parks or monuments she should have been able to see from the subway. It was impossible. Just lumped, huddled concrete rubble in perfect squares. The roads between each demolished city block were the only sign that any human— that any living *thing*— had ever been there. That they hadn't suddenly emerged from the subway onto the surface of a barren planet.

"How did it spread so far? Even without firefighters— it should have burned itself out."

He touched the bubbled glass mound in front of them with his fingertips. "This wasn't just a fire. Bomb maybe. Not the first. This was a shelter. That's why those people blocked off the tunnels, to keep from getting sick. Sandbags were here too, that's what the glass is."

"Why? Who would bother? Everyone was already dead."

"Maybe they were scheduled to go off if everyone was dead. What was the word? A dead man's switch? Or maybe an accident. Or maybe someone was in a facility playing with buttons and pushed the wrong one."

"Or someone wanted to finish the job?" asked Nella.

"Maybe. It happened after the Plague, that's for sure. I bet the people downstairs were refugees. Someone built the shelter. Someone warned them to use it. A government? Just a smart survivalist? I don't know."

Nella was silent for a long moment. "This is why, isn't it? They're all going to be like this. Empty craters, everyone dead or scattered. How did we get missed?"

"We don't know that. The capitol of any country is the first logical place to attack in war time. Maybe they were auto-targeted here. Maybe this is the only place that got hit. We can't assume this is the reason we haven't met anyone."

"Then what's your theory?"

He sighed and turned back to the stairwell, pulling her gently back the way they had come. "I think more people died in the Plague and its aftermath than we realized. We were very lucky, Nella. We lived to see a Cure. Almost everyone else has had eight years to fight the Infected, to suffer the breakdown of order and kill or rob from each other, or just to starve. It was silly of me to expect help here, just a dying instinct left over from Before."

They stepped gingerly past the gray bundles on the platform and back into the subway tunnel. Neither one wanted to explore more. *What do we do now?* Nella wondered, but she couldn't bring herself to say it. They walked back to the pawn shop in heavy silence and camped there again, not even bothering to pull the security gate down behind them.

CHAPTER 9

Most of the freshness had evaporated from the morning by the time Ruth reached the hospital. The bulbous bellies of the clouds above her and the wind rushing past as she rode her rust-spotted bike had fooled her into thinking it would stay cool. Instead, she was heavy with sweat by the time she'd hidden the bike in the overgrown shrubs.

She looked up at the building. It sprawled over the grounds like the clawing roots of a great tree. An old Kirkbride model, it must have housed almost a thousand patients at some point. But it had been abandoned even before the rest of the world emptied out. The stone walls, once naked and clean, were overgrown with climbing trumpet creeper, in some places several inches thick, so that even the outline of the structure was softened. Parts of the far wings had collapsed and the hollow sockets that had been patient rooms were carpeted with moss and rotting leaves. The whole building reminded Ruth of a corpse mid-decay, half melted back into the earth, with all the secret parts glaring out at the world.

The central building had survived, and it was here that Juliana had brought her almost seven years before. The glass in the doors had been covered with large sheets of plywood and the doors were barred with a long piece of heavy scrap metal. Ruth thought it looked like an old beam axle. She wondered where the small woman had found it and how she had gotten it to the hospital.

There was a loud screech of rubbing metal whenever Juliana opened the door, and the shrieks would start immediately. Seven years ago, it had shocked and horrified Ruth. It had been a sort of hell to walk into the place surrounded by screams. Now, though it shamed her to admit the thought, it felt more like walking into the local dog pound. The thick vines and shadowy stone made it look cool and peaceful from the cement walk. Ruth tried to persuade herself that it wouldn't be so bad, helping Juliana, if Father Preston just stayed away.

The door was unbarred now, which meant Juliana was inside. Ruth wondered what would happen if a fire started while Juliana was gone. There were people out there who would do it. People who thought the hospital was insane and dangerous. People who actively hunted the Infected.

Ruth had met them. Some of them tried to idolize her. One of them had even showed up to the police station a few years earlier. He'd passed a string of blackened, leathery lumps through the receiving window without saying anything.

"What's this?" she asked, staring at the string. It was looped, like a necklace, each lump knotted into place so they wouldn't slide.

"It's for the bounty," hissed a reedy voice. The window was too smudged with greasy prints to see who was out there.

"What bounty?"

"The bounty for the Zombies. Joe Mackey said you'd pay a can for each ear. I caught these in a back alley where they had cornered a bunch of wild dogs. I sliced them off the ones that I took care of myself. Amateurs might try to pass you ears they've swiped from corpses, but Gray will always bring you the real deal."

Ruth jerked her arm back from the receiving tray. She wiped her hand down the side of her pant leg. "N-no, that's not me. I don't pay bounties. I don't hunt people either. And I don't know any Joe Mackey."

"Now don't be like that. You want fresher ones? Next time I'll bring them in quicker. You're hard to track down and—"

"No. I don't want *fresher* ones. I don't hunt people. I don't pay bounties. I offer a way out for the chronically ill when they no longer have someone to take care of them."

"Listen, lady," hissed the voice and the owner drew close enough to the glass for Ruth to see dark leather clothing but nothing else, "I don't care how you get to sleep at night. You want me to tell you I put them out of their misery? Fine, I ushered them into heaven with a soft kiss. Would you rather I saved a pack of school kids from ravening hordes of Zombies? Then next time, those are the ears I'll bring you. But I came to trade and I did a lot of work to get you that little bauble and I expect to be paid." The voice was a rumble now, quiet and vicious. Ruth pressed her hand against her hip, looking for the gun she had locked in the safe.

"Take your trophies and leave," she said.

"Not until I'm paid."

"I told you, I don't pay bounties."

"Joe Mackey told me you did. So either he's lying or you are. I don't really care much who is, but you're here and he's not and *somebody* is going to pay me, or the situation is about to get really nasty."

The overt threat snapped Ruth out of her unease. "The glass is bulletproof. So are the doors. I'm locked in here. There's nothing you can do, so take your stuff and leave."

A sleeve swiped a few times across the glass and its owner's eyes appeared an inch outside. The man's gaze darted around the small office, resting at last on Ruth. The corners of his eyes crinkled with his slow, sleazy smile.

"You can't stay there forever. You have no supplies and no water. I can wait." He turned and leaned his back against the glass and began whistling.

The man was right. Ruth was not prepared for any type of siege. This was simply where she spent her days until someone needed her. She couldn't shoot him. She'd never shot a healthy person before. Besides, the glass was just as bulletproof for her as it was for him. There was a back exit, but even if she slipped out when he wasn't looking, then what? He could just wait her out and attack her when she came back.

Ruth sighed. "A can for each?" she asked.

The man whirled around, his leather jacket brushing more of the grime away. She could see most of his face now, but didn't recognize him anyway. The sleazy smile was back. "That's right, twenty cans for twenty ears."

"And then you leave and never come back."

"I swear," he said, making an x over his chest, "I will never darken your door again."

Ruth hesitated, but then reached under the desk for the pile of tin cans she had put there. The labels were torn off, but Ruth knew what they were. She'd picked them up at a vet's office when she raided it for medicine. She'd used them to make the wild dogs around the station friendlier. She hoped he wouldn't know they were dog food until he was long gone and far away. She piled them, a few at a time, into the receiving drawer and then pushed her side closed.

"What is this?" asked the man, holding up a shining can.

"Food," she snapped, "Take it or leave it, it's all I've got."

He scooped them up and dropped them into a backpack.

"Don't forget your...memento," she said, pointing at the pile of shriveled skin and tendon. The man sneered as he reached into the drawer. Ruth grabbed his arm and yanked. His shoulder hit the edge of the drawer with a meaty thunk and he yelped. "You're thinking that maybe I'm not so tough," she said, "That you could have taken more with a little more pressure. You think I'm scared right now, and you think maybe you'll come back later and try for more."

He was struggling, pulling against her, trying to free himself. Not paying attention. So Ruth slammed her hip against the drawer, catching his wrist with the sharp metal edge. He howled, but she kept the pressure on while her free hand grabbed a sharp pair of scissors off the counter top. "Listen closely," she said, smacking the scissors onto the glass in front of his face, "I survived *hordes* of slime like you. And I'm not talking about the Infected. The looters that came through are all gone now. Most of them dead. I'm not. And I'm not frightened of you or of anyone else. If you *ever* show up here again— I don't care if it's because you think you can extort more from me, or because Joe Mackey told you something even dumber, or if you're just 'accidentally' passing by— if I ever see you here again, I'll rip *your* ears off with this and string them up next to the others for you to wear." She let his arm go and he stumbled backward. She expected him to swear at her, maybe try to throw one of the waiting room chairs at the window. But he only went very pale and picked up the pack. He stared at her for a long moment and flexed his arm. Then he walked out. And Ruth quickly sat down in her chair so her legs would stop shaking.

She hadn't seen him since, but she knew there were dozens like him out there. Ruth blinked and realized she was still staring at the hospital door. She had always assumed that Juliana kept the doors barred to keep the Infected from breaking out and running rampant into the city. Now she wondered if it were to stop people from getting in to harm the Infected instead. She opened the door without knocking to prevent a fresh round of shrieks from the Infected. It was much quieter than she'd expected.

Juliana must have just finished feeding time, she thought, as she always did, and was immediately ashamed. She knew they weren't animals. They were special to someone, or they wouldn't be here. They'd all been somebody's children. But deep down, in the part of her that society didn't regulate, she thought of them like wild dogs or bears. They were dangerous and unpredictable, unable to recognize anything beyond their own hunger and rage.

Father Preston wandered out of the admitting office holding a bible and mumbling to himself. Ruth thought about darting back outside, but she'd promised Juliana help, and she was worried about her friend's increasing fatigue.

"Good morning Father," she said, knowing he'd seen her.

"Why do you come here, Ruth?" he asked, looking up, "Are you making a list of future victims? Is the hospital just a catalog of anticipated thrills for you? I have tried to tell Juliana that it is only a matter of time before murdering the Afflicted becomes routine and boring for you. Then you'll move on to healthy people and it will naturally be she and I who are first—"

"Save the fire and brimstone, Father. There's no Congregation here to win over. You know that I'm not killing for pleasure. Certainly, I think that what I do is kinder and more rational than what you are trying to do here. But the Infected, sorry—*Afflicted*— who are here aren't my family. I can't make that choice for them."

Father Preston closed the bible around one thumb to mark his spot. "And are you certain the people that you've already killed would have chosen to die? How many *have* you killed?"

"Fifty-seven," she answered, not certain whether he'd be shocked that it was so many or so few. The number meant little to her, just an internal clock of sorts. In her mind, she only did what she had to.

"Fifty-seven," repeated Father Preston, "And you don't think even one of them might have chosen to keep waiting for a cure, despite their pain?"

"There *is* no cure," snapped Ruth.

"I'm living proof that there is. *You* did it. With your own hands. You could do it again if you just tried. But you won't, because it would mean you killed your son and all the others for nothing."

Ruth could feel heat rising into her face and the force of her anger made her dizzy. "Why do we keep arguing about this?" she cried, "You weren't cured by anything except sheer, dumb luck. Your body responded to a secondary pneumonia infection and stumbled on the correct antibody for the December Plague. Someone else's body would react differently. I can't just go around infecting people with pneumonia and hope it works out—"

"But you can give them my blood instead—a, what's that called? An anti-something."

Ruth sank onto a nearby bench. The old argument had worn a rut in her, a fragile, over heated streak that weakened a little more every time. "Even if an antiserum would work, it would take a team of experts and some high-tech machinery to create it. If there had been time in the beginning, someone should have done it with the blood of an immune person. But everything fell apart so fast. It was already too late. I'm not a hematologist or a microbiologist. And I had trouble even keeping my own lab sterile enough to test already existing antibiotics."

Father Preston stood over her, unrelenting. "So study. The library is still here. You've had almost seven years to figure out how to use my blood, but you prefer to shoot people instead."

"You don't think I tried? I've not only ransacked the public library, I've been to every medical school, doctor's office and even vet clinic in a hundred miles. It's taken me years to check them all. I've been chased by Infected, shot at by looters, I've even risked getting too close to wild fires to get the information. But there are so many pieces missing. Just gone."

"What do you mean, 'gone'?"

"So much of our lives weren't written down. Or at least, not on paper. So much of humanity was what passed between people. I can read the pieces that are left, but I still don't know what a lab tech would know, because I wasn't shown. And I've yet to meet a surviving lab tech. I could fumble through with a book and maybe kill some more people before I found a proper method, the way I would have if Juliana hadn't been in the conservatory to show me which plants were the ones I was looking for and which were dangerous look-alikes."

"It's better than shooting them without trying. As long as there's hope of finding a cure, how can you claim to be on the side of mercy if you keep killing them instead of trying to cure them?"

Ruth ran a hand over her face and sighed. "Have you forgotten what it was like to be Infected, Father? The uncontrollable rage, the need to harm someone, anyone, even your loved ones? The unceasing urge to eat, even if it's human flesh? I've never pried, Father, because it's your life to share or not, but certainly you must have harmed people to survive before you were brought here. These people have endured seven more years of unrelenting madness and pain than you did. Every day is agony, not just for them, but for their caregivers too. Sure, Father, there's *always* hope. But sometimes that just isn't enough."

Juliana cleared her throat and both Ruth and Father Preston jumped when they realized she'd entered the room. Flustered, Ruth blushed and walked quickly over to her. Father Preston merely nodded and walked toward the patient rooms. Ruth disliked him even more for being so cool after her own agitation.

CHAPTER 10

It was Vincent's fault that he was here. Even after all those years, Father Preston still had not forgiven him. He knew it wasn't just this city. As soon as he had recovered, almost at the moment Ruth had tried to smother him with a towel, Michael Preston had known with overwhelming certainty that the Plague had wiped out most of the world. It was like another sense— like trying to scratch a phantom limb. The months when he was ill had been a bloody blur punctuated with sharp memories of violence and guilt. He wasn't going to tell that to *her*. She was not his judge, not even his peer.

He stood at the long window, its thick glass netted with silver diamonds and his gaze dissolved somewhere beyond, somewhere in the waist high brush and grass that seemed to swallow up the edges of the great city, to erase it. He hadn't noticed the silence of the city when he first recovered, or the darkened lights like faded gems. He'd been too consumed with his own memory to notice the world outside. But before he'd even seen the notices and billboards peeling, dissolving, tumbling in the wind like old leaves, he knew that the whole world was gone. That millions must have died, entire continents become empty. Still, in his heart, he blamed Vincent for it all.

And why not? The monastery had been isolated enough. Without Vincent, they might have avoided the outbreak altogether. Michael Preston had been a very young priest then. Very young and consumed with passion for his calling. But Vincent had returned from his missionary work in mid-

November that year, a defeated man. He had been gone many years and Father Preston didn't know him well. Brother Vincent had suffered a breakdown of some sort, unable to face the interminable famine and drought a moment longer. So he'd been ordered back to the seclusion and quiet routine of the monastery to rest and recover. Some of the novices envied Vincent, he had an air of something ancient and exotic, as if he were a broken relic that had made miracles once and was now sent home, powerless.

But Michael Preston could see the melancholy in the man, and he scorned the ragged edge of a fraying faith that Brother Vincent displayed in his despair. Father Preston had avoided him whenever possible, afraid to be infected with doubt. But Vincent brought more than doubt with him. He brought the December Plague back with him too, though no one knew until far too late.

It had been so slow and creeping at first. There was no television or radio at the monastery, no papers were delivered. Only the brothers who worked at the monastery's shop knew what happened outside, and they got it in rumors and gossip from the customers. By the time the Plague had spread far enough to gossip about, most of the customers had stopped coming in and the shop stood empty.

Vincent had complained of dizziness and exhaustion. The elder brothers thought it was still a product of his mental breakdown. They dismissed him from chores and the early prayers so he could rest. A few weeks later, he woke the brothers with shrieks from his small cell and bit the first man who ran to his aid. It was thought his mind had simply snapped and a doctor was called in. But the December Plague was just beginning to be felt. It wasn't even a rumor in the mouth of the world. So the doctor had given Brother Vincent a sedative to calm him, and recommended moving him to a hospital for treatment of psychosis, but the elder brothers refused. The monks would give him the care he needed and tranquility and solitude would bring him back to himself. So the doctor had shrugged and written a prescription for a sedative to keep Vincent calm.

But Father Preston knew then, and was still convinced years later, that Brother Vincent had been stricken because he committed some grave sin of despair or heresy in his heart. For a few more weeks the monastery went on as usual. Each man completed his daily tasks and shared quiet meals, each tried to pray although Vincent's shrieks occasionally punctured the thick silence of their meditations. But then the brother assigned to care for Vincent became first erratic, then angry with everyone, and finally as violent as Vincent had.

The doctor was called again. This time he didn't arrive alone. Men in thick plastic suits arrived within minutes of the call. A few were carrying guns. The Abbot protested, but the men in the suits, while apologetic, entered anyway, guns and all. A few more of the brothers were complaining of dizziness or stumbling by this time. The men rounded them up with Vincent and his unfortunate keeper and put them all in a large bus where they sat, restrained. Those who weren't yet mad were frightened and stared at their quiet home through the dusty windows.

The doctor tried to explain through his ventilator, but even he didn't know much. It was a disease, spreading through the air. Nobody knew how many were already infected. The soldiers would take Brother Vincent and the others to a facility in the south where they would receive the best medical care the government could offer. The doctor was hopeful that removing them would stem the infection of the monastery. The Abbot looked worried, but Father Preston was relieved to be rid of them, Brother Vincent in particular. Ill or not, Father Preston had been uneasy to know a doubter shared their community, now he would not have to worry about Vincent's cowardice spreading to the others, or himself.

A few days longer, the serenity and smooth flow of monastic life reigned, even though the missing members meant more chores for the remaining brothers. It fell to Father Preston to deliver the sermons to a local church while the brothers were gone. He sat late one night composing his first, choosing a grim passage that would compare his flock to the people of Moses during the plagues of Egypt. The hallways were quiet, the evening prayers long past. Hunched over his small desk, the swift pen shooting aching cramps through his clenched fingers, Michael Preston was in bliss. If ever heaven could exist on earth, for him it was when the passion and fire of faith flowed through him, made him a conduit and he felt as if he spoke with a divine voice.

Father Preston's belief was never gentle or

nurturing. He had no patience for the weak or the wavering, because he didn't understand it. He was young enough to hold to not only the spirit, but the letter of the religion. Anyone who did not, he was convinced, would never feel the searing righteousness that he did. It was his comfort when forced to hear confessions. He would listen and mouth the words of atonement and forgiveness, but they never touched his heart. It was unjust, he thought, that the weak should be admitted to heaven. It wasn't enough, his secret heart cried, to be merely good. Any old sinner could turn good in the face of fear. It required so much more devotion to be truly deserving and blameless. To be like him.

There were few people whom Father Preston looked up to, or evoked affection from him, beyond the pallid warmth that came from Christian duty. Even his own natural family had fallen short. Even in the monastery he'd chosen, Father Preston admired none except his Abbot. The Abbot had been even younger than Michael Preston when he became a monk. He had not stepped foot beyond the monastery gates in the fifty years that followed. He had little contact with the outside at all, only receiving those visitors who were absolutely necessary, such as the doctor. He wrote and received no letters and the only news he heard was from returning missionaries, like Brother Vincent. He expressed no longing for anything beyond what the monastery provided.

It didn't occur to Michael to wonder if he were truly keeping to the laws of the faith or if he had fled to the arms of the church to escape temptations that were too strong for the Abbot to resist. In Father Preston's eyes, the elder priest was wholly and unswervingly devoted. Perhaps he lacked the acid zeal that bubbled in Michael's heart, but Father Preston chalked it up to age rather than weakness or wavering. He revered the Abbot. It was as much for his approval as that of a distant deity that Father Preston diligently performed abhorred tasks or spilled his heart into his sermons and meditations.

It was the Abbot, mostly, that he thought of as the December night blew in between the loose panes of his room's small window, curling around his cramping fingers and turning his breath to smoke over the burning words he wrote. A loud thud reverberated against the wall in front of Father Preston. He glanced up from the page as the thud was immediately followed by a harsh yell and then a wet, gurgling shriek that trailed away. Father Preston leapt up, the chair clattering to the stone floor behind him. He tore open his door and was at the neighboring cell in a few strides. The door was cracked open, but the interior was utterly dark. The brother who lived there had retired hours before. Father Preston hesitated. Silence was supposed to be kept until morning prayers. But a snuffling moan from the cell broke his paralysis.

"Brother Andrew, are you ill? I heard a disturbance." He took a step into the dark room and his bare foot slid in the slick warmth of a spreading puddle. "Brother Andrew?"

His eyes adjusted a little to the dark interior. A shadow darker than the room was hunched over in front of him. It rocked gently and its breath bubbled and slurped as if it were emerging from water. Father Preston reached for the light switch, half of him still outside in the hallway. Other doors were opening now and brothers peered sleepily out at him. The electric light blazed and the thing on the floor reeled back shielding its face with two wrinkled, blood-blackened hands. Brother Andrew lay on the floor, his head tilted back to look at Father Preston with the blank whites of his eyes. His neck was a crater, a sudden volcano still trickling. Father Preston realized he was standing in a thick sludge of blood. He stumbled backward with a yell. The other brothers flung their doors open the rest of the way and hurried toward him. The thing on the floor was a man. He ignored Father Preston and hunched over Brother Andrew again.

"What are you doing?" cried Father Preston, "What have you already done?"

But the man didn't turn. He put his face down onto Brother Andrew's chest. One of the others had reached the room. It was Brother Matthew, the Abbot's attendant. His eyes grew large but he splashed through the blood to kneel beside the man, thinking him overcome with grief. The man's head jerked to the side and Andrew's body twitched. Father Preston realized what the man was doing just as Brother Matthew reached up to gently touch his shoulder. Father Preston lunged forward to stop him just as Brother Matthew said, "Reverend Father, are you injured?"

The corpse jerked again as the man whipped around to face Brother Matthew. A strand of stringy flesh hung from the Abbot's teeth. The silver cataract in his right eye flashed as he sought out the source of the voice. The stubble on his cheeks was stiff and dark with gore, each whisker standing like a needle with its own droplet of blood. The Abbot snarled like a lion interrupted mid-feed. He leapt at Brother Matthew who flung his arms over his head to protect himself.

"Please! Reverend Father—" cried Brother Matthew. Father Preston heard a chorus of gasps behind him and knew the others had arrived. The shock was too great to feel disappointment or anger with the Abbot, but a pang of sorrow pierced him at the thought that the others were seeing his idol fall. He leapt forward and tackled the older monk just as he was about to close his teeth on Brother Matthew's arm. The Abbot writhed beneath him, arms grabbing and scraping at Father Preston, but his strength had mostly gone with his youth. Father Preston wondered how he'd gotten the better of Brother Andrew at all. Perhaps only because of surprise.

"Calm down, Father," Preston begged him in a low whisper, trying to hold him still. "Please, it's me, Michael. The others don't know yet, they didn't see. Calm down."

But the Abbot just growled. The brothers were beginning to murmur behind him and Brother Matthew began to rise.

"Shh," urged Father Preston in a shaky voice. He held the Abbot's head still with his hands and kneeled over his chest, pinning his legs. The Abbot's nails scratched at Father Preston's face and arms. "Shh," he urged again, but the Abbot's chest rumbled with a deep and resonant roar. Father Preston glanced back at the others. They craned to see over each other and muttered amongst themselves. Brother Matthew took a step toward the Abbot. Father Preston whirled back again, desperate. Instead of the warm, noble guide he'd worshiped, Father Preston saw only a wild beast, a struggling animal cornered and vicious.

"Please," Father Preston hissed, but the Abbot only continued to roar. So Father Preston slapped him.

He had lived in awe of the Abbot for so long, had such a dread of altering the hierarchy that he had expected the entire world to stand still, to teeter for a moment on that slap. But nobody stopped, time did not slow to a crawl and the guttural shout of the Abbot didn't fade into the background. Nothing changed, except that now Brother Andrew's blood was smeared over Father Preston's palms too.

The lack of response, the permanence of the scream despite his best effort to stop it, sent an icy quake of fear through Father Preston. It quickly melted into anger. Father Preston raised his hand again. But Brother Matthew had reached them.

"Don't, Brother Michael. He's sick. He doesn't understand. He— he can't stop himself."

Father Preston glared at him for a moment. "Sick? This isn't sick, this is madness. This is possession," Father Preston lowered his voice, "He *was eating* Brother Andrew. This is evil. Some demon has taken up residence in the Reverend Father's mind—"

Brother Matthew shook his head. "You heard the doctor. This is what the Plague does. There's nothing supernatural here. Just illness."

"Then the Reverend Father has committed the gravest of sins. Brother Matthew, this is a man we've followed for decades. He cannot be a murderer— an— an abomination."

"He's *sick*. He doesn't know what he's doing. We don't have time to argue this, Brother Michael. Our Abbot needs medical care and Brother Andrew lies unattended and exposed. Help me get the Abbot back to his room so I can call the doctor."

The Abbot snapped his teeth together, trying to bite, as they lifted him to his feet. He struggled but they kept a tight grip. The circle of monks who had gathered around Brother Andrew parted for them, but no one spoke. Father Preston could feel their eyes on his back during the entire agonizing trip down the hall. He tried to be gentle, but the awkward writhing of the Abbot exhausted him and Brother Matthew both. They dropped him onto the narrow bed and fled out of the room quickly. Father Preston pressed his back against the door to prevent it opening as the old priest flung himself at it over and over, as if he were a small child having a tantrum.

One of the Afflicted banged into the cell door nearby, and Father Preston shook himself. It took him a second to realize he wasn't in the dark abbey but standing in front of a sun drenched window in the only operating asylum in the world. His thumb ached and he looked down. His thumb still marked his place as the rest of his hand clenched the book until it nearly folded around the thick finger. He forced himself to relax. He looked around to make sure he hadn't been seen, but Ruth was nowhere in sight.

CHAPTER 11

Ruth stood up from the bench as Father Preston walked away. She forced a smile for her friend. "Here I am, as requested. Just point me in the right direction," she said.

Juliana gave her a hesitant smile. "I tried to keep him out of the office this morning. He must have slipped by me while I was serving breakfast. Sorry."

Ruth shook her head. "You don't have to worry, I'm an adult and still semi-civilized at least. I can handle Father Preston. So, what's first?"

"I thought you could help me with bathing and rebandaging. I think I've got one with gangrene too."

"I'm sorry, Juliana, I should have realized. I didn't bring my kit."

"I have what we'll need." Juliana began walking down the hallway.

"But all we have here are bandages and sedative," Ruth called after her, "I'll go back and get the tea tree ointment from the station. Do I need any instruments?"

Juliana turned around and shook her head. "No, it's spread too far. He was picked up a few days ago, been living off rats in a garbage pile near the old garbage transfer station."

Ruth shuddered. When the world stopped working, lots of survivors had piled their trash in vacant lots and near transfer stations for the first few months, thinking it would get picked up any day, when things got back to normal. As people died, the trash piles stopped growing, but there was no one left to clean them up. Ruth had treated several survivors who had been desperate enough to scavenge in the hills of plastic bags. The rats and the wild dogs were bad enough on their own, but she'd told everyone she could find to steer clear, the threat of rabies was one of her worst nightmares.

She'd never dreamed a human could survive for six years in one of those trash piles. As larger prey grew scarcer and more wary, the Infected must have moved to smaller, more dependable sources of food. She wondered how many Infected had burned to death in the massive tire fire a few years earlier.

"Is that why I'm here?" she asked, catching up to Juliana.

"I wouldn't ask you to do something I refuse to," said Juliana, "I asked for help because this has gotten too big for me. Or maybe I've found myself smaller of late, I don't know," she explained tiredly.

Ruth put a hand on her friend's arm. "What are you talking about? You haven't been yourself lately. Are you feeling all right?"

Juliana waved her away. "Yes, I'm fine, just tired and constantly playing catch up." Ruth followed her to the kitchen, watching carefully. She couldn't see anything alarming about the other woman, but she promised herself to persuade Juliana into a checkup when they finished for the day.

The sink was filled with breakfast dishes and Juliana looked utterly defeated when she saw them. "I asked Mrs. Baird to do these," she said quietly.

"Don't worry," said Ruth, manning the hand pump with some vigor, "I'm no stranger to dishes.

You get the bandages and then come sit down at the table and dry for me."

Juliana disappeared into the pantry. "Who is Mrs. Baird?" Ruth yelled after her.

"Part of Father Preston's Congregation. When I suggested that they were more interested in protesting outside the police station than in helping those they claimed to be defending, he made some of them volunteer."

Ruth snorted. "Then they should all be here today. There's nobody to protest today. I'm conveniently nearby."

Juliana emerged from the pantry with a load of linen and bandages. She dumped it on the table and picked up a towel. Ruth placed a stack of dripping bowls on the table and pulled a chair out for her friend. "Oh, they're here," she sank into the chair and picked up a bowl. "Sorry," she offered with a half-smile.

"Well, what are they doing?"

"It's time for the morning reading."

"The what?"

"Father Preston has decided that the patients need to hear the bible. So each of the Congregation goes and stands in front of each door and shouts a bible passage through it every morning."

"They couldn't think of a better way to demonstrate religion?" asked Ruth, scrubbing scratches into the plastic bowls in frustration, "like empathy or charity in caring for these people? Or mercy—" she fell silent for a moment, "sorry. I didn't mean to say the last one. Does he think they can even hear it over their own screams?"

Juliana shrugged. "I don't know. I think it gives him something to do. And it keeps him out of my hair for an hour a day. I use the Congregation for things around here when they are willing. I don't trust them with the garden. The relatives of the people here do that. They have the most motivation to take care of it and help Bernard guard it when I'm not there."

Ruth finished the dishes and piled them in front of Juliana. "How many patients do you have now?" she asked, her tone gentle.

"Seventy-nine. There's hardly any on the street anymore, I'm not sure how they'd survive. That one from the transfer station is the first in years. But there are still people out there caring for their relatives. They trickle in. I don't think it will ever stop."

Ruth shook her head and turned back to the pump, filling buckets with water for bathing. "You can't keep taking them. It's too much. They'll starve or you'll drop dead from exhaustion."

Juliana rubbed the last of the dripping bowls with her towel. "What if you stayed here?"

"You mean for good? With Father Preston and his 'flock' just down the hall?"

"I'll ask them to leave."

Ruth stopped pumping and the spout gurgled its last. She turned around. "You've never offered to make him leave before."

"I need help. More than shouting bible verses through doorways." She picked up the pile of clean diapers and bandages. "Just think about it, Ruth. I'm not asking you to stop— you know, your *services*. I'm just asking you to *help* me," she lowered her voice, though there was no one around to hear. "If nothing changes, we'll starve this winter. Or freeze. All of us in the hospital. I'm frightened. More scared than I've been since the first few weeks of the Plague. I don't see another way."

"I don't know if I can do— all this again. I don't know if I can relive this—" Ruth stammered, blushing.

Juliana stood up. "You don't have to decide now. Just think about it a while. I'll be grateful even if you only help today and never again. Just promise to consider it. Please." She walked out of the kitchen into the noisy hallway. Ruth followed her with the buckets of water, trying to mask her panic.

The man from the transfer station was in the room at the end of the hall. The same one Father Preston had been in when Ruth had spent the night breathing for him through a blue bulb at the end of an ambu bag. The room was no different from the dozens of others on the ward, but the sight of it always made Ruth shudder. It was the death room to her. Even Juliana seemed to sense it, always putting the patients in the worst health in that room, without realizing it. Ruth could smell the man from outside the door. The rotting sewer smell clung to everything, like a sticky, invisible sweat. Ruth pulled up her face mask. "This is going to be really bad," she muttered through it.

"I know," said Juliana, "I don't know what to do for him."

Ruth opened the door. Her eyes teared up at the strength of the reek, even through the mask.

She could hear Juliana retch behind her. She knew that she should tell her to go, but something hard inside of Ruth made her want to force Juliana to see the pain the man was being put through. To see the consequence of her decision. His eyes were dark craters in his face and his skin had turned a dull gray. Juliana scuttled past Ruth when she saw him lying in a puddle of his own filth.

"I swear, I just changed him. Not even an hour ago. He just keeps going. Sometimes it's bloody. I don't know what to do anymore."

"That isn't gangrene," said Ruth. She helped Juliana turn him to his side to clean him. His lips curled back in a partial snarl but he was too weak to do more. She gently pinched a section of the skin on his arm. It didn't sink back when she let go. The thrum of his pulse was too fast and too distant in his wrist. "It has to be dysentery. Or cholera maybe. But from what you told me, he's been living in a garbage pile for years. For all I know, he may have the plague too. The bubonic one. He's probably been bitten everywhere by the rats—" Ruth shuddered thinking of the rats trying to devour him, and him trying to devour the rats. "There's nothing I can do for him. I have no antibiotics. And even if I did, he's already dying from dehydration."

"We can try an IV," offered Juliana.

Ruth sighed. "Even if I could find a saline pack, I have no tubing and no catheters. Everything is gone, Juliana. Short of spoon feeding him liquids, I don't know what we can try."

"Let's try, please," said Juliana instead of answering.

"He's eating food that could go to someone that might survive."

"We aren't starving yet."

Ruth sighed and shook her head. "We can't just give him water. We'd need sugar and salt to make the right solution. How many years has it been since you've seen either one?"

"Look at him, Ruth. Someone cared about him once."

Ruth thought for a long moment. "I can't give him what we don't have," she said, putting a hand on Juliana's shoulder, "and if it's dysentery it could spread to the others very quickly. It just takes one unwashed linen or us not disinfecting ourselves enough before doing something else. He's dying. Whatever we do will only prolong it a few hours or days. This isn't like the others. I don't have to guess whether this man is actually in pain. The rat bites on his arms and legs are infected. He's starving because everything is passing right through him. The dehydration is causing cramps throughout his body. It's not just his mind that's sick. He doesn't have years of good health in front of him, so I don't want you to think I'm saying this because he has the December Plague. I think the kindest thing for him and the safest thing for the others is to give him a sedative and let him rest."

"You mean give him an overdose of sedative, don't you?"

"Yes, Juliana, I do. Think of what you would want if you were in his position."

Juliana nodded. "I'll think about it," she said. They left the man's room and relief washed over Ruth as she shucked the mask and breathed clean air again. But Father Preston's Congregation was waiting for them in the hallway. They watched the two women in silence for a moment. Father Preston stepped forward as if he were shielding his flock with his own body.

"You are going to murder that man aren't you?" asked Father Preston, "right there where you were going to murder me."

Ruth gasped. In seven years, he'd never mentioned what Ruth had done. She had no idea he had remembered it. She flushed, feeling confused and cornered. Juliana glanced at her with obvious curiosity. But instead of asking, she said simply, "Ruth is treating that man. He is infectious and you should all stay away."

"Don't fall for her tricks, Juliana," said Father Preston, "She'll tell you she's here to help but she'll slip him poison when you aren't looking. Or suffocate him." Father Preston was shouting now and he whipped an old tattered towel from his back pocket and flung at Ruth's feet. It was the same towel she'd held against his face.

Ruth bent over and picked it up. The Congregation was completely silent, their gaze like the heat of an August sun. But the Infected began wailing and screaming in the rooms beyond Father Preston as he shouted. "I was trying to *help* you. I only wanted to ease your pain," said Ruth, with surprising calm.

"I didn't want to die, Ruth. None of these people do. You can't play God."

"Why not?" Ruth asked, the volume of her voice rising as the agony of the Infected overwhelmed the hallway, "If He's not going to do

His job, why shouldn't I pick up the slack?"

The women in the Congregation gasped. The men crossed themselves. "You can't speak for these people," she continued, "Only their families, who know them, who know what they would have wanted can. You're playing God as much as I am. If you had left them where you found them—"

"Left them where we found them? Many were starving or freezing. How is that kinder than what you've done?" shouted Father Preston, his cheeks reddening.

"At least it would have been quicker," said Ruth.

"You aren't fit to be a physician," spat Father Preston.

"I wouldn't trust you to care for a beast," shouted one of the men behind him. Juliana held up her hands to stop the fight, but Ruth lost her temper.

"It would be easier if I *were* a vet!" she cried, "at least they put animals out of their misery when necessary. Nobody questions them. It's the humane thing to do. What has happened to you people? Where is your mercy? Where is your simple decency? You used to treat *dogs* better than you treat the Infected. At least a dog is allowed to die when it has suffered enough. At least a dog gets fresh air and sunlight and grass. If you kept dogs chained as tightly as you keep these people restrained, you'd have gone to prison. At least a dog doesn't have to be trapped in its own filth until someone changes it." She pounded on the door behind her, "These are *human beings*. Can't you hear them? You think they shriek like that for fun?

They are more than a cause to shout about or a mythical 'heathen' in need of bible study. They are *people!* Once they had mothers and fathers and spouses and children. And maybe they lived good, decent lives. Maybe they were artists who created beautiful things. Or maybe they were policemen or soldiers who protected you. Or maybe they were just normal people who got up every morning and kissed their loved ones and went to work and had picnics. Maybe some of them even showed up to your church on Sunday. They at least deserve the respect and dignity you'd give to an animal. Not— this."

Suddenly, Juliana raced down the hall, pushing her cart ahead of her and almost knocking Father Preston over. Ruth immediately regretted falling for the bait and shoved her own way past the people in front of her. Some of them spit on her, but she didn't pay attention, following her friend instead.

"I'm sorry, Juliana," Ruth called after her. Juliana stopped on the front walk. "I'm sorry. I wasn't talking about you. I didn't mean what you were doing—"

"Never mind," said Juliana, "I shouldn't expect you to understand. I do what I think is best and you do what you think is best, and we can still be friends, right?"

"Of course," said Ruth.

Juliana pushed the cart out to the manhole in the middle of the cement walkway. Volunteers had rolled the metal cover away years ago and recovered it with chain link fencing. Juliana began dumping dirty water into the sewer. She stared for a moment at the mountain of soiled diapers and bandages. She sat on the hot tar and began to cry. "What is it?" asked Ruth, sitting beside her.

"I ran out of soap a month ago. We ran out of toothpaste and baking soda over a year ago. They are *all* going to get it. The dysentery or the cholera or whatever he has. I can't get the linens clean enough. Their teeth are rotting even though I brush them every night. They have barely enough protein from the garden, and this winter we'll have none at all. Half of them are probably developing scurvy or rickets. You're right, Ruth, I treat them worse than animals. And it's only getting worse."

Ruth thought for a moment. "I shouldn't have said what I did. I'm sorry."

"No, you are *right.*"

"Yeah," said Ruth, "but if I were being fair instead of blowing up at Father Preston, I might have said we were treating them like animals, but I also would have said that *we* are living like animals too. Juliana, you didn't run out of soap just for *them*, the Infected, you ran out for you too. Sure, their teeth have some plaque. So do mine," she started grinning and pointed to her friend, "So do yours, for that matter. There's two bits of good news: *Everyone's* teeth are rotting, so nobody's going to stare."

Juliana gave her a weak smile. "And the other good news?"

Ruth shrugged, "We so rarely have sugary or starchy food now, that our teeth will rot slower. As long as we keep rinsing their mouths and brushing until the brushes run out, their mouths will be as healthy as ours. All I meant was that Father

Preston's people treat the Infected like they aren't human. Like they are just an excuse to hold a tent revival. If this were Before, they'd all have 'Save the Afflicted' t-shirts. They'd go to their rallies and write a check once a month and never otherwise think about the Infected at all. They might not have the bumper stickers anymore, but they are doing the same thing. They come in, shout some verses and feel they've done some good. They come to the station and shout some curses and feel that they are righteous. Then they go home and loot from their neighbors or hoard things that are desperately needed here, all the while feeling perfectly pure and sanctified. If they were really thinking of the Infected as people, if they really *cared* about what happened to them, they'd be here, every day, doing what you do without being asked. You give everything you have to the people you care for. You eat after they eat. You wash after they wash. You sleep after they sleep. None of that — scene was meant for you."

Juliana was silent, her gaze far off, lost in the sway of the tall summer grasses. "Is it the linens you're still worried about?" Ruth asked. "You didn't give that man dysentery. What he was living in all these years did that. I'm still floored he lasted this long. And we can boil the linens, it's as good as soap for disinfection. We'll start drying them in the sun instead of over the kitchen stove. That should kill anything that makes it through boiling. Honestly, though, if an outbreak is going to happen, there's only so much you or I can do. We're all drinking the same groundwater and not everyone is as careful about their waste as we are."

She waved at the grate over the manhole.

Juliana shook her head. "Where are we going to get all that fuel to boil the water? It's hard enough to get wood for the winter as it is. It just keeps getting harder. Everything is falling apart."

"This isn't like you. What is making you so sad? We've been through worse times. Remember when that hail storm took out half the garden? You didn't even blink. Or when those trees fell onto the roof? You had someone fixing it in days. So we burn some tires in the old boiler instead of wood this winter. No one's going to be complaining to the city. And we'll be a little thinner in the spring. We'll make it. I thought of a few more places to try for canned goods anyway, and I treated a guy with a broken arm a few months ago. He was just passing through and he told me about an orchard about twenty miles outside of the city. I'd need a few helpers and a couple of days, but we could bring back cartloads of fruit before the snow. I've made my decision. I'll stay Juliana. I'll go get my things tonight and I'll be back in the morning. Okay?"

Juliana smiled. "Okay. That will help." She got up and dusted off the backs of her legs. She looked at the pile of laundry. "Do you want to cook dinner or—"

Ruth groaned. "Just give me the laundry," she scowled and pushed the cart into the kitchen.

CHAPTER 12

Frank crouched next to the cabinets counting water bottles. He tried not to listen to Nella as she spoke calmly over the radio to the people waiting at home. It was like calling a friend to let them know a loved one had just passed away unexpectedly. But worse. He'd never dreamed the capitol would be wiped out. Not really. No one would expect that. It was going to crush all hope of returning to any kind of normal life for anyone who still clung to it. Frank couldn't do it. He had reasoned that Nella was better at it, that she was trained to know what to say. But nobody was trained for this. She'd made the radio call so that he didn't have to.

He closed the cupboard and flopped back onto the bunk, looking up at the map he'd pinned above it. Unless they could find a clean source of fresh water, they would only be able to go another week before turning around. Was it even worth going farther? He shut his eyes. The truth was, he'd been terrified when they'd sailed out of sight of the City. Every town they'd landed in had been an aching stretch of adrenaline from the minute they touched the solid ground. He'd expected an ambush from every empty doorway, or thieves to take the boat and strand them. He thought about telling Nella, but she'd been nervous too. So he'd held his tongue, waiting for the safety of the capitol. It had been the first thing he thought of each day as they lifted the anchor. Every hope had hinged on the thousands of people he had expected to find. What was he to do now? What were any of them to do?

Nella appeared beside him and sat on the edge of the bunk. "What do they want us to do?" asked Frank.

"It's really up to us. Things aren't so hot at home."

Frank sat halfway up. "What do you mean? We've only been gone a few weeks, what could have happened already?"

"The people we left at the farmhouse— the ones we cured," said Nella, rubbing the dark jagged scar on her shoulder, "they made it to the City. They were unhappy— and not just them. Lots of the Cured are unhappy. It's not fair, the way things are. Several dozen people, both Cured and Immune, picked up and left a few days ago. They're starting a new settlement near where we found them."

"Was there fighting?"

Nella shook her head. "No, it was completely peaceful— so far. They only took what they'd earned and just walked out the front gate. But a lot of them were from the electric plant and the farm. The governor is very angry. Sevita doesn't think he'll let them go. She says it's getting tense, and there's been talk of closing the Barrier and only allowing people out who have permission."

"We aren't the City's slaves!"

Nella put a hand on his shoulder. "I'm on your side, Frank."

"I know you are. If we had only found another group, maybe the people at home would realize the wider world is out here, that how they treat us will tell others a lot about the kind of society we have. Maybe things would be better.

Maybe they would treat us like equals instead of criminals."

Nella slid down next to him. She traced the rough, sunburned bitemarks that scarred Frank's arm. "No, I don't think that's what would have happened," she said. "Nobody else has the Cure. Just us. The other Infected must all be gone now. There is no other group of Cured people. Other groups would see us and wonder why we bothered. They'd take notice of how we treat the Cured, but it wouldn't be to condemn, it would be to imitate. The best thing that can happen, is happening, as hard as it might be. The Cured are taking matters into their own hands, standing up for themselves. Creating another community where it is normal for everyone to be equal. Maybe *they* will set the standard instead. You said if we wanted to rebuild modern civilization, we had to act as if we are already part of it. We have to be the ones to put it all back together."

"You want to turn around and find this new settlement they're making?"

Nella shook her head. "No. We still have a job to do. There are still people out there waiting for someone like us, I know it."

"We don't have a lot of fresh water left. I haven't even looked at the food situation yet. A week, maybe two, and then we'll have to go back either way."

"One more try then." She pointed to the largest red splotch on the map. "Here, don't you think? There have to be people left there, it's one of the biggest cities in the world."

"What if it's been wiped out by a bomb too?"

Nella was quiet for a moment. "Then we'll know that we can stop looking at least. We won't have to wonder any more, if there are other big groups out there to help or to threaten us."

"One more try then," he agreed. He wrapped an arm around her and closed his eyes again. He didn't know if he wanted to know about all the people in that scarlet dot. He'd been isolated or mad with Plague for most of the outbreak, and when he was Cured he'd woken in a diminished world. He'd seen the empty houses, miles of crumbling road being swallowed by fields and woods. He had imagined the paltry crowd of humans that could barely fill up a large courtroom would be almost everyone he would meet for the rest of his days. But now he knew there was nobody coming. The capitol was gone. The coastal towns were silent. If he turned around now, he could pretend that there were others gathering somewhere, filling skyscrapers and making laws and teaching kids how to survive for another few years.

Going to find those people, sailing farther from the only place they knew was safe— Frank felt like the first astronaut watching the earth fall away beneath him, facing only the blank, unexplored dark. He'd never felt so lonely in his life.

CHAPTER 13

Ruth was surprised at how many things there were to pack. She'd spent almost six years at the police station, but in her mind she had a simple life, almost ascetic, if there were such a thing after the Plague. But she'd gathered far more from trading services than she'd realized. She didn't take much for her time, food mostly, and that was consumed as soon as she received it, either by herself or left in small anonymous packages at Juliana's door. An offering of penance, maybe. It wasn't the ones who wanted medicine who paid the most though. They had to keep some back, to live upon. The people who asked her to kill for them, they gave her anything. Everything. Many of them took Nick's planned route afterward. They didn't have to worry about scrounging or bartering or defending themselves any longer. The gun itself had been from the wife of an Infected.

She had made three trips already, all at night. She hadn't wanted anyone to see what she was moving or where. But it was broad daylight now, the thick windows already steaming behind her. Ruth was exhausted from her trips, and she knew the hospital meant another full day ahead. She was just locking the empty clerk's room when she heard shouting outside. She pushed open the front door and squinted against the thick gold fog still burning it's way up from the street. There was a chorus of shouts mixed in with the unmistakable roar of an Infected. And underneath, a constant metallic shudder. The sparkling end of a shopping cart burst through the edge of the fog. There was a boy inside it, screaming with hunger and anger. He had been bound to the metal with dozens of straining bungee cords. The hinged flap at the back of the cart was gone, because the boy was too large. His legs stuck out of the hole and thrashed under the handle bar. A middle aged man was running behind the cart, alternately pushing it and trying to turn to watch the people yelling at him. He saw Ruth leaning out of the police station and dragged his feet until the shopping cart skidded to a stop. The boy was still screaming, and the man was pleading with him to stop, though he must have known it wouldn't help. The kid must have been about thirteen, not more. His face was still round, even though he was so skinny that Ruth could see his ribs between the rainbow of rubber cords that circled him. She should have been giving him his meningitis vaccine and warning him about mono. "Can I help you?" she yelled over the boy, certain the father was in trouble.

There was a shift in the wind and the sun blazed through the street as the fog swirled away. Father Preston stood at the end of the block with a dozen of his Congregation. The light glittered over them, hard and spitting sparkles, a sharp burning halo that made Ruth instantly furious. It made her feel as if she battled God, Itself. "It's them chasing you isn't it?" she shouted, nodding her head toward Father Preston's group.

The man just nodded and tried to catch his breath.

"You're wasting your time," she yelled, loud enough for Father Preston to hear, though she meant it for the man too, "I don't do kids." She turned her back on all of them and locked the police station door. The man came up next to her and clung to her arm.

"Please, lady, just hear me out," he begged, "it's my wife. My new wife that is. She's very pregnant."

"Oh," said Ruth, turning to smile at him, "you're here to ask me to help with the delivery. I thought you were here about the boy. Those people probably did too."

"No, you don't understand. My wife thinks the boy will try to kill the baby. I've tried everything. At first, I put him in the garage. But it's cold in the winter. He got frostbite and the ends of his toes rotted off. And it was still too close. So in the spring I moved him into the house across the street. But we're running out of food and my wife says we need to save it for the baby. Winter will be here too soon, and I won't be able to find enough wood to heat both houses. My wife wants to leave the city after the baby is born— how can I travel with a new baby and, and that?" He gestured to the cart.

"Is this boy your son?" asked Ruth, shocked at how little sympathy he seemed to have for the boy and how much he wanted her to have for his own hardship.

"Yes, by my first wife. I saved him from her, when she turned. I had to. But then a month later, he got sick too. I've cared for him so long, but he never gets any better. My new wife tries to understand, but she says we have to look forward now, that it's kinder to let him go."

"I'm sorry you've come all this way, but I don't do children."

"Why not? They suffer as much as we do, don't they? More I'd think."

"I just— I can't."

"What am I supposed to do?" the man asked angrily.

"Why don't you take him to the hospital?" asked Ruth, though she knew she was only adding to her own troubles by saying it.

"You see the people back there?" he pointed at Father Preston's group who were slowly but surely closing the distance to Ruth. "They say the lady at the hospital has come down with the big C. And nobody can help her now. They say she'll be dead by winter and the people in the hospital are starving anyway. They said they'd take my boy. That they were starting a *new* place for the sick people, that my boy could earn his keep. But they want him to haul logs like a horse or guard their home like a dog. He may be crazy, but he's still my son. I'm not giving him into slavery and misery. My wife's right, it's better to let him go now. He's suffered long enough. Only, I can't do it. He's mine. I've tried, lady, trust me..."

But Ruth was reeling with shock and didn't hear the rest. "I told you, I don't do kids," she said absently as Father Preston arrived in front of them, his expression a nauseating seesaw between compassionate pity for the man and triumph over Ruth.

The boy was still shrieking while his father stammered questions at Ruth. The Congregation began singing some strident hymn that Ruth didn't recognize. Everything was a blur of heat and sound. The cords around the boy writhed and blazed their bright colors in the morning sun. Ruth's mind felt aflame too, jittering and popping, all the thoughts just beyond her reach for just a second too long. Only Father Preston was silent, his smile settling into a gloat. He was like a gleaming crystal pillar that focused the meanness and cruelty of the others onto Ruth.

Just then, the boy's father finally snapped. "I can't do this anymore!" he shouted. He pulled at his hair and paced next to the cart. He leaned over the boy and kissed the top of his head. "I'm sorry Connor." He wailed and spun around to face Ruth. "I can't do this anymore," he said and then bolted down the street before she could stop him. She watched him disappear, leaving the boy between her and the priest. She sighed and squatted down to take a can from her pack. It was tuna fish, her favorite. She hadn't seen one in years. Canned meat had been one of the first things to disappear. She'd had it locked in the safe and had meant to share it with Juliana. But the boy was hungry. So hungry. She pulled open the tab and it made a low popping noise underneath the screams and the singing. The smell of unspoiled meat drifted into the air. The Congregation fell slowly silent as it reached them. The boy shrieked even louder and thrashed so hard that the shopping cart would have rolled away if Ruth hadn't stopped it. Everyone stared at Ruth and the can. She could almost feel them licking their lips around her, but she ignored them. She freed one of the boy's hands from the cords and put the open can on his lap. He didn't waste time and fell silent as he ate. There were audible sighs as the others watched.

Father Preston finally spoke into the quiet. "So, Ruth, it seems you have a choice to make, since even *you* can't kill a child. Juliana is ill. I'm sure it can't have missed your trained medical eye," he said, but his gloating smile told Ruth he knew she was shocked. "There's nobody to properly care for the boy at the hospital. And there isn't enough food set by to get even the Afflicted who are already there through the winter. Juliana denies it, but she may be forgiven for the deception, for her concerns now lie in a better world. I believe she expects to be singing with the angels before the snow flies."

"What's your point?" snapped Ruth, feeling more and more like a cornered rat.

"You don't want to be burdened with the hospital after she's gone. I know you're itching to leave this city behind. They aren't your family. You never volunteered to care for them. It isn't fair for Juliana to foist them onto you."

Ruth shook her head. "What are you talking about? She hasn't even mentioned the hospital—"

"Oh, but she will. She'll expect you to take over after she's gone. To care for all those *strangers* and their most intimate needs. You don't want to change diapers every day. Or toil in the fields to scratch out enough food for them."

"How do you know she won't ask *you* to do it?"

Father Preston's face purpled with suppressed rage. He waited a moment to calm down. "Juliana's path has diverged from ours. I will not judge her harshly, because she is a good woman who is very frightened of dying. I hope she will change her mind before the end."

She did it. She made him leave, thought Ruth.

"So the Congregation and I are beginning a new home for the Afflicted. One where they will be cared for by many hands and will also have the opportunity to participate in God's work, even in their illness. Give us the boy, he will be well looked after. And when Juliana passes, turn the hospital over to us and be free of this place, confident you fulfilled her last wishes."

"What do you mean, 'God's work?'" asked Ruth, glancing at the boy who was sucking on the rim of the empty can.

Father Preston turned to the Congregation and crooked one finger. A man slid out from the small crowd. He rubbed his right elbow self consciously as he walked forward. Ruth stared at him trying to place his face. "Brother Gray wandered the wilderness for many years," said Father Preston. "He has come home at last, but his trials have not been without worth. In the south, he found a community that thrived by caring for its Afflicted and giving them honest jobs that they could do even with their reduced intellect. They defended their communities as guards and carried the burdens of those unable to do so, or provided the power for machinery that improved the lives of all. Please, Brother Gray, enlighten Ruth."

Gray shrugged and wouldn't meet Ruth's eyes. "They pulled the plows or turned the stones in the flour mill. It kept them in shape."

"You see? It keeps them healthy and gives them a purpose," Father Preston rumbled like a contented cat.

Gray glanced up and Ruth finally recognized him. It was the man with the ear trophy necklace. Her hand dropped to the gun on her hip and she saw him flinch. "Just how did this miracle come about *Brother* Gray?" she asked, slowly pulling the shopping cart back toward her.

He shrugged again and glanced at the priest, who frowned, waiting. "Um. People just led them."

"Led them. You mean they chased people. Because they were hungry. And they were made to move something heavy at the same time."

"Yeah, I guess. Except the guards, they didn't carry anything."

"I bet they were kept hungry, too, though, just in case an enemy— I'm sorry, a *rival* wandered in. That about it?"

Gray nodded. Ruth fought a sneer of disgust and ignored him. She turned to Father Preston. "You're talking about slavery. I'm not letting you take this boy or anyone else."

"You wanted us to treat them like our neighbors and friends. Like they were human beings with value. I don't disagree with you. Decent human beings contribute to their society. They work to better everyone's life. That's all that we're asking. In return they'll get lifelong care."

Ruth snorted, "You mean by keeping them just above starving? By killing them slowly with too much labor while you sit back and reap the rewards? Are you going to loan your Infected out too? Have them work the local farms for trade while you build yourself a church? Unleash them on anyone who disagrees with you?"

Father Preston reddened again. "I will not

waste my breath answering such outrageous accusations when I've done nothing but show the Afflicted kindness. They are my brothers—" he stopped and took a deep breath. "It's very simple Ruth. If you really care what happens to this boy, you'll let him take his chances with us. You'll let them all come to us. Otherwise, they'll suffer a very long and painful death through starvation and freezing this winter when you have too many to feed. It will be *you* torturing them then Ruth, you who advocate mercy. There isn't any other choice."

She knew he was right. She'd seen the meager garden and the bare pantry. She doubted whether there was even enough to get them to harvest, even with extensive scavenging missions. She'd comforted Juliana the other day, but in truth, she saw no way for them all to survive. The boy was chewing dents into the can and beginning to kick again against the cart. He was still hungry. *They're always so hungry*, she thought. She glanced at Gray who was whispering to Father Preston. His clothing had changed into a plain, unassuming church goer's outfit, but she knew what he was. He'd drive the Infected as hard as he could and then sell them to someone else who would treat them even worse. And as long as Father Preston could pretend it was good for their souls, he'd never stop it. The boy might survive the winter with them, but it wouldn't be much longer than that. What on earth could she do? He was right. There was only one choice. There was no way out that she could see. She couldn't watch him starve. She couldn't watch any of them starve. It was too much.

She stared at the multicolored bands around

his chest and arms. "Well?" rumbled Father Preston. Ruth selected a red bungee cord. She carefully unhooked it and draped it over the community board that held all her photos. "I'm sorry, Connor. I really, truly am. You didn't deserve any of this. Better luck next time around, kid," she said, looking at the boy. His gaze slid away and flitted over the rest of the crowd and then back to the can.

Father Preston smiled. "That's not necessary Ruth. I assure you we'll take good care of him. We can get him safely out of his bindings—" He stopped and the color drained from his face as Ruth pulled her gun from its holster. Gray ducked behind the priest. The others gasped or shrieked. Ruth hesitated for one more second. *It's for the best,* she thought. She heard Bill's voice in her head again. "It's time to let him go. It had to be today." She pulled the trigger and the boy's head rocked backward. The shopping cart rolled a few feet away from her and caught on the edge of the community board.

There was time to hear the tin can clatter against the metal bars of the cart and then the cement. Then someone screamed. Then someone threw a stone. It landed in front of her. She turned and saw a look of utter shock on Father Preston's face. Behind him, the Congregation was a seething mass of fury. She saw more stones in their hands and she ducked. A few hit her anyway. They were small, street rubble. In a few seconds they'd find the heavy stuff. She didn't want to be there for that. She thought of her gun, but she knew they were too outraged to react to a simple threat.

She grabbed her pack and began to run. A large rock plowed into her hip and she stumbled but kept to her feet. Another smashed into her back. And then she was gone. She regretted leaving the boy's body. They'd never let her go back to bury him. They might even attack the hospital. She knew Juliana would never understand what she had done. She would die hating Ruth. But Ruth had to try to explain. And she couldn't abandon Juliana especially now. She made her way back toward the hospital, hoping she'd beat the mob.

CHAPTER 14

The cord glowed red against Ruth's hand. Like the blood of martyrs. More real than anything around it, more real than the boy or Ruth or the Congregation at Father Preston's back. She draped it over her foul trophy board. He'd have to give a sermon on the pride of the wicked. That would encourage his reluctant flock to do something about it.

Ruth murmured something to the boy.

He was cheerful now that he'd won. The moment of triumph had been years in the making and it was all the sweeter when it finally arrived. Now she would see that he had been right the whole time. She'd hand over the hospital Afflicted and then leave. Not that it mattered, they'd be sloughing off this foul city as soon as Juliana passed anyway. He didn't much care where Ruth went, as long as it was away. He smiled and said, "That's not necessary Ruth. I assure you we'll take good care of him. We can get him safely out of his bindings—" The words shriveled in his mouth as Ruth raised the gun in front of her. Father Preston didn't even have time to understand what was happening. The boy was dead, his head dark with blood, the silver cart rolling farther from them.

A woman behind the priest screamed. He just stared at Ruth. He had expected her to give in. It wasn't supposed to end that way. She had *rules*, damn her. Even *she* had limits. He'd counted on it, driven her to them on purpose. A chunk of asphalt flew past him and hit Ruth's hip with a thunk. He didn't move. Couldn't move. Another rock sailed past and hit her in the back and she turned to flee.

A crawling burn formed in his gut as she disappeared. It mushroomed into fury and finally broke his paralysis. He turned around. Most of his Congregation had run off, chasing Ruth down the street. But the new convert, Gray, was watching him.

"She'll kill the rest," Gray hissed, "Our community can hardly thrive without the Zom— I mean, the Afflicted, Father. We have to stop her before she takes more innocent lives."

It had been a mistake to tell her about Juliana. He was convinced her friendship was the only thing that restrained Ruth. But Juliana had pushed him out, left him with no alternative. He couldn't let the hospital fall into Ruth's hands. It was his calling to minister to the people left in the city, all of them, the sick and the well. He had been released, recalled from madness to perform this holy work.

He knew better than Ruth or Juliana what the Afflicted experienced. He knew the good the morning readings must do. Locked in their insanity, the Afflicted could not ask for guidance, but they would remember it when at last they were cured. He had. He remembered everything. How a word or act of kindness, though it fell upon a man blind and deaf with rage, was now the sweetest medicine for his spirit, something he looked back upon with all the relief it ought to have created at the time. And the guilt of his own violent actions drove him to amend, to repair, to strive to forgive. He could not abandon his Afflicted brethren to someone who didn't understand, who had no faith in a coming cure. He couldn't let Ruth have them.

Anything, even violence, was preferable to that.

"Father?" whined Gray, "have you forgotten your flock?"

Father Preston shook himself out of his dark thoughts. "We must get to the hospital first. Juliana won't be so willing to have Ruth stay there once we tell her what has happened here. Don't worry, Brother Gray, the Afflicted will know salvation yet." He smiled and the man ducked his head in agreement. "See how many of our people you can round up," Father Preston continued, "I will go have a talk with Juliana. In the meantime —" he glanced at the shopping cart, "bury the boy. And destroy this place of evil. Salt the earth beneath her. I don't want Ruth to have anywhere to come back to when I'm finished. I want her out of this city for good."

Gray's face split into a slow smile and Father Preston felt a slick worm of doubt twist in his gut. He ignored it and began walking toward the hospital, rehearsing the story he would tell Juliana.

CHAPTER 15

The hospital was in uproar when he arrived. The immense iron bar that was usually seated next to the door had been flung into the tall grass of the yard and the front door stood wide open. The Afflicted were shouting and banging and a mangy dog stood in the foyer growling and snapping. It looked like the gardener's dog, but Father Preston couldn't see Bernard anywhere. The dog, nervous at the noise of the Afflicted, turned toward Father Preston and growled.

The priest backed out and walked around to the kitchen rather than risk being bitten. He called for Juliana but no one answered. He wasn't sure if anyone would be able to hear him anyway. The kitchen door was closed and the meal carts were empty, though Father Preston knew it was past lunchtime. He shrugged and pulled the door open. Maybe Juliana had already cleaned the dishes. But she'd had no volunteers that day, not from the Congregation anyway. They'd all been with him.

Maybe it was Bernard, or a family member helping her. Or maybe Ruth had beaten him there after all. Father Preston tasted a dry, bitter flash of fear. Was that why the Afflicted were screaming? Was she slaughtering them even now? His heart rattled against his ribs. He slunk into the kitchen and cautiously peered down the hallway. Just the dog, continually barking. There were thuds on the stairs just beyond the door. Father Preston pulled his head back and pressed himself against the wall. The kitchen door sprang open, almost hitting him. It was Bernard with a small bucket. He lumbered over to the sink, not seeing the priest behind the door. He threw the handle of the hand pump up and then slammed it back down, frantically trying to fill the bucket. Father Preston glanced around the door to make sure no one was with him. Then he slid out from behind it.

"What's happened?" he asked. Bernard jumped and twisted around. The skin under his eyes was red, as if he had been crying and his hair was raked and pulled in half a dozen places. He grabbed the priest's hand and pulled him toward the door. Father Preston pulled back. "Is it Ruth? Is she here?" The gardener shook his head. He pointed up and began pulling Father Preston toward the stairs again. "Where's Juliana?" he asked Bernard, but his arm was only pulled harder, so the priest reluctantly climbed the stairs, wary of any ambush that might be waiting. It took three floors to house all of the Afflicted now. Juliana stayed in one of the attic offices. Father Preston had stayed in another until the Congregation rebuilt the local church and its parish house. It was suffocatingly hot in the attic, even in midwinter. It was almost unbearable when Bernard brought him to Juliana's room. She lay on top of the neatly made bed, dust from the garden crumbling from her boots onto the covers. Her face was ashy and beaded with sweat. She was unconscious. Bernard patted her hand and gently shook her shoulder but she didn't wake up.

"Go back and get that water," ordered Father Preston, "It's too hot in here."

Bernard tromped back to the stairs and disappeared. Father Preston opened the window. It was one of the few perks of living up here, the offices all had windows that could open. The kitchen was the only other room that had them. He sat down in a rickety folding chair that Juliana kept beside the window. Bernard came back with the bucket of water. He placed it next to the bed and began soaking a cloth in it.

"Has she been unconscious long?" asked Father Preston.

Bernard shook his shaggy head.

"Was she feeling ill this morning?"

He shrugged. He put a sopping washcloth on Juliana's head. She took a sharp, surprised breath and opened her eyes.

"Did you find Ruth?" she asked.

Bernard shook his head again and pointed with a grimy thumb toward the priest. Juliana struggled to sit up and see who was there.

"I came to see you about Ruth," said Father Preston in a grim tone. "I'm sorry to have found you so ill."

The gardener helped her sit up. Juliana smiled. "Nonsense, I just got a little dizzy from this heat. Bernard brought me back. I'll be fine in a minute or two."

"I'm afraid you are overtaxing yourself. Let me handle the hospital for a while. I know what needs to be done." *This is almost too easy,* he thought.

"That's okay, Ruth should be back shortly. We'll be fine."

Father Preston let the gentle smile on his face wither into a grave expression of pity. "Ruth has done something terrible— I would say unforgivable, except that I save judgment for God."

He shook his head slowly and looked at the floor. Juliana rubbed her temples gently and huddled closer to Bernard, who put a protective arm around her. Father Preston didn't wait for a response. "There was a boy— a young boy, perhaps twelve. His father didn't want him anymore. I begged him to give the boy to me, but he refused and brought him to Ruth. I thought she had rules about this sort of thing. She's never harmed a child before, not even an Afflicted one." Juliana looked up at him. "I asked her to give the boy to the Congregation, told her that we would care for him, that she didn't need to worry about straining the hospital's already depleted resources, that our church had enough and some to spare. She just— snapped. I didn't think even *she* could harm a child. She had *rules*." He reached for Juliana's hand and enveloped it in his own. "She shot him, Juliana. Right there, in front of all those loving, caring Christians who were just trying to help him. She shot him and then fled. I know that God forgives all of our sins, no matter how heinous, but I'm afraid human justice isn't so forgiving. I tried to hold them back, begged them to show her mercy, but the Congregation was outraged and filled with zealous wrath. They scattered and even now seek out justice. I would have followed them, in order to stop any violence, but I was worried she might be headed here and in her unstable condition, well— I'm glad to find everyone here unharmed."

Juliana sat for a long moment in silence, her eyes closed. Then she turned to Bernard. "Will you find Ruth for me? I need her to come back. I need her help. Make sure she's all right."

Bernard nodded and tromped down the stairs again. Father Preston waited until he was gone.

"Are you feeling much pain?"

Juliana shook her head. "I just get tired and the occasional headache. I can manage."

"I'm sorry such trouble has disturbed what ought to be a time of rest and peace."

Juliana laughed. "There's not much peace around here, regardless of what Ruth or you do."

"You needn't work so hard, you know. You could retire, live out the rest of your days in tranquility. I will care for the Afflicted. We are starting a new community, they will be well fed and attended to. They will be healthy with us until a cure is found."

Juliana frowned. "Father, I'm past believing comfortable lies. We both know that there isn't a cure. There won't ever be one now. But we've already discussed this," she waved a hand at him, "I want to talk to Ruth first, before I decide what happens to the hospital when I'm gone. You can fight like dogs over it if you want then, but let me think that my request will matter while I'm alive."

Father Preston released her hand. "Of course your requests will be honored. I know we both want what is best for the Afflicted. But I now know what Ruth is capable of. I can't possibly allow her to commit the same atrocity again. But she is your friend. Indeed, we ought to all be a friend to Ruth in her time of despair. You will want to hear what happened from her own mouth. I understand that impulse. I urge you only to be cautious. And know that I will be nearby if you need assistance, with

Ruth, with the hospital or just to sit and read with you."

Juliana managed a dim smile. "Thank you Father. Now, if you'll excuse me, there are lots of very hungry people waiting for me."

Father Preston rose. He looked down at her, as if he were about to say something else, thought better of it and gave her a nod. Then he strode out of the hospital, leaving the shrieks and clawings of the Afflicted behind him and turning his thoughts to the future of Ruth's police station.

CHAPTER 16

Ruth had run through the baking streets for several minutes before the sizzling in her lungs forced her to slow down. She kept glancing around her, sure the mob was chasing her, but her shadow was the only thing that moved in the windless concrete. She ducked into the cool dark of a small alley expecting an ambush but only the echo of her own feet followed her. Her hip and back were sore and hot where the rocks had struck. She was limping badly and knew she'd never beat the others to the hospital. She'd only end up being overtaken by them if she tried. And then what? A lynching? A fire at the hospital? They weren't going to stop once they found her. She'd seen the complete surprise on Father Preston's face. He'd been sure she'd never kill the boy. He'd probably told the Congregation as much. If he hadn't pushed so hard— if he'd let her think for a moment...

Ruth sank against the brick wall of the building behind her. She had time to think *now.* Had there been another way? The people in the hospital would never survive the winter. She'd seen the pantry. The bins were only a quarter full, even while they were harvesting the early crops every day from the garden. The shelves were empty except for the very back. A few cans, a few jars of preserves Ruth had made herself from another distant orchard the year before. Family members stopped in less and less, and when they did, they brought very little. Ruth had watched as they, too, lost weight over time. The whole city was in its death throes, not just the hospital. Even if the boy had somehow survived, if she could bring them all through the winter, what was it for? He'd still be sick. Still be suffering. It was just Charlie all over again. It always was. Every day, every contract. She was just repeating and repeating the same hell, watching people wither and die for years and years. Was she really going to do this for the rest of their lives?

Ruth leaned over and threw up the thin oatmeal she'd had that morning. The boy's face became Charlie's in her head. It cracked where she'd shot it and then splintered away. She wiped her mouth with the back of her sleeve and focused her gaze on the peeling back door of the restaurant across the alley, counting splatter stains until the image in her head went away.

There was no way she could have given him to them, not knowing what they intended to do with the Infected. Father Preston didn't understand. He couldn't. Ruth knew he was dogmatic and stubborn, even willfully stupid. He could be downright nasty in his righteousness. But he wasn't cruel for the sake of it. If he really saw what the bounty hunter wanted, he'd never go along. Gray must have painted a picture of paradise for him. A vague camp far away that thrived in the wasteland. A utopian dream of the Infected and the healthy as peaceful, benevolent neighbors. But by the time Father Preston admitted the reality, it'd be far too late for the Infected. Still, it was life. It was a chance at a cure. Was it so different from the people in the hospital?

There is NO CURE, she thought, *stop fooling yourself. There're no more labs, no more doctors, no lost vial of relief waiting out there like a grail.*

There's no cure. Just this never ending loop of misery.

She had given up long ago wondering what the right thing to do was. Now she only worried about what the *kindest* option was. She let herself examine the memory of the boy one more time and then let it rest. She pushed off the wall and began limping toward the greenhouse, hoping Juliana would meet her there instead of risking the mob following her to the hospital.

She was surprised to see the vegetable patch empty and unguarded. Juliana never let it go untended lately, not with so many thieves. Though volunteers had diminished, there were always one or two at least that showed up faithfully. And Bernard should have been there, at least. He had become a caretaker of sorts. Juliana,Ruth and Bernard had converted one of the conservatories into a cozy house for him. He slept there, guarding the food supply, and taking care of the medicinal plants for Ruth. She checked his rooms but he wasn't there. His dog was gone too. She tried to tell herself he was out scavenging, but the stillness in the garden sent a painful chill through her core. She called for him, but not very loudly, afraid of who else might be nearby.

He had been dropped on Ruth's doorstep four years ago. He'd been beaten unconscious. His wounds were serious and he took months to recover, even with Ruth's help. She had no idea who he'd been before, if he had deserved the beating or not, if he'd been a good man or evil, and neither did he. Or if he did, he couldn't tell her. He couldn't speak and made very little effort to communicate through other means, though she could tell he followed at least some of what Juliana and she said, and would laugh at a simple joke.

Bernard took care of himself and had been pleased to be trusted with the garden. He was big enough to be scary to people that didn't know him. The dog had adopted him a year later. They hunted pigeons and crows together, the only game to be found in the massive city.

Ruth went back to the vegetable patch. She put her pack down and tested her bruised hip and back gently with one hand. The plants were withered and brown. Ruth looked at them for a moment, swearing under her breath. No one had been there for hours. She checked the gun and tightened the holster on her hip, then she grabbed some buckets and headed for the pond.

The water was so low that the painted concrete winked through the algae and shone up at Ruth. The summer had already been very dry and even hotter than usual. Even the swampy marsh behind the hospital had dried up and become a dangerous, brittle mass of tinder. Ruth was dreading July and August. *If it doesn't rain soon, we may have to resort to the brackish stuff in the subway.* She scraped the buckets along the bottom of the pool and began carrying the scummy water to the dwindling pea vines.

CHAPTER 17

Bernard hadn't thought to check the garden until almost sunset. He'd checked the police station first, where a handful of men were already smashing windows and piling everything flammable they could find in front of the door. He stayed far away, not wanting to be seen. He worried that Ruth might be inside, but since none of the men were really guarding the door, he moved on, hoping she had, too.

He checked Ruth's old home and the clinic where she had treated him when she had found him. The clinic had been ransacked, the door torn from its hinges, chairs and desks gone, burned to keep someone warm. Her house was caving in, a leak in the roof had become a cascade, and her living room was now a small, rotten pool fringed with moss and mold. Bernard left those places to their quiet fates and let the dog lead him,not sure where to try next.

The dog eventually led him home, where he found Ruth weeding the garden, slick with sweat and crying in great whooping gasps. She didn't even look up when Bernard's shadow blanketed her. The dog leapt up in front of her and licked her face. She slumped into the soft ground between the rows of tomatoes and said, "Is she okay?"

Bernard looked confused and scratched at his thick beard. He crouched beside her.

"Is Juliana hurt?"

Bernard shrugged, then shook his head. He pointed a calloused finger toward the hospital.

"I can't go back there. She can't know what's happened."

Bernard pulled her to her feet. He pointed back to the hospital. There was a shout from the far end of the park. A cluster of shadows was forming at the edge of the tall grass.

"They've found me."

Bernard waved toward the hospital and picked up a heavy rake. Ruth shook her head. "No, if I leave, they'll destroy the garden or burn down your cottage."

He shoved her in the chest with one large hand and she took a few stumbling steps backward. He pointed to the hospital again. She glanced toward it, though she knew it was out of sight. He gave her another shove, but gentler this time.

"Okay, I'll try," she said. She picked up her pack from the end of the row and began to run. She glanced back and the gardener was facing the other way, his legs planted carefully and solidly between the rows. He held the rake across his body, ready to use it if he had to. The dog's back bristled as it stood next to him, growling. Ruth hoped they'd be all right. The park's rustling grass gave out onto cement and she slid into the shadows between buildings, still running.

When she reached the snarl of brush that surrounded the hospital, she dropped down into a crouch, afraid that Father Preston or his mob were waiting for her there. But there were no angry people waving torches by the door or screaming protesters along the path. The scene was serene, the lamps in the hospital beginning to shine out of the occupied wing just as usual and the slow plaintive echo of a mourning dove calling its mate home to nest. The ordinariness badly frightened

Ruth. Part of her suspected a trap, but a voice inside her was convinced that she was in a changeless Hell. The hospital would always be there, a bleak battleship half-sunk in an ocean of scrub and tall grass. The walls would forever be decaying, the Infected would never stop screaming, and she and Juliana would continue to scrabble and starve for them for eternity. She struggled against the burning weight of shame and despair as she thought about fleeing.

But then the front door opened and Juliana rolled out her cart. It was piled high with dishes and laundry and buckets of filthy water. She was just a shadow in the dusk, so Ruth couldn't see how tired she was. But Juliana struggled as she lifted one of the buckets, almost dumping it on herself. Ruth's hesitation evaporated and she hurried to help her friend.

"I wasn't sure you'd come back," said Juliana as Ruth emptied another bucket.

"And I wasn't sure you'd want me to. But if what Father Preston said is true, I can't leave you to do all this work alone. So I'm staying. Even if you hate me."

"What was it that he told you?"

"That you've got an active cancer. That you don't expect to see the spring."

Juliana sighed and sat down on the front step. "I should have told you first, but the time was never right. And then I had a very bad night. I was scared. So I asked him for counsel. He promised not to say anything."

"Why didn't you let me treat you? Are you certain it's cancer? The symptoms are similar to other—" but the words died as Juliana shook her head.

"This isn't the first time," she said. "I've been so lucky, it's been gone so long that I thought I'd forgotten what it felt like. But that was only me trying to fool myself. I persuaded myself that it wasn't back for a long time. And when I admitted that I was sick, I *thought* about telling you. So many times. But there's nothing to be done. Even *you* can't stop this, though after the Plague you seem like a miracle worker."

"I could operate, we can find what we need, somewhere. Maybe we can trade for it."

"It's spread, Ruth. I'm getting terrible headaches. Sometimes I lose consciousness. Bernard brought me home from the garden today because of a bad spell. I don't think it will be too long now." Ruth hugged her, not sure if she were comforting Juliana or herself. "Don't fret," said Juliana, "I've had fourteen more years than I expected. There wouldn't have been much more that could be done even before the Plague. Maybe I stuck around to run this place. Maybe it was to meet you. Maybe it's just luck and clean living. Whatever it was, I've had extra time to be useful. To make some very loyal friends. I've had a decent, fulfilling life and I'm not done with it yet."

The crickets hummed around them in the dark. *A decent, fulfilling life. But she didn't say happy. Nobody says a happy life anymore,* Ruth thought, *it's just too much to ask for.*

"Is that why you didn't bring the boy here? You didn't want to be stuck with them all when I die?" Juliana's voice was calm, but Ruth could sense the panic underneath.

"You want me to promise to take care of them all. To keep the hospital just as it is until I find someone else who will do it or they are cured or we all die. I'm not sure why you want *me* to do this, when Father Preston seems so willing— eager even, to do it. But you don't know what you are *really* asking."

"I *do*, I understand. I know how badly you want to leave the city and I know what I'm asking will put that off indefinitely. But the truth is, I don't trust Father Preston. He seems to have no empathy for the Infected at all. It's like he's forgotten what it was like. Maybe he has."

"Juliana, it doesn't matter who you ask. They aren't going to last through the winter. There's almost no food left and very little wood."

"You said we'd find a way. You said you knew where there was more, the orchard—"

"Because I thought I had time to find it. Yes, there's an orchard. But it's far away. Two or three days away. Yes, there's probably a few overlooked places for canned food. But I thought I had time to look. I can't leave you here by yourself. You can't do this alone, not while you're sick. And even if you could, I don't think I should leave. The people out there— they'd as soon steal what they found for themselves as help us. You're asking me to watch a hundred people starve to death around me. To do nothing while they die a very slow and painful death, when I have the power to stop it. It's too much, I can't do that even for you. That's why I shot the boy. I had a choice, Juliana. Three actually. Father Preston offered to take the boy, for his new community. But there was a man with him, a man I met years ago. He used to hunt the Infected for bounties. Now he sells them to slavers.

"Father Preston doesn't understand. But the boy and any other Infected they get their hands on would be starved, beaten, uncared for. They'd be no better than guard dogs or mules until they were worked to death. I could have brought the boy here, too. Could have watched him freeze or starve with the others and then have to shoot him in a few months anyway when none of us could take it anymore. Or I could save him the utter misery of both. That's what I chose. Is that who you want to run this place when you're gone?"

Juliana dodged the question. "They won't starve. Something will turn up. Someone will help them, it always has in the past."

Ruth shook her head. "No Juliana, it hasn't. We've always had a plan, always had more than we needed. When the garden was almost wiped out a few years ago, you had a pantry full of cans. When winter lasted long after we expected I found places that still had wood and food. I had to go a long way. It's been years since then. Those places are gone. People outside the hospital are getting desperate. They are getting bolder with their thefts. There's nothing for them to eat either. I can't blame them for wanting to feed their children. More of our food will disappear before we pick it. What we have in the kitchen right now is almost all that we will have. A month's worth? Two if we stretch it as far as it will go? If a miracle is coming, it better hurry up and get here," she glanced over at Juliana, "for all of our sakes."

Ruth began to see flickering lights at the far end of the overgrown lawn. She stood up. "Go inside, Juliana."

Her friend stood beside her. "Maybe you should be the one to go inside," she said.

"I don't want them to do anything stupid, like burn down the building to get at me."

Juliana reached for her hand and squeezed it. They stood on the front step together as the flickering grew into a cluster and then a wave of light closing in around them. The field rustled and lay prostrate in the wake of people dragging heavy steel beams across the grass. Grim looking women followed the beams, each carrying heavy tools or draped in coils of rope. There were almost a hundred people. More people than Ruth had seen in one place outside of the hospital in almost a decade. All of them were silent, staring at Ruth and Juliana. They stopped at the edge of the grass, just in front of the hospital doors. They stood there and waited.

"Can we help you folks?" asked Juliana with a sour smile.

The crowd of people shuffled and Father Preston emerged with Gray. Gray had lost his penitent expression and didn't avoid Ruth's gaze any longer. He hefted a sharpened fire ax in one hand while he dragged a large chain over his other shoulder. Whatever the chain was attached to was lost in the dark beyond the mob.

"I think you know why we're here," Gray sneered, but the priest held up a hand and he fell silent.

"I'm here to beg Ruth to submit to justice, to

prevent more bloodshed." Father Preston held his hands out toward Ruth as if expecting her to leap into his arms for protection from the crowd.

Ruth just laughed. "Justice? This is just mob brutality. I thought you left judgment up to your God," she said, clinging to Juliana's hand. She tried to calm her breath but deep down, she wasn't sure she'd survive the next half hour.

"Your actions are crimes against both man and God's law, and both require redress. Submit to us of your own accord and no one else will have to suffer in your place."

Juliana stepped in front of Ruth, half shielding her. "She's harmed none of you. What she's done, she's done out of kindness. Not malice, not for gain or because she enjoys it. Her punishment is already severe enough. She carries it with her everywhere. Nothing you do can be as terrible as her own guilt."

"What guilt?" A voice in the crowd shouted. "She shot that boy in the street in broad daylight. She has no remorse for the people she's murdered!"

Juliana faltered. She glanced back at Ruth. "She was trying to prevent more suffering. The truth is, there isn't enough food here. Not for anyone, but especially at the hospital. That boy would have starved to death in a few months along with the rest of the Afflicted. After all this time, the hospital is failing. We can't care for all of these people. And starvation is a terrible, painful way to die."

Ruth knew it broke Juliana's heart to admit how much trouble they were in. Gray took advantage of the opportunity. He slunk forward as

Juliana was speaking. "We offered to take the boy. He would have been safe, well fed with us. We can take them all. All of the Afflicted can stay with us. We have enough. You don't have to break your back any more, Juliana. We can help now—"

"You mean you can use them as slaves, as beasts of burden and as human shields," interrupted Ruth. "I won't let you do it. You may have all these people fooled, even Father Preston. But I know what you are. The last time I saw you, you swore never to return. If we are truly seeking justice, why don't we talk about how many Afflicted *you've* killed Gray? And for what? A couple of cans of dog food." Gray raised his axe, his face a twisted snarl. Father Preston restrained him. "You cannot judge me," continued Ruth and she looked out at the crowd of people. "None of you can. Who among you hasn't killed someone in the past eight years? An Infected that was attacking your loved ones? A looter trying to take your goods? An attacker trying to violate a family member? Maybe you've been lucky. Maybe you avoided all that. But you saw your neighbors die to the same things and did nothing. Or they became infected and wandered out into the street and died on your doorstep from hunger or exposure. Or you knew about someone else's stockpile and you took just a few cans of food or a couple of boards or books for warmth. And then you took what remained when they died of want. None of you are fit to judge me or anyone else." She looked out over the crowd. "Go home. Forget the Afflicted. Forget this place. Let us starve in peace."

"No," growled Gray.

Ruth looked down at him and began speaking quickly and quietly. "I know you want the Infected. They are valuable to you. This is the only place where you'll find so many together. Do you really want to create a frenzy? These people are a few words away from burning the building down around us. You want to risk all that stock? Think of the trade you'd lose. You could have it all in one job. Drugs, electicity, gas, whatever you wanted with this many slaves. Or you could let it all go up in smoke."

"You aren't going to give them to me anyway. What do I care if they burn?"

"Maybe you'll get lucky. Maybe I'll die first. Maybe you'll outwit me. But if the hospital is destroyed, you'll have no more opportunities to try. For now, it's a truce."

"Wicked deceiver!" cried Father Preston, "do not bargain with this woman, her tongue is as forked as Satan's own. No truce!" He held up a handful of photos. They were bound in the scarlet bungee cord she'd taken from Connor's shopping cart. "Someone has to pay for the innocent blood that has flooded these streets. If you will not submit, someone will have to pay that debt for you." He nodded at Gray who gave the chain a mighty yank.

There was a groan and some jangling. The crowd separated and began moving the steel posts as the chain became slowly slack and slithered in the grass around Father Preston. Two men crawled slowly forward, moaning with pain. A badly hewn section of telephone pole was lashed to their backs, long splintery shards slicing their shirts and skin as they dragged themselves into the light. The others ignored them, busily chopping the brush and dirt away from two small sites.

Golden sparks sprang from the end of a few welding torches as they worked on the steel beams and the rope was uncoiled and cut into long pieces, shining like silver on the dark grass. Gray hauled the man on the left to his feet. The man screamed and thrashed feebly, too exhausted to do much else. There was a heavy dog collar around his neck that the chain passed through and his hands were bound to the telephone pole with rope. His face was swollen and dark from repeated beatings, Ruth didn't recognize him. "Please," he gasped, "my wife is pregnant. We're having a baby. You have to let me go, she'll be all alone—"

Gray wrapped the chain once around his hand and pulled the man closer to his face.

"You're lucky she's not up here too. From what I understand, she's the one that wanted your son dead. Count your blessings and stay quiet." He shoved the man backward. He fell and his head snapped against the pole at his back with a thud. He lay there weeping. Father Preston held up the red bungee cord. Gray took it and wrapped it around the man's chest. Ruth finally realized that it was Connor's father. She took a step forward but Juliana grabbed her arm and pulled her back.

"They're already dead, Ruth. They'll kill them now whether you try to save them or not. It's no use you dying alongside them. That man's wife will need help. You're the only person for hundreds of miles who can." Her eyes were streaming, but Juliana's face was hard and frozen.

One of the beams was lifted up by a small surge of hands. It sank into the crude hole that had been hastily dug in the yard. A few men held it upright while others packed the dirt back in around the beam. The other man was dragged to his feet, but he said nothing. His nose was bloody and smashed, but Ruth remembered the loose band-aid on his cheek. Father Preston plucked a photograph from the bundle he was holding. Ruth didn't have to look to know it was a photo of Emma and the man in front of her was Nick, Emma's father.

"You know," said Father Preston, gently tapping the edge of the photo against his chin, "I'd hoped for some divine hand to strike the police station with lightning or a tornado or some other terrible force so that it would be gone. So you could no longer revel in your misdeeds. But I'm glad that prayer went unanswered. Because your board of trophies has given us a way of tracking down every wicked soul who ever resorted to your services." He handed Gray the photograph while staring at Ruth. "How many did you say over the years? I think it was more than fifty anyway. Well, it's going to be a little tricky finding fifty steel beams that will suit the purpose, but we'll manage. You can have a new trophy board," he raised his hands to indicate the field as another beam was lifted into place. Juliana sobbed but clung to Ruth's arm to prevent her from surrender.

Nick looked up at her. His lips were broken and swollen but he managed to stretch them into a smile. "I buried Emma yesterday. She looked so peaceful. I slept today. Wanted to plant some flowers before—" His smile faded and his eyes sparkled in the torch light, "I just wanted to say thank you. Whatever the cost is, I'm paying it willingly. Happily. It was worth it just to see the calm in her face."

Gray kneed him in the gut. "Shut up, baby killer. You think this is the price for what you've done to your daughter? You're going to hell, you'll pay for an eternity."

Nick doubled over and then laughed, a wheezy, shaky rattle. "At least I'll have a friend," he managed and caught Ruth's eye.

"I'll see you soon," she said and Nick nodded as he was pushed backward toward one of the beams. Twin stepladders were opened on either side of each post. Nick was relieved of the telephone pole, only to be rebound with his arms above his head in the center of it. A man stood on each stepladder holding one end of the pole, awaiting direction.

"This man is a murderer," said Father Preston loudly, "he requested and paid for the slaughter of his own child. Since the one who carried out the deed will not submit to justice, he must answer for both his own sin and hers," Father Preston turned to Ruth, "He is dying for *you*. It may be a pale reminder, but let it soften your pride and lead you back to the path of the righteous. Repent and put aside your wicked disobedience."

"Blasphemy," spat Juliana, but Father Preston ignored her.

He raised his hand and the men holding the beam started up the ladder. Nick closed his eyes as his feet rose off the ground. His body twisted slightly to the side as he dangled. Ruth watched the muscles in his arms tighten. The beam was put in place on a welded bracket and the photo of Emma was stapled to the wooden beam. Nick hung from his wrists directly below it. He tried to brace himself with his feet against the steel post. The men saw what he was doing and made a grab for his boots. He didn't fight them as the boots were removed. His arms shook and his face began to redden. There was a hollow pop and he cried out before biting his lip. Ruth saw Gray's slow smile smear his face and turned away for a moment. She shut her eyes. The sweet, green smell of the crushed grass made her dizzy. There was another pop and Nick screamed. Ruth took a deep breath and turned back so he could see a friend's face as he died.

Nick began to gasp, panting out his breath as his feet slid against the smooth post behind him, trying to push himself up. He was drowning in the cool night air. He kicked and finally planted his feet on the post. He pushed himself up for a second and gasped before falling again, his torso twisting to the side.

Juliana sobbed and tugged on Ruth's arm. Ruth turned to look at her. "Where's the gun Ruth?" she asked in a whisper so that no one else could hear.

"The gun?" Ruth asked, too shocked to understand.

"You can't leave him like that."

Ruth glanced back at Nick, who had pushed himself up again. He was steady and his breath was coming in great whoops. She could see his legs shaking with the effort. The quarter moon emerged from the shattered clouds and cast a cool light on his face and over the crowd, turning them to marble.

"Ruth," he said quickly, "it's okay. It's done." He sucked in one great deep breath and then shoved off with his feet. He held his breath, kicking only once, wildly. After a few moments, his eyes rolled back and his head dipped forward. Ruth heard a few struggling wheezes and then there was nothing more. One of the men climbed the ladder and checked the pulse in Nick's dislocated wrist. He nodded briefly to Father Preston. The first notes of a hymn spilled into the soft summer air, a woman's voice, high and sweet overwhelming the crickets. The rest of the crowd joined. The Infected heard and began shrieking. Juliana turned and vomited. Ruth held her up as her body shook with the violence of the expulsion. "Go inside, go lie down. You don't have to watch this," Ruth said in her ear.

Juliana shook her head and wiped her mouth. "If I leave, they'll grab you. Come inside with me. You don't have to watch either."

But Ruth did. She was somehow responsible for all of it. She had to be there. "If I don't, they might do something worse," she whispered.

The hymn evaporated, and the crowd became ominously silent again. Ruth turned around. Gray was walking over to the other bound man, the father of the boy Ruth had shot. The stepladders were moved.

"No!" cried the man, "No, have mercy! Please, my wife is very pregnant. I was only trying to protect my baby. What choice did I have?" He wept while they arranged him on the telephone pole and rebound him.

"You could have left the boy with us. We offered to care for him for the rest of his days," said Gray and turned back toward Juliana, "an offer I extend to everyone inside as well."

"You would have worked him to death," the man sobbed, "You would have used him up and starved him or beaten him. I've heard of those camps to the south, I know what they do to the Infected there."

Father Preston looked sympathetic as he leaned over the man. "We aren't like the heathens to the south. I wouldn't allow anyone under my care to come to harm."

The man struggled and ignored the priest. He turned to the men tying him down instead. "What do you want?" he asked, "You want food? I'll show you my stockpile. You need shoes? I've got good boots. Just let me go back to my wife. I won't cause any more trouble."

A thought seized Ruth. Nobody but her had heard what his request was. Nobody knew he had abandoned Connor but her. "It isn't his fault," she said loudly over the man's cries. He stopped and stared at her. "He asked me to bring Connor to the hospital. I told him there was no room. No food. That he'd have to take the boy back with him. He said the boy had tried to kill his wife, that he was afraid he'd get loose and kill the baby. He couldn't bring him back. He didn't know I'd make the choice that I did."

The man looked confused for a moment but

quickly jumped on the thread of the lie. "I didn't know she'd murder my boy," he cried, "I asked her to take him here. That's all. You can't do this!" The people binding him paused and looked at Father Preston, who was frowning and staring at Ruth in consideration. He turned to the man.

"Ruth is well known for what she does. You must have known when you brought her the boy."

Lie, Ruth willed at him, *keep lying. You're almost free.*

But the man hesitated a fraction of a second too long. "I don't believe you!" shouted Father Preston, "You stand upon the doorstep of death! Yet you compound your sin by lying. Finish it," he waved a hand at the men on the step ladders and they began raising their victim onto the post.

"Please," yelled the man to Ruth, "please, my wife, my new baby. They'll starve. Don't— "

The man groaned as he was lifted from his feet. Ruth sprang away, darting into the hospital, leaving a weeping Juliana on the step. She sprinted down the hallway, sliding and banging into room doors which caused fresh fury from the Infected. She flew up the steps and tore open her pack. The gun gleamed with the reflection of the moon. She checked the last remaining bullet and kept the safety on as she raced back down the stairs and out onto the walkway.

Juliana was covering her face with her hands, but looked back when Ruth came tumbling out of the doorway. The man was screaming in pain and terror, so nobody else paid attention to her when she came out. Juliana's eyes widened as she saw the gun, but she sobbed and nodded. Ruth aimed, but her hands were shaking. She took a deep breath and fired.

The screaming stopped and she grabbed her friend before the mob realized what had happened. She pulled Juliana through the door and closed it, locking it from the inside. She handed Juliana the gun and ran down the hall to the kitchen. The mob was shouting and rounding the corner of the building as she slammed and locked that door too. There were a few smashing blows, but then someone called them off and the crowd retreated. Ruth returned to Juliana in the hallway. They watched the mob scatter, their torches like stray sparks swirling from a fire into the dark. Rain began to fall on the field, dropping heavily on the hospital's patched roof in a soothing roar.

The Infected stopped screaming one by one, dropping off to sleep. The dead men creaked as their ropes twisted and rubbed against the wet wood. At last, exhausted and numbed by grief and terror, the two women wandered up the stairs to bed. Juliana was pale and shaking as she crawled onto the bed, but she fell asleep quickly in the cool, damp air. Ruth slumped against the wall outside her door and fell asleep at the top of the stairs with the gun on her lap, her hand clenched around the grip.

CHAPTER 18

Ruth peered through thick spirals of gray fog at Nick's body. There was no breeze and the corpses didn't rock or twist on their beams. She wanted to take them down and bury them in a quiet place. She wondered if she should try to find the other man's wife. She didn't even know his name. *How many pregnant women can there be?* She thought, but she had larger problems at the moment. Gray had not left the hospital unguarded. A woman was crouched over a campfire between the two crosses. She pulled a dead gull out of a pot and began to pluck it, occasionally scanning the hospital for movement. Another man made a circuit along the path, parting the fog every few moments only to disappear again into it. They both had weapons. Ruth had no doubt they'd been instructed to use them on her.

The cart of dirty dishes and laundry still sat in front of the door on the walk. The place couldn't function without the things on it. Ruth checked her gun. The bullet she'd used last night was the only one she'd had left. It had been the one Nick had given to her. But she was the only one who knew that.

Gray had gone a step further and bolted them in with the heavy crossbeam Juliana used when she left the hospital. There was a crank to pull it back up, but Ruth knew it would move too slowly and loudly to surprise the people guarding the yard. She glanced down the hallway to the distant kitchen door. The fog was thick, but it was a long way around the building and she'd have to walk right by the woman and her fire. That left waiting for Juliana to do it or going through the ruined wing, and Juliana was exhausted and ill.

Ruth had crept down the stairs so her friend would keep sleeping. She looked at the boarded up door to her right and then glanced back outside. The male guard was lost somewhere in the gray. The woman was deeply intent on scraping pinfeathers from the dead bird.

The boards came off smoothly with one twist of a hammer. Ruth was surprised. The structure had to be rotting faster than she'd thought. She pushed on the door gently. It scraped over some rubble about halfway open. She stopped and held her breath. There were no sounds from outside. She slid through, her belt buckle clinking the edge of the door. She stopped to clear the bits of wood and drywall that had stuck under the door. She didn't want to retrieve the cart only to draw attention to herself on the way back in.

This side of the building was a mirror image of the other, except that it ended abruptly in gray fog halfway down, where the walls had collapsed. She edged her way down. The floor seemed solid, but the roof showered her with dust as she moved toward the opening. She could hear the footsteps of the male guard scraping over the cement outside. They died away and she slid carefully down the rubble hill and into the long grass.

The front of the building was lined with hedge. They had been small once— neat, squared, hip-high things. Eight years of wild growth and tangling with the building's heavy curtain of ivy had made them a snarled nest of dead branches and rabbit warren under a skin of green. Ruth crawled under the edge of the hedge. She had to scrape along the dirt to avoid being snagged in the dry, brittle claws of the brush and it bothered her that she could see nothing of the guards or the cart until she got much closer. She froze as the footsteps returned and then multiplied. She tried to peer through the dusty covering of leaves, but she could only see boots.

"How much longer do we have to stay? I got kids at home waiting for food. I can't spend all day here," said a man's voice.

"I hear you, brother, but we can't let that murderess escape. Who knows what she'll try next. Maybe she'll come after us for revenge, or our families. You saw her yesterday, she's capable of anything." It was another man. Not Father Preston. Gray perhaps?

"But I have to feed my kids—"

"Relax, you and Breanne will be relieved shortly. We found another of her accomplices and the construction crew will be here shortly. Besides, I don't think food will be a problem for much longer. Father Preston says time is running short. He wants to press things along. If they don't cooperate in a few days—" the voice paused and spoke lower, but Ruth was closer than he knew. "We'll take out that garden. In fact, if you want to get out of guard duty early, you can go take care of that dog the caretaker keeps. We don't want them to have any chances to stop us and a dog could be a problem. I've got rat poison in the wagon."

"Where am I going to find dog food?" scoffed the guard.

The other voice laughed a grating, hate-filled

sound that made the pit of Ruth's stomach grow chilled and tight. "That bitch passed off cans of dog food as regular food to me once. She doesn't know I still have a few. It'll be like sweet karma." Gray laughed. "Or you can bean it in the head and we can roast it up with Breanne's bird. Have a regular feast." The other man laughed too. "C'mon," resumed Gray, "let's get you set up with the supplies you'll need. Breanne, the construction crew will be here shortly. Care to help us unload?"

The woman grumbled but Ruth could tell the request was not optional. How badly these people must hate her, to go to all this trouble. *No,* she thought, *it's not me. It's the whole world. They hate what their lives have become. The choices they can't make. I'm just a symbol of it.* She heard scrabbling as the woman shuffled over to them and they began walking toward the road. Ruth waited until the footsteps were almost gone, then pushed her way through the thick brush, scraping her arms on the jagged branches. She darted for the cart and swung the bar up on the door, surprised at her own speed. Once inside, she pulled the cart down to the kitchen. The Infected heard and began yelling. Instead of starting breakfast though, she paced the kitchen.

Bernard had to be warned. The dog was his reason for existing. But there was no way she could leave now. The guard would be back now, or would come back when she heard the noise of the Infected. And the construction crew— Ruth spared a pitying thought for whoever they had captured. All those families, just trying to do the right thing. Would they all be Father Preston's victims? How long could she allow this to go on? There was an obvious solution and Ruth was avoiding it.

She dumped the dirty bowls into the sink and started pumping water into the basin. Yesterday had been chaos. She'd been frightened and exhausted, angry and grieving. But in the cold morning stillness, she knew she couldn't let anyone else die for her. She scrubbed furiously at the dishes, wanting just this one task to be really, truly done. Done for Juliana. Just one thing really finished, not left trailing and looping like her whole life, before the steel beam rose up in the field and she gave in to them.

All these years, she'd struggled on, afraid to die, but suffering the whole time. She was kinder to strangers than she'd been to herself— than she'd been to her own son. The seven years since Charlie and Bill died hadn't been living; they'd been a continuous, hopeless streak of hell. When Juliana died, there'd be no more kindness left in the world. It was fitting that someone like Preston should win.

Ruth swiped the clean bowls with a frayed towel, not really seeing them. She slammed them onto the table one after another. The Infected wailed without pause. *No peace, even in my last half an hour,* she thought. But there would be silence soon enough. She wandered into the dark pantry and felt the hot bubble of a sob burst in her chest. It spilled into her throat before she could stop it. She leaned over a large empty bin and let the cry out. She sank down to the floor and closed her eyes. The wooden bin still smelled crisp and sweet like the apples it had held long ago. The sounds of rage from the hospital were muted.

Ruth felt a cool hand on her shoulder and opened her eyes. Juliana crouched next to her.

"They are going to keep killing people," said Ruth.

Juliana nodded.

"And I heard them planning to raid the garden and poison Bernard's dog."

"That's not entirely unexpected," said Juliana calmly.

"Eventually, they'll get tired of waiting and burn this place down or storm it. I have to go out there, before anyone else is hurt."

"No, Ruth, you can't. It won't make any difference. A group that angry is never satisfied. It has to burn itself out. It's like a pressure cooker; it has to spend its steam for a long time before it's all gone."

"I can't just let them keep crucifying people."

"We won't. You were right about the hospital, Ruth. These people are all going to die. There's nothing I can do to stop it. And if you're right about what that man with Father Preston intends to do with them... I can't just abandon them. But I can't just— I can't ask you to do what you've been suggesting with them. I know there's no cure coming. I know they'll probably starve or freeze. But I have to give them a chance. And I have to give *you* a chance."

"What are you talking about?"

"We're going to let them go. We're going to fight for our lives and for theirs."

"But they'll run rampant over the city!It's been years since the Infected were loose in the city.

The people who are left think they're safe!" cried Ruth.

"You think they're any better off with these zealots in charge? They aren't going to stop. They'll judge and crucify anyone they don't approve of. This is just the start. Look at what we've been through. We survived the end of the world, Ruth. All the chaos and murder and looting and violation and suicides that happened with it. We fought it off. We built this place—"

Ruth shook her head. "*You* built this place. My only purpose these last several years has been murdering other people's loved ones. I couldn't even help my own. My life's been pointless and cowardly."

"Ruth, I've thought for a long time about what you do. Sometimes, when the people here scream or scratch their faces bloody or chew away their own skin, I think you're right, that you've been right all this time. But I keep hoping, and I keep going. Not once, in all these years, not even after Father Preston recovered, have I thought of what you do as pointless or cowardly. And this place wouldn't be here without you. Don't think that I don't know where our supplies came from or who has been caring for the garden when nobody else will. We built this place together. And I'm not going to let a bunch of slavers and murderers walk in and take it over. Someone's got to stand up to them. The people that aren't with them are frightened. Or will be. They're scattered and lonely. You and I have what might be the deadliest army left on the face of the earth. Is it better to let them starve when I'm gone? Or live out the rest of their lives being beaten and worked to death? At least this way they'd have a chance. Not just to survive, but also to do one more good thing with their lives, to use this terrible Plague against people that want to hurt their families."

Ruth was silent for a moment. "Wouldn't we be just as guilty of using them as Father Preston would be if we gave them to him?"

"I'm not going to force them to kill or starve them so they want to. I'm just going to let them go. I hope some of them run away and live. But I know some of them will attack the first thing they see. It's what they do."

"How do we stop them from tearing each other apart?"

"We have the poppies," Juliana said. There was a distant screech of metal as another steel beam was set in place. Ruth nodded grimly.

"When?" she asked.

CHAPTER 19

Father Preston was calling for her to come out. A woman outside moaned in pain and the Congregation's hymn floated over both in eerie harmony. The kitchen was hot and thick with sickly-sweet dust. Ruth's back ached as she divided the straw into individual portions and then wrapped them for the kettle. They were a dozen doses short.

"We don't have enough," she said and glanced up at Juliana. Juliana rubbed a greasy arm over her sweaty forehead. It left a brown smear of poppy dust behind.

"Isn't the early crop ready?"

Ruth shrugged. "I didn't get a chance to check. But we need to warn Bernard anyway."

"I wish we could save the food." Juliana sighed and cut another disk from the coffee filter.

"I'll get what's ripe, but it's still pretty early. And we had to plant late this year."

Juliana sighed. "I know. I think about it constantly." She plunked down into a nearby chair and rubbed her eyes with the palms of her hands. "A week earlier or a few extra feet plowed or a couple more hours of weeding and watering and we wouldn't be here. Everything would have been okay for another year."

"No. Don't think that way," said Ruth, wiping her hands on a damp cloth. "A hundred people weren't meant to be kept alive for this long by a dying woman and a handful of casual volunteers. It's an impossible task. You can't clean them, groom them, feed them, nurse them when they are sick, maintain their shelter and raise all their food. It's astonishing how much you've managed for so long. It's time for all of it to change. Do you know what a *krìsis* is, Juliana? It's where we get the word 'crisis.' It's the point in an illness where every option has been exhausted. It's the point where the patient either succumbs and dies or their body rallies and fights off the infection. The city is at its krìsis. And we are at ours. The Infected will either free us to finally begin rebuilding a world of a decent, kind, helpful society, or Father Preston and Gray will win and people like us will pass away, and human civilization will at last be over. Either way, the interminable stagnation is done. You've done your duty, Juliana. More than. Now allow your kindness to be repaid and, I hope, pass on to all the people who are hiding, terrified of the Congregation and people like them." Ruth peeked out of the kitchen window at the group on the lawn. The woman on the third cross writhed and struggled and the tense Congregation were like cats watching their victim.

"I should go now. Before they have a chance to find someone else." Her heart cried for mercy for the woman, but she had no bullets left. At least she could use the distraction to slip away and warn whomever she could find.

Juliana stood up and pulled a scrap of coffee filter from her pocket. She'd scribbled a list on the ragged leftovers. "We need more than the poppies. We can't just put them out there the way they are. They need clothes and boots."

"I don't know if I can find a hundred sets of clothing Juliana, let alone shoes."

"We have to give them the best chance that

we can. Bernard can help. He and that dog know all the unlooted places."

Ruth shook her head but took the list. "I'll do my best. Don't expect me until late." She stared intently at Juliana. She was pale and swayed a little. Even Ruth was a little dizzy in the heat of the kitchen. "Maybe I should get you to bed. You have time to rest. Don't push yourself too hard."

Juliana nodded, too exhausted to argue. Ruth made certain the doors were well blocked and secure before helping her up the stairs. The attic rooms were cooler but the open windows carried the agony of the yard into the room. Ruth started to close the window when the wails abruptly stopped. A few seconds later a fierce, joyous hymn took its place. Ruth slammed the window shut in disgust. Juliana cried for the dead woman, but she was already dozing by the time Ruth crept down the stairs and into the abandoned wing.

She eased along the length of the hall, avoiding the large, brightly lit collapse she had slid down that morning. She could see the Congregation milling around through the thinning tops of the hedges and knew she'd either have to hurry or wait until they dispersed completely. Fearing she wouldn't reach Bernard first, she tried to speed up without making too much noise. She came to the end of the hallway; the front of the building crumbled away, the remaining jagged outline like an empty socket where the tooth had splintered away. Orange and red Indian Paintbrush pushed up through the tumbled stones and a large snake lay sunning itself on the dusty cobble. Ruth crouched to make herself as small as possible, but she knew she was still plainly visible to anyone who turned her way. She slunk to the edge of the broken wall and peered out.

The day was warm and a light breeze blew over the brush and long grasses toward the other side of the hospital, but Ruth could still smell the older bodies beginning to rot. They were bloated and blackened against their shining beams. Ruth felt only sorrow and pity, but she promised herself she'd take them down and burn them with the hospital once Gray and Father Preston had been run off.

The Congregation had diminished, at least temporarily. There were only about fifty circling the third corpse. They had stopped singing and Ruth could see Father Preston standing before them, his hands wild and emphatic, his face a deep, hot red. His flock, however, seemed more interested in picnicking than in listening, lounging on blankets and passing bowls of food to each other in the shadow of their latest victim. Ruth found the scene nauseating. She turned away and ran quickly to the thin fringe of trees that separated the hospital from the highway. She took one more quick glance back at the hospital hoping Juliana was asleep and would be all right until she returned. Then she threaded her way through the dry, brittle branches of the pine trees at the edge of the field and out onto the baking highway.

The city was barren once she left the hospital. Everything was waiting, even the birds were mostly silent. It felt to Ruth more like the breathless afternoons in July that ended in terrific thunderstorms, rather than a mild morning in mid-

June. Though it had hardly changed in eight years, the silence felt suddenly oppressive and filled with predatory ears. Even the gardens seemed ominous as she approached, the sun glittering off the greenhouse like signal fires to someone she couldn't see.

Her pulse doubled as the screech of metal rubbing against itself reached her from the vegetable patch. There was nowhere really, to hide. Bernard enjoyed clipping the grass with the push mower, so it was one of the only places without even any bracken to duck into. She had no real weapon either, just a bulletless gun that she might be able to bluff with if pressed. There wasn't really a better approach than the one she was on; she was still below the crest of a hill and not visible to whatever was up there. There was another screech and Ruth froze. *I have to at least try to help him,* she told herself and pulled the empty gun out of its holster, hoping she looked calmer than she felt.

The sun prickled on her back, seeping through her thin shirt. Her breath was deep and rasping as if she'd sprinted from the hospital instead of walking briskly and carefully. She licked the salt from her lips without realizing it. She was at the top. Bernard was standing there, his back to her. A rusty barrow filled with dark soil sat beside him. A dirty shovel leaned against it.

"Oh no," Ruth cried, "I'm too late."

Bernard was startled and spun around. But he wasn't holding his dog. It was just a sack of carrots. Ruth sighed with relief. Bernard flung down the sack and grabbed her arm. He pulled her into the cottage and shut the door. The dog lay in the sun pooling under the window, he thumped his tail halfheartedly as they entered and then fell back asleep.

"What—" began Ruth, but Bernard put a large, dirty hand over her mouth and shook his head. He pointed out the back window toward the greenhouses. A shadow flickered behind the glass of the closest structure.

"They're already here?" she asked, "but how? They were busy at the hospital when I left."

Bernard shrugged.

"We have to stop them. They'll steal all the food. They want to poison your dog."

The gardener held up a hand to make her wait. He pushed the small bed aside and pulled up a board. Ruth leaned over and peered in. The hollows for as far as the light reached were filled with food, everything that was even close to ripe from the garden. He gently placed the board back and pushed the bed back into place. Then he pulled her to the small attached tool shed. There were trays of seedlings on every surface, all the plants twisting their faces to the bright slit of window above.

"You knew to do all this? But how?"

He pointed to an ear.

"You heard? Oh, of course. You would have come to check on Juliana after her fainting spell."

He looked anxiously at her.

"Juliana is okay," said Ruth, "but we have to make sure she rests more."

The crash of breaking glass interrupted them. Ruth darted back to the window. The closest greenhouse was black with soot and a sheet of flame billowed and snapped in a light breeze as it poured from the broken panes. She could see one of the willows inside glow from the ends of its leaves to the trunk as its vines curled and twisted in the heat before dropping away.

She hadn't expected them to hurt the greenhouses. They held no food. Medicinal herbs, astringent plants, but nothing most people would recognize or know how to use. There was no reason to destroy them, except spite.

A small knot of people were already heading for the other greenhouse while a larger group drew closer to the cottage and Juliana's garden.

"The rest of the poppies," Ruth cried and leapt for the door. Bernard grabbed her and shook his head.

"You don't understand, they'll destroy everything. We need those, I have to stop them." Ruth pushed back, but he refused to move and shook his head again. He held up his hands and made a cross with his two forefingers. Then he pointed at Ruth.

"I'll die anyway if they burn everything. We all will."

Bernard shook his head and pointed to the floor where the food was hidden. There was a banging on the cottage door. The dog sprang up from where he had been napping and snarled deep in his throat. Bernard's eyes grew wide and he grabbed her by the shoulders. He put a hand over her mouth again and then pointed under the bed. Ruth shook her head. Bernard pushed her down to her knees next to the bed. She struggled silently. There was another bang at the door.

"Open up if you aren't in league with that she-devil!"

The dog began barking and his back bunched and rose. Bernard shoved her again and she relented, sliding herself under the low bed frame. Bernard kicked a pile of dirty clothes gently into the crack. Ruth pushed them around so she could see without being discovered. Bernard gave the dog a soothing pat and then opened the door.

"Where is it? Where's the food?" came an angry voice.

Bernard shrugged and then staggered backward as he was struck.

"Don't play dumb." There was a snicker from someone else and Ruth's face went hot with anger and embarrassment. "You take care of the place, you must know where it's gone." Bernard pointed in the direction of the hospital.

"No, now I thought you might say that. I know the food's not at the hospital, because we've had the place surrounded for days. Try again, Joe." Ruth recognized Gray's sneering tone.

CHAPTER 20

"What's wrong with him, Boss?" asked the other man.

"Joe? He and I were buddies, a long time ago. We used to... well, we used to keep the streets safe, didn't we Joe?"

Bernard had turned slightly and Ruth could see Gray was hitting him gently in the shoulder with the flat of the ax he carried. "And people would pay us to keep it safe for their families. Lots of looters in those days. And Afflicted without people to care for them. Joe here heard there was a woman who would pay us really well down at the police station. So I went to have a chat. But it turned out to be that she-devil. She almost broke my arm, didn't she Joe? I guess he didn't hear so well, cause she wasn't interested in paying. But his tongue worked well enough back then. We became reformed men after that. Brought the Afflicted to places that could care for 'em. Places where they could do good. A long way to the south, isn't that right Joe?"

Bernard was shaking his head, his face perplexed. Ruth wondered if he could remember any of this, if it was all lost in the severe beating he had taken, or if Gray was just lying for his audience. Gray continued. "There's a city to the south. Another one. Smaller than this, but lots more people. They have it made there. Electricity, military, there's even a rumor of a cure for the Plague. Poor Joe. He was always such a sucker. He believed the rumor. Wanted to take the Afflicted there, to be cured. So he tells me this whole story of the cure and the city and how we could live there as heroes. 'Joe,' I told him, 'There isn't any cure. If there was, and this military that the city has is real, don't you think they would be out delivering this cure to people? Starting up the government again, getting folks organized?' These people were just sitting behind a cement wall, taller than a three-story building. They just cowered in there, scraping by. So I said, 'Don't you understand, Joe? They are persuading people there's a cure so they'll bring their sick relatives. That way they don't have to go out and round them up. And when they get to the city, they probably get taken to a hospital, just for show. But they're just taken out back and shot. No more zom— Afflicted.' But Joe wants to find out for sure. 'Just go ask,' he says. I told him no, even a hint of what we were doing could put the operation — the *Afflicted* in trouble. Like I said, he didn't hear so well then.

"Good old Joe Mackey, just had to go his own way, no matter what anyone else thought. So he brought a soldier into our camp on our way by. Did it really casually, when we were packing up to move on. Well, the soldier would have killed everyone in that camp. We had to defend ourselves and the people in our charge. And Joe— well, let's just say his tongue doesn't flap so free anymore." Gray reached up with surprising speed and pinched Bernard's cheeks, forcing his mouth open. The other man gasped at the stump Ruth knew he saw there.

Her head was whirling. Bernard was the man that had sent Gray to see her in the first place. Without him, none of it would have happened. And there were rumors of a cure? How could there be a cure? Her mind rejected it almost immediately, though she didn't believe Gray's version either. He was right though. If there were a cure, word would have spread, even over a great distance and even given the scarcity of people. Wouldn't it? It was like the Holy Grail. How many rumors of cures had she heard in the past eight years? How many old wives' tales? All false, all mirage.

"Now tell me where the food is," Gray growled and he pushed Bernard backwards toward the bed. Bernard simply shook his head, his face pale and stony. "Get the dog," Gray snapped. Bernard grabbed for his dog with a loud groan, but Gray was too quick. He brought the flat of the ax blade down on Bernard's shoulder. It hit with a meaty thunk that Ruth could feel in her teeth and she guessed that at least one bone had broken. Bernard howled in pain and staggered back a step as the dog leapt at Gray, snarling and biting. His teeth closed around the hand holding the ax and Gray swore loudly.

"Get it off, you fools!" he roared, and two men hurried forward to pull the dog off. Bernard had recovered and punched Gray in the jaw with a massive fist. He barreled through the other men. The dog let go and sprinted after him. There were too many people waiting outside. The dog escaped but they dragged Bernard back in to the cottage and forced him into a chair near the plain wood table. He was smiling as Gray fumed about the dog.

"I want that mutt found," shouted Gray. "Whoever kills it gets to take it home to their family. Must be enough meat on that thing to eat for a week."

The chorus of cheers that erupted at this announcement made Ruth both nauseous and profoundly sad. Even Bernard's smile dissolved into a look of deep pity, and she knew he was wavering about giving them the food. So was she.

"In the meantime," Gray said, walking over to Bernard, "You're going to tell us where the food went."

Bernard took a deep breath. He pointed again to the hospital. Gray shrugged.

"If thy right hand offend thee, cut it off. You're lying Joe. Or your hand is. Hold him down."

But it didn't take much to pin his broken arm to the table.

"I'm going to give you one more chance to redeem yourself and tell the truth. Where is the food?"

Ruth held her breath, but Bernard didn't even betray her with a glance. He pointed immediately back to the hospital. Gray raised the ax over his head. Bernard shut his eyes.

"Brother Gray," said a nearby man, nervously, "If you cut off his hand, he'll die. Even if he doesn't bleed to death, he won't be able to work. You've broken his arm. The only doctor in town is that heathen who is bent on killing people. It'll never set right on it's own. He's already going to have a hard time plowing. He'll starve if you take it completely."

"Better he should die than continue to lie for that murderess. Better he should starve than *your* children. He knows where the food is. Don't you want it?"

"Well— well, yes," stuttered the man and the others around him nodded. "But surely we should be merciful and give him a chance to repent. Take him to Father Preston. I'm sure he can help this man see the light."

Ruth watched Gray's eyes narrow with hate when Father Preston was mentioned. He kept his voice smooth, in control. "Father Preston has already spoken on this. He's said that anyone in league with that devil-woman was to be cast out of our company, unworthy of being in our presence."

The others still looked doubtful and there was an uneasy shuffling in the small cottage. Gray realized it, too. He twisted the blade around as he spoke. "My brothers are right. We should always strive to be merciful. Still, I think the path to righteousness sometimes needs a little *prod*." He grasped Bernard's broken arm and brought the blunt side of the ax down on Bernard's hand. It hit with a wet crunch and Bernard screamed, his uninjured arm flailing even with two men holding it down. Ruth tasted the coppery salt of blood and realized she'd bitten her own lip.

"I've heard the pinkie finger isn't really good for much, but it seemed to prove useful this time. Now, where is the food from the garden?"

Bernard raised his good hand. He was shaking, but he pointed to the hospital.

Gray shrugged. "Well, you've got four more chances anyway. Plenty of time to change your mind." He smashed the ax down again. Bernard whimpered this time.

"Where's the food? Careful now Joe, or you're going to start losing fingers that matter."

Bernard just shook his head. Gray grinned. Ruth realized that he didn't really care where the food was. Maybe he didn't even care where *she* was. The longer he was in control, the more he could *hurt* people, the happier he'd be. It sent a spiny shard of fear through her limbs.

"Which finger should be next? After all, we want to be as merciful as possible. The thumb should be last of course. But should we take the middle finger next? It would only make a foul sign if it were left alone. Or should we take the forefinger, since its twin keeps pointing to a lie? What do you think brothers?" He spun halfway around to see the others.Most of them were pale and uncomfortable.

"Maybe it's really at the hospital," offered one.

Gray sneered. "Is *that* what's troubling you? No. It's not at the hospital. The hospital has been under constant guard. I know that *I* didn't shirk my watch. Did *you,* Brother Michael?"

A skinny man in the back twitched as all the eyes in the room swiveled onto him. "No, no of course not, Brother Gray."

"How about *you,* Brother David?"

A man she recognized as the guard in the fog shook his head quickly.

"Well, there's your answer then. *We're* not the liars and sinners here. And if we aren't lying, then Joe here must be." Thwack! The ax crushed another finger. Tears streamed down Bernard's face and he sobbed.

"Just tell us where it is and all this can stop. It can all be done, Joe. You're in control of this whole thing."

Bernard groaned, but he didn't shake his head again. Ruth ached with dread. She knew he couldn't last. He was going to tell them. What could she do? She was trapped. And once they had their hands on her—

"Where's the food, Joe?" Gray asked again, his tone almost friendly.

Bernard whimpered like a dying dog. He raised his good hand again. It hung in the air as Bernard sobbed again. Every eye watched the hovering hand. Bernard slowly raised his forefinger and pointed to the hospital.

Gray slammed the ax down twice, in quick succession. Bernard screamed. Gray turned away from him in disgust. "This man still refuses redemption. Throw him in the cart. He can face the cross like the others. Maybe Juliana's misplaced affection for him will make her give up that bloodthirsty whore, to save him and he can end all this misery."

A few of the men lifted Bernard from his chair and pushed him out of the door. Ruth's mind raced. If they'd just wait until dark, maybe she could rescue him. But if he didn't stop bleeding he'd probably be in shock by then. She had to find a way to treat him, and fast. Her muscles tensed, ready to spring up from her hiding spot as soon as the rest of the group moved on. But Gray had other plans.

"You," he said, pointing the ax at one of the men standing in the doorway, "stay here and keep an eye on this place. Juliana will send someone out here eventually to find the food she needs for the hospital. If it's that baby-slaughtering doctor I want you to hold onto her until I come to get you. Do what you like with her, just be sure she's alive and conscious for the cross."

Ruth shuddered and tried to crunch farther into the shadows beneath the bed. A few more of the men lingered to search the cottage. The rest followed Gray outside. There was a bustle and the sound of breaking plates as the men swept the small kitchen clear, looking for food. It wasn't long before one of them found the seedlings in the shed. He called the others over. "Well, shit. I actually believed the gardener," said one, peering in.

"If the plants are here, where's the edible stuff?" asked another.

They all piled into the small shed. Ruth glanced at the front door. It was still ajar from when the others had left. She couldn't see anyone outside. Nobody was looking. Soon they'd tear the rest of the place apart. They'd find the loose floorboards, and they'd find Ruth. She took a deep breath and pushed herself up by her hands, the back of her hair just catching on the underside of the bed. She glanced at the storage shed door to make sure their backs were turned and then tensed to spring out from beneath the bed.

"We better tell Gray," said one of the men and turned around, Ruth froze. She'd moved too close to the edge of the bed. He'd surely see her if he looked.

"Wait a second before you go off running your mouth," said another and came out of the shed after him. The other two men followed. "Listen, Gray doesn't have a family. He's only got to look out for himself."

"And?" asked the first man, his eyes narrowing.

"We can't feed everybody, no matter how bad we want to. Your kids are hungry, John. We're neighbors, I hear 'em crying at night. Mine too. I do what I can for the Congregation, but scavenging hasn't gone so well these past few months. There's less and less in the city. Me and Martha— we've talked about leaving, lots of times. But this is our home, always has been. And we figure any help would come here first, to a big city where there might still be people left to need it, not out in the wild. So if we can find a way to stay, we're going to."

"But Gray said—"

A third man interrupted. "Gray said we should let him know if we find the food. This is just seedlings. He's burning the greenhouses. He doesn't care about plants. He's no farmer. But we could do something with them."

"What about the rest of the Congregation?" asked the last man.

"You heard Father Preston, they're leaving as soon as they get the Afflicted out of the hospital. I don't know about you, but I don't want my newborn sleeping next to a zombie, no matter what the Father says. I'm staying. And if I'm staying I have to feed my family."

Ruth took advantage of the confusion as the men argued amongst themselves for a few more minutes and drew herself farther into the shadows. She'd have to wait for another opportunity. She worried about where they would take Bernard and whether he was still holding onto consciousness or not. Part of her hoped not. At last they agreed that one of them would go find a wheelbarrow while the others reported back to Gray.

"What if that woman comes while I'm gone?" asked the man who was meant to guard the cottage.

One of the others scoffed. "She's locked up tight in that hospital. There's almost fifty people in that field. There's no way she's coming here."

They left together, closing the cottage door behind them. Ruth sagged against the floor in relief. She only waited a moment and then darted to the door. She peered out the window into the bright afternoon. She'd never get across the garden without being seen. The guard had found the barrow and was wheeling it back. She pressed herself against the wall so she would be behind the door when it opened. She grabbed a sharp trenching shovel that was leaning nearby. Bernard had used it to start building an irrigation canal early that spring. It hadn't been completed.

She realized she was going to have to incapacitate the guard and a wave of anxiety sent cramps through her gut. Despite what Father Preston proclaimed, she'd never considered herself a murderer. The man just wanted to feed his family. He believed she was evil. She knew that. Deep down in their hearts, all the people that followed Father Preston were convinced she was truly bad. Deep down in her own, she desperately wanted to believe she was not. But she knew she was about to do something worse than everything that had gone before. *By the time the day is out, you'll have to do it again,* said a little voice, but she pushed it away. No time for thinking or even justifying now.

The wheelbarrow's rusty wheel creaked as it came to a stop outside the cottage. The man clumped up the few steps and opened the cottage door. He headed for the storage shed, leaving the front door open. Ruth gave it a gentle shove so it would shut but not slam. The light changed as the door began blocking the sun and the man began turning to see why. Ruth leapt at him before he could see her. She brought the heavy point of the shovel down on his nose, shattering it and spraying a heavy splash of dark blood over the floor. The man reached up and began to yell, but she jerked the shovel back and drove it into the front of his throat before he could bend over to cradle his broken nose. The man tried to gasp and only gurgled. He toppled and lay on his back, his hands still holding his broken nose as he struggled to breathe through the slice in his throat.

"I'm sorry," Ruth sobbed and brought the shovel down on his neck once more. She dropped the shovel and ran to the door. She looked through the open crack but didn't see anyone. She slid out of the door and shut it behind her, hoping nobody would check on the guard until she and Bernard were long gone. Where had they taken him? There was a low whine from behind her. Ruth whirled around thinking the guard was still alive, trying to reach her. But the door was still closed. The soft whine came again and Ruth crouched down and tried to see into the crawlspace beneath the cottage. Bernard's dog crept forward and thumped its tail.

"Good boy," she said quietly, stroking the dog's muzzle, "find Bernard. Good dog. Find him." The dog was a mutt, probably a stray long before the Plague. But it knew Bernard, and even if it couldn't understand Ruth, it naturally sought him out. She followed the dog as it snuffled its way over the muddy patch that used to be the garden. She crouched and kept glancing around, but there was no one in sight, no sounds of anyone else. Ruth ached to be well past the open park land, even though the grass was high enough in most places beyond the vegetable patch to hide her if she stayed low. But the dog took its time, untangling Bernard's old, familiar footsteps with the recent ones. They came to a wide opening where the grass had been heavily trampled. It lay, gold and green in a matted path, the sweet smell of the broken blades at odds with the grief and fear that grasped at Ruth's chest when she saw it. It was something that belonged to an earlier time. A smell for sports fields and late summer evenings. It made her even sadder. She hurried down the path the men had made, leaving the dog to follow behind her. She stumbled out of the grass onto the blank flatness of the street. She took a quick glance around and then darted into the shade of a bus shelter. The dog followed her and stood in front of the bench. She pressed herself into a peeling ad on the wall and took a long look around.

The building across from her, an old glass case that used to be offices leaned against an adobe church nearby, closing the alleyway to a sliver. On the other side was a lot, a construction site with a naked metal frame of a building. Saplings grew in its center and weeds covered most of the gravel. Bird nests clung to the beams. It looked almost undisturbed. But there was a tarp that had been thrown back from a pile of steel beams. The metal gleamed too brightly, it flashed in the summer sun unlike the rusting beams of the structure.

Nearby, a few telephone poles were stacked, the bottom two dark and rotting. The top pole had been freshly sawn, sections of it strewn over the lot. It had to be where the Congregation was getting their materials. Ruth was surprised it was so close to the garden.

How long had they been planning this whole thing? *Just Gray,* she told herself, *the others are going along. Even Father Preston, though he doesn't know it. He's not in control. Gray is. And he's probably been planning something since I threw his ear trophy back in his face and humiliated him years ago.* She knew she should be frightened, overwhelmed at the forethought that had gone into it, but a bright flare of rage flickered in her head instead. Bernard had to be near the construction site. She had to find him.

She didn't see anyone guarding the site, and she had followed too quickly for them to have picked up the beam and the section of pole and taken off already. She didn't like running across the open road, but she hadn't been on this side of the gardens for a long time. The roads around the site might be blocked with debris or buildings like the one across from her. She didn't have time to make a lot of detours. She took a deep breath and then raced across the road, careful to stay clear of the broken glass that had fallen from the windows above her. The dog padded after her, his tongue hanging out in the heat of the afternoon.

She made it to the construction site and threaded her way through the debris and rusting tools. There was still no sign of anyone. On the far side of the site was a squat brick building with a blacked out door. It hid between the other buildings, once it was a squalid little mole at the base of shining towers and bright, clean sidewalks. Now it was the survivor, a great swollen mushroom thriving as the others toppled and shrank. Ruth could hear voices inside as she got closer. They rose and fell, but they were garbled and confused behind the brick. Ruth snuck around the building, trying to find a window to peer through.

She didn't see the dog's hackles rise until she heard it growling beside her. She tried to calm it but the animal pulled away and continued its low snarl. It was facing the rear of the building. Ruth slowly leaned out to look around the corner. There was Bernard. He was lying in the back of a police car, unconscious. He was shut in the car's cage, but the front half was missing, shorn away in some accident, jagged, rusty edges left of the roof. Someone had welded a kind of metal yoke to the sides and its two stalls were occupied by two restless people. They were bound to the metal, their arms lashed to their sides and a football helmet jammed down onto each head. Only their legs were free. The car was anchored to the building with a thick tow cable so that even when the people in front pulled, it stayed put. Ruth didn't have to get close to know the two were Infected.

How could Father Preston not see how badly

things had twisted out of control? How could he possibly justify what Ruth saw as pure slavery? The Infected had heard the dog. They were trying to twist in their harnesses. She could hear their teeth snapping and grinding in a futile effort to feed. They began to moan with anticipation and Ruth knew she didn't have much time. She ran to the car and opened the door. Bernard opened his eyes as cooler outside air hit him. He was covered with sweat and drying blood. Ruth helped him scoot forward out of the car.

"Can you walk? Just a little way, we have to get out of here."

He nodded but swayed as he stood. Ruth supported him. The Infecteds' cries were growing. She gave one glance at them, wishing there was something she could do, but she knew there was no time. She pulled Bernard down the alley as quickly as she could. The dog bounded after them. The Infected began shrieking as Ruth helped Bernard into the only dark place she could find.

CHAPTER 21

The subway was pitch black and the smell of sewage mixed with seawater was overpowering even after almost a decade. The dog whimpered beside them. Ruth scratched him gently behind the ears. "Don't worry boy, we aren't staying long." She could hear shouts above them and decided the mouth of the stairwell wasn't the best position. If they were in luck, the guard station might still have its emergency med kit and she could treat Bernard while they waited out their pursuers.

"Stay awake Bernard, we'll have you feeling better soon. We have to move now, but not far." She fished the music player out of her pocket, thankful she'd remembered to hook it to her little solar panel days before. The screen lit and a cast a dull gray circle around them. The tiled floor was damp but free of standing water. Ruth felt better until she heard a stealthy scrabbling from a distant wall. She flashed the player toward the sound, but it was far too weak to light up anything at a distance. She wondered what else had taken refuge in the subway station. She looked down at the dog, but its hair lay flat and it thumped its tail gently. Trusting the dog's instincts more than her own, she pulled Bernard down the slippery tunnel.

The gray circle began reflecting in shimmery waves a few feet farther in and she felt cold water seeping in through a hole in her shoe. She struggled to keep her footing as rubble and debris cropped up in little piles below the water. Bernard was slow, but he seemed steady enough. By the time they reached the bank of turnstiles, the dog was swimming in the muck and Ruth was wet past her knees. The garbage and weeds turned it into a kind of pulpy rot instead of water and she made sure to keep Bernard's injured hand far above the surface.

They followed the line of turnstiles toward one wall. The dog began to growl and swam frantically wide of the metal posts. There was a bang and a howl close to Ruth and she jumped. Bernard perked up and tried to back away. Ruth lifted the music player. The feeble beam showed her a bone-thin arm laced with old scars and then a hand with long jagged nails, three inches of filthy, cracked claw. There was another howl and the arm was replaced by a naked chest, so emaciated that Ruth couldn't tell if it was male or female. It smashed against the other side of the turnstile, stopped by the locked metal bar. The Infected leaned forward, its mouth gaping with want. The weak light got lost in the hollows of its face and made it seem a skull with a thin covering of vellum or plastic. Its mouth was bloody with the last prey it had caught and its skin peeled and puckered with old bites and infections. Ruth wondered what it had been eating. Rats, she supposed. It was too weak to push through the bars and not intelligent enough to go under, but she still didn't like it being there. It might attract other, worse things.

She nudged the dog up some shallow steps and away from the Infected. The water sank away to ankle level as they reached the guard station's roll up door. In the first few chaotic days of the Plague there had been several attacks in the subway. The government assumed that was where the Plague started or that the subway's dark tunnels attracted the Infected for some reason. In reality, it had only been more noticeable on the subway because of the number of people crammed into the trains and waiting on platforms. But rumor and panic had won, and the police had shut down the stations very early. The guard station's security gate had been closed and locked. That it was still intact gave Ruth some hope that the emergency kit was still inside and whole. But how was she supposed to get the gate open?

She let Bernard lean against the wall. He was pale and beginning to sweat even in the cold dark of the subway. Ruth knew he was going into shock. She had to stop the bleeding. The little music player's light flicked around the metal gate, the dirty tile wall, the turnstiles and screaming Infected. She turned to the other side of the gate. The light shone on an old, greasy fire extinguisher that still hung on the wall.

"I need you to hold this, Bernard. We're almost there. Just hold this so I can see the lock." She handed the player to him and fumbled in the dark for the extinguisher. It was heavier than she expected, but she had adrenaline on her side. She swung it as hard as she could, and missed. It shattered a few of the tiles on the wall with a loud crunch, but that was it. She pulled back and tried again. It slammed into the metal slats, making a dent. She was swinging too hard to keep it up too many more times. Her arms shook, but she swung it again anyway. Another miss. Bernard's hand wavered and he slumped slowly into the wall. The dog whined and the Infected kept shrieking. She couldn't concentrate.

"Shut up," she muttered through clenched teeth. But the starving creature went into a long wail instead. "Shut up," she said turning towards it. The Infected couldn't understand. She knew that. But panic and anger and sorrow made a bomb in Ruth's chest. "Shut up!" she screamed back and sloshed down the steps, the extinguisher still in her hands. Bernard slowly rolled himself towards her and followed her with the light. The Infected scrabbled at the metal post, trying to crawl up it and reaching for her with its driftwood arms. Its voice was a terrible drill in the echoing station. Ruth stood in front of it. "Shut up," she said once more, "I can't take it anymore. You can't take it anymore. I don't know who your family is. I don't know who you are. I'm sorry. But you're in pain and I'm in pain. No more." She waited until the creature reached for her again. She grabbed its arm, half hauling it over the stile. She let go and it dangled there for a second. Using both hands, Ruth brought the extinguisher up and swung it back, crushing the Infected's head between the heavy tool and the metal side of the turnstile.

It was easier than it should have been. The screaming stopped instantaneously. The Infected dropped into the sludge and Ruth set the extinguisher down beside her. She bent and held the body underwater for a few minutes in case she hadn't finished it as completely as she thought. She let her heaving breath calm, and then fished out the extinguisher she had dropped in the water. The light sparkled as it hit her and she was surprised to find it was because she was crying.

She trudged up the steps. The dog backed

away from her. "I'm sorry," she offered. Bernard folded the player into his hand and curled his good arm around her in a tight embrace.

"C'mon," she mumbled, "we have to get you fixed up. We've got a long night ahead." He let her go and she backed up again. One more time she swung the extinguisher and it popped the lock with a clunk. She pulled off the pieces and then slowly pushed up the heavy rolling gate. The floor was flooded and the walls were damp with mildew, but Ruth found the medical kit without much trouble. It was still sealed in its plastic container and she almost laughed with relief to see the contents untouched by the damp or the filth.

She helped Bernard sit in one of the decaying office chairs and helped the dog jump up onto the other and out of the water. "You, my friend, are going to have better medical care from this little package than anyone's had in almost five years."

Bernard offered her a weak smile. She pulled a flashlight from its spot in the cabinet. The batteries were still good. She put it on the counter and began her work, relieved to be concentrating on something she felt competent at.

"Are you really Joe Mackey?" she asked quietly.

Bernard nodded and hung his head. She finished cleaning the dried blood off of the wounds and began opening splint packets and gauze pads. When she was all set up she asked as casually as she could, "Is there really a cure?"

Bernard put his good hand on her shoulder and she looked up from her work. He stared at her for a long moment and then very deliberately nodded. Ruth tried to swallow but there was a hard, dry lump in her throat.

"But you never said anything. Why didn't you say anything?"

Bernard just shook his head and opened his mutilated mouth. Ruth nodded but her eyes filled with tears. "You saw it?" she asked, "You saw the cure?"

He looked confused and then made a cross with his fingers again. It took Ruth a few moments to understand him. "You saw people like Father Preston? People who had recovered?" she guessed.

Bernard nodded.

"How many? How did you know they were cured?" Ruth gripped his injured fingers too tightly and he winced. She let go remembering why they were here. "Never mind," she said, "I guess that part isn't important. Could you find it again? The place with the cure?"

Bernard stared off into space for a long, long time. At last he made a frustrated sigh and shook his head. He pretended to punch the side of his head.

Ruth nodded sadly. "It's gone, isn't it? When they hurt you, you lost some memory." She went back to concentrating on her work, her hands no longer shaking with excitement. She knew it wouldn't have mattered. Even if she'd known back when she met Bernard, it was far too late for Charlie. And it could hardly help now. Juliana was trapped in the hospital and Ruth and Bernard would be killed on sight. But it would have made Juliana happy. And the Infected— all the ones she had killed, all the ones in the hospital— what about them? Had Father Preston been right all this time? And what they were about to do, how would she justify that if the cure were within reach? She looked up at Bernard. His eyes were filmy and unfocused and his breath labored. She knew it was the pain of his broken arm, but she couldn't shake the image she'd had of him. He was simple. Gullible. Probably had been before the beating too. After all, he'd sent Gray to her for a bounty, hadn't he? Maybe he imagined it. Maybe he was taken in by people that intended to take advantage of him. Maybe it was just like Gray said, a front for killing the Infected off.

By the time she'd wrapped the rest of his hand in bandages, Ruth had half convinced herself that Bernard had been wrong about the cure. But doubt still slithered through her gut. Bernard had seen what Gray was really doing, he'd known it to be wrong and tried to stop it, something even Father Preston seemed unable to realize. That wasn't simple or gullible. She told herself to focus on the immediate problem. Time for guilt and regret later.

It was past sunset when they finally crept back out of the station, but there was nobody in sight or earshot. Ruth was worried about Juliana, but she knew the best way to help was to go on with the plan. Bernard was weak and in pain, even with the basic pain killers that had survived in the kit, but he was stable and she had let him rest for a few hours after she did what she could for him.

The plan was insane. So much had gone wrong already. She'd worn a deep, panicked rut in her mind trying to find another solution, but nothing came close. She began leading Bernard toward the harbor. It was a long way on foot, made even longer by Bernard's injuries and Ruth's exhaustion. She talked it through both to fill time and to try to solidify it in her own mind.

"We're letting the Infected go, Bernard. We have to. Even with the food you saved today, they'll starve before the end of the winter. And if we let Father Preston take them, the way he wants to, they'd end up like those two poor souls who were dragging that police car back there." She glanced at Bernard. He seemed to be listening but his gaze was somewhere far ahead of them. "And Juliana—Juliana is very sick. She can't take care of all of them any more. She's going to need us to take care of her, Bernard."

A few tears rolled down the large man's face and he nodded but didn't look at her. Ruth waited a few moments before continuing. "I know you are thinking of the cure, but I don't know how to get it. We don't have time. Juliana needs our help now and I can't leave her to go look. We can't take care of them anymore, but we can give them whatever chance they have left. We can let them go free where maybe they'll live an extra couple of weeks. Who knows? Maybe they'll wander to the place you found and someone will cure them. Maybe they'll get lucky. At worst,they'll die the same way they would in the hospital this winter."

She looked up at Bernard, not sure what she was expecting to see. Judgment? Anger? Sorrow? But his face was impassive.

"But it will be dangerous for us when we

release them. So we've got to warn everyone. Well, everyone that isn't attacking the hospital anyway. And we have to get Juliana away. I was coming to ask you to find a boat and to get it ready. I didn't know what Gray was going to do to you. If I'd known—"

Bernard shook his head and squeezed her shoulders.

"We're going to find a boat together and then I will warn as many people as I can. But I don't know how to get stores down to the boat. I had to kill the guard they left at the cottage, but I'm sure he's been found now. Even if I could get back there without being seen, I don't have time to make many trips back to the harbor. They'll have figured out that I've escaped before long."

Bernard let her go and stood up straight for a moment. He pointed to her and pretended he was steering with one hand.

"Do I know how to drive a boat?" Ruth guessed.

Bernard nodded.

"No. Do you?"

He shook his head.

"Ah well, no matter. We won't be able to use a motorboat any way. I was hoping to find a sailboat. Even if we just anchor farther out in the harbor for a few weeks until things die down and then I swim back for a row boat, we should be safe. The Infected won't be in boats."

Bernard looked troubled but just leaned on her again as they continued. The supplies tormented Ruth. She had counted on Bernard's help, but he was in no condition now to carry heavy loads or even to protect her while she did. She couldn't just shove Juliana on an empty boat. She had no idea how to fish, besides the need for clean water. Her original thought had been to simply sail somewhere better. But it was a dream, not a plan. None of them knew how to work a sail boat, and even if one of them had, where were they going to go? Everywhere would be as bad. Maybe they would get lucky and find easy pickings somewhere empty or maybe they'd run into a gang worse than Gray's. Or a pack of feral dogs. Or just empty, cleaned out homes for miles and miles.

But it was the only plan she had. Bernard hadn't had time to think of one at all, and she knew Juliana expected them all to die in the onslaught between the angry Congregation and the freed Infected. Ruth was stubbornly hopeful, so she stuck to the plan even though she knew it had already gone seriously awry.

It was about midnight when they reached the docks and both of them were stumbling with exhaustion. A quarter moon covered the rotting boards with pale shadows, but it was still far too dark to find what they needed. Like it or not, Ruth would have to wait until morning to return to Juliana. The area was strange to her, and she was wary about moving too far from the docks now that they were here. She helped Bernard sit on a metal bench while she and the dog limped down the pier to find some shelter. She kept a close eye on the dog, but it sniffed its way down the road, unconcerned. Ruth relaxed a little in her strange surroundings. She settled on an old restaurant at the far end of the docks. It was thickly carpeted and still dry, its windows still intact. She helped Bernard inside and lit a few of the candles that were scattered over the tables. She pushed the furniture back. Bernard clumsily folded old tablecloths with one hand into lumpy pillows. Ruth took a quick glance out the front door again to be sure they hadn't been followed and then collapsed next to Bernard and the dog.

"It'll be okay," she said into the dark. She smiled and turned to look at Bernard, to make him feel better. But he was already asleep. The circuit of worry sparked one more time in her head. "It'll be okay," she said again. The panic faded and she dropped into a deep sleep.

CHAPTER 22

The morning sparked like fire on the glass door of the restaurant. Ruth squinted at it in silent protest. Bernard was still sleeping heavily but the dog thumped its tail as Ruth sat up.

"Want to go out, boy?" she whispered. The dog's tail wagged faster. Ruth stood up and opened the door for it. She would let Bernard sleep and heal while she found a boat. She rubbed her eyes and stretched as she walked out into the restaurant's weedy parking lot.

Then she took a long look around the harbor. The sight made her heart sink even further. Half a dozen boats sat in the water near enough for her to reach. A few of them listed to one side. One of them was mostly sunk, its prow poking through the gray water and crusted with green growth. A few others had snapped masts that trailed into the water behind them, still clinging by a wooden shard. A steel tanker had ground itself on the beach and lay blooming bloody rust pits in the sun. None of them was usable.

Ruth had only been to the docks a few times as a little girl, but she remembered there being dozens and dozens of boats, large and small. She tried not to panic. Where would they have gone? Looters? Maybe some, but she doubted they were all yacht experts. She had an idea that a lot of people fled the city in boats during the Plague, thinking it would protect them, but they were already infected. It occurred to her that the Plague had hit hardest in December and January. Most of the boats would have been stored for the winter. Ruth felt calmer.

She walked down the long harbor looking for a storage facility. There would have to be dozens. She decided to just work her way down the harbor until she found a boat that she could slide into the water. The first place she came to had dozens of boats sitting in racks or covered in dusty cloth. But even the smallest were too large for her to push herself. They'd been designed for trucks to carry. She wandered through the dim building peering carefully at each boat, tugging on the trailer hitches to see if they would roll even the slightest bit.

She thought her luck had come through at last when she found an electric forklift at the very back near the manager's office. Spare batteries for it were neatly stacked against the wall in a "charged" shelf and a "depleted" shelf. She didn't think the one in the lift would work, but she climbed in anyway and turned the key. She was shocked when it turned over. Ruth had never been inside a forklift. She tried to ease forward but she lurched a little to the left. She twisted the wheel, but it turned slowly instead of the way a car would. She looked worriedly down at the panel trying to find out how much battery she had left, but she couldn't tell which dial it was. She shrugged. No good worrying about the battery if she couldn't figure out how to drive the thing. She took a slow practice loop around the edge of the building. After a few rough patches she felt confident enough to try the forks. She lifted an old desk that was sitting in the back. When she was satisfied she knew what she was doing, she switched the lift off and got out. She scanned the aisles until she found a boat that would be large enough for all three of them. Or at least, that's what she hoped.

It took another forty-five minutes of tense tries and a battery change to get the boat out. She inched it out without dropping it, though, and backed slowly out onto the road. The boat was too large to see going forward, so the forklift bumped up over the curb and across the road, sliding toward the water. She let the water come up to her waist before dropping the forks. The boat bobbed on the water, but the lift shorted out. She swam the few feet to a ladder on the boat's side. Excited, she pulled the covering off as quickly as she could. Before it was halfway off, she jumped in and tried to use the wheel to steer her toward the restaurant and the docks. She banged her head on the stored mast. The boat turned, but it made no advance. She let go and the boat sat in a bare foot of water, its bottom making dull clunks as it scraped the rocks. She pulled the cover off and let it fall into the water. She tried to pull the mast up, but it was a tangle of wires. She was taking a close look at the pins meant to hold the mast in place when the boat finally drifted far enough to move freely. The front tilted quickly and then the boat started tilting sideways. Ruth clambered higher up the deck, but she could hear water rushing in. She watched in dismay as the boat sank, inch by inch until it hit the bottom again and straightened out, no better than a jagged stone sticking out of the shallow water. She jumped off and swam back to shore, the water as bitter as her mood. Bernard had come to find her. He waded partway into the water to help, but she waved him back.

"It's no use," she wheezed as the ocean dripped from her onto the pavement, "Everything has gone wrong. Every inch I gain is countered and beaten back. We have to find another way. Unless we can carry it and paddle it, we won't be able to use it. Which leaves— what? A dinghy? A canoe, if we got lucky?"

Bernard suddenly brightened. He waved for her to follow him. "You found a canoe?" she asked, but he just shrugged. He led her back toward the restaurant and past it, where the harbor widened and the docks collapsed from their rotting wooden stilts. The water was as empty as the richer side, but pulled up on the shore were dozens of small humps hidden by tattered plastic tarps and rotting nets.

"These will be rotten Bernard— nobody has cared for them in years."

Bernard shook his head and walked on. There was a huge stone building set back from the shore. Its back to the ocean, its base was still covered in green seaweed that the high tide washed up. Bernard went around to the front. The metal sign in front had fallen sideways and been half eaten by the salt air, but Ruth could still see "Maritime Museum" fairly clearly. Her temper improved immediately. She followed the dog and Bernard inside the dark, solid building.

She pulled the heavy curtains that were over the window open to let in the sun. There were small canoes and kayaks lining the lobby, but Bernard walked right past, following a path only he knew. They climbed a set of stairs and came out in a long gallery with a musty display of small boats of the world.

Ruth felt a pang of homesickness. The gallery had obviously been abandoned long before the Plague, one of those small exhibits that never changed and were a perennial favorite of school trips. Charlie would have loved it. How many things she had missed doing with him. Bernard stopped in front of a bright red boat that hung from the wall. Wide and flat, the placard said it was used for carrying goods to floating markets. There were some long handles paddles propped next to them. She looked doubtfully at the boat. "Do you think it will hold all of us?" she asked.

Bernard pointed to her, pointed to one end of the boat, then pointed to himself and the other end.

"And Juliana?"

He looked sober and pointed to the length between.

"You think she'll be too sick to sit?"

He nodded sadly.

"There's not much room for supplies," she said. "That is, if I can even find any."

Bernard smiled and put a finger to his lips. He pulled up one of the floorboards in the boat and showed her a shallow compartment that ran the length of the boat.

"This is where you got the idea to hide the vegetables?" she asked.

He nodded and grinned. Ruth scratched at the back of her neck. There wasn't much room and she didn't know if it would even float after hanging for what must have been decades in the museum. Still, they probably kept it restored. And it was better than anything else she had. She struggled to pull it off the wall. It was awkward and pretty heavy, but she could still get it to the beach.

"Can you get the paddles?" she asked Bernard and headed slowly down the stairs, letting it slide gently down to the lobby. They wouldn't be able to stay in it for long. It wasn't the floating fortress she'd imagined when she thought out the plan, but it would work for a fairly quick getaway.

She tried to feel relieved as Bernard happily paddled the boat onto the bright water, the dog panting in the bow, but she felt the minutes creeping by and knew she had no more time to improve the plan. She called him back into the shore.

"I have to go. I have to help Juliana and the Infected. I'll try to send friends with supplies but—I don't know what else to do. I have no time. There are probably a lot of people who would help Juliana left in the city, but no one is going to helm *me*. What I've done hasn't left many survivors," Ruth exhaled. "I'll try to save what you paid so dearly for."

Bernard shook his head and hugged her with his good arm.

"I don't know what will happen. But it will happen tonight or tomorrow morning. Can you guard the boat until then? Will you be all right here?"

He nodded and pointed to the dog.

Ruth shook her head. "I've left you with nothing. No food, no water. And no way to get it, now that your hand is mangled."

Bernard pulled the boat up onto the rocks with his good arm and placed the paddles inside.

He tied the rope to a sturdy wooden post and then led Ruth back into the restaurant. He pulled her into the dark kitchen and opened the back door, letting in some light. There was a dead refrigerator case half full of bottled water. He tossed her one and she grinned. The lukewarm water washed the salt off her lips and tasted like nothing she'd had in years. He tapped her on one shoulder and pulled out a plastic bin from beneath the cook's stainless steel line. She peeled off the cover and he slapped her on the back. It was full of oyster crackers. The mice hadn't been able to get at it in the bin and the looters either missed it or never hit the place. It wasn't much; even taken together it'd never get them through more than a few days, but Ruth felt a palpable ease wash through her. At least they had that. At least they would have a couple more days to find a better place. She hugged Bernard and told him to stay out of sight. Then she started back into the sweltering city to handle the toughest part of the task.

CHAPTER 23

They had begun seeing lights about a week from the capitol. Here and there, just a campfire or two. They had been far apart at first, maybe the people that made them weren't even aware of each other, but from the boat Frank could see them all. The little lights had cheered them, but with stores dwindling, Nella didn't want to risk delaying if there were a big group ahead. They had sailed past the solitary camps waiting for the tiny string of fires to become a cluster. As the miles slipped by, they could see planted fields and little markets near the shoreline. In the evening, the windows of the houses shone with lanterns more and more often, sometimes grouping in small squares.

Many of the small harbors were blocked with wreckage. Boats or buildings tossed around in a hurricane years before littered the water around the coast. Rotting wood and jagged metal made the shallows a murky labyrinth, even for the rowboat. Nella regretted passing the groups of people, but it was too dangerous to attempt a landing. The coast fell away behind them and a few days later Frank steered them into a wide bay. Skyscrapers huddled on the banks, their shadows hanging over the water the only relief from the bright glare of the summer morning. The shore roads were all empty, shimmering in the blazing sun. The only movement was the hundreds of seabirds crying and skittering down the sand or wheeling over the road and between the shattered windows of the buildings. One of the largest cities in the world and there were no people walking on the roads, no sounds of industry, no heaps of recent trash. No signs of humanity beyond the decaying structures.

"Do you see anything?" Frank whispered, afraid of setting off an endless echo.

Nella squinted against the sun and pointed to a thin cloud far inside the city. "Is that smoke?" she asked.

Frank framed his eyes with his hands. "I think so."

"Well, we didn't come all this way just to turn around without looking," said Nella.

"We don't know who's in there. We should wait until dark so we can get a look without them seeing us."

"But we don't know this place. We'll just get lost."

Frank thought for a minute. "I don't see a good place to conceal the boat. I think we should wait until dark and then take the rowboat to one of those little shops on the beach. We can camp out there and then in the morning, we'll go exploring. I don't want to draw attention to ourselves until we see what kind of people are in there. Also, if there are Infected—"

"It's been eight years, Frank. I don't think there are any Infected left, even in a big place like this." She tapped the cases of cure darts in her pack. They jingled. "I'm not even sure why we bother lugging these around."

"We thought there were none left a few months ago and one got you. I don't want to risk that again."

Nella sighed and rubbed the scar on her shoulder. "Okay, you win, we'll go tonight."

Frank stared at the wisping plume of gray.

Let it be people, he thought, *let there be SOMEONE in there.*

CHAPTER 24

"She's loose." Gray scowled and scraped the ax head over the concrete floor of the old pool hall.

Father Preston regretted using the building while the church was being restored. There were other, cleaner places. Especially now that they would be moving to a quieter farming community and would never get to use the old Spanish cathedral anyhow. Father Preston was beginning to regret many things. That ax Gray had adopted was another.

Father Preston hadn't said or done anything to rein Gray in, reasoning that the more dangerous a man appeared, the less real harm he had to do to prove his reputation. But now, he regretted Gray altogether. The man seemed insatiable, bent on vengeance. *Justice*, Father Preston internally corrected himself. Even when that justice had little to do with Ruth. He had been the one who brought the pictures to Father Preston in the first place. He had volunteered to track down their owners in the vast emptiness of the dead city. And then there was the debacle with the gardener.

"Yes, I know she is loose," Father Preston sighed. "She was probably trying to get to the garden. Thought she could wait us out if she could bring back enough food. But she's not going to go far. She'll be back for Juliana before long. And back to finish off the Afflicted while they are vulnerable in their cells. Juliana may be more persuadable while Ruth is away."

"If she's away then we don't need to fear that she'll carry out mass murder. We can take— we can *rescue* the Afflicted while she's gone. We don't have time to waste negotiating with Juliana."

Father Preston shook his head. "No. I will talk to Juliana. She will listen to reason. I won't risk her coming to harm in the confusion."

Gray shook his head. "This is foolish. We should be breaking ground on the new mission right now, not sitting here at the whim of two old women. We're going to run out of time before winter. It's almost July, summer is flying by. Would you let a hundred of your own people freeze and starve just to humor the feelings of one woman? Why is *she* so much more important than the rest of us, who have faithfully followed you? Than the Afflicted she locked away?"

Father Preston clutched the front of Gray's filthy, sooty shirt and pulled him close. "Because she's *good,*" he hissed, "and I don't know if there's another soul alive who is. I know *you're* not, though you think you have me fooled. God knows *I'm* not." His voice dropped to a mumble as he released Gray. "She saved my life. And all of theirs too. She deserves to be at peace in her final days. She deserves to believe that we will care for the Afflicted as well as she has done. I owe her that much."

Gray shook his head but raised his hands in surrender. "Have it your way, Father." He began walking toward the door.

"And suspend the executions until I say otherwise," commanded the priest. Gray paused and looked as if he would turn to say something, but he shrugged and continued out of the building.

He had surprised himself. He was accustomed to thinking of himself as "good." *Better* than other men. But Gray had forced the admission from him. Why had he changed his mind? And when? Juliana was weak. As weak as Vincent had been, maybe. Close to as broken. But she was still better than Father Preston. Still more *worthy*. The thought wriggled inside him, taunting and biting like a poisonous centipede. He tried to stomp it out. She wasn't *better*. She was just untested. Father Preston though, he had been through the fire. Him and all of his brothers. Only he had emerged. Only *he* was worthy. Chosen all those years ago in that barren December. He'd known he would survive that very first night. He'd known he had to take the Abbot's place as a leader of the faithful as he had pressed his back against the Abbot's door to prevent it opening.

The old priest had flung himself at it over and over, as if he were a small child having a tantrum.

Brother Matthew had shaken his head. "He's going to hurt himself," he said.

"There's nothing we can do. If we let him out, he'll hurt someone else. Find something to bar the door."

A large oak pew was brought and slid in front of the Abbot's door. Time did no good, hours later he was still flinging himself against it. Both the doctor and the police were unreachable. As the monks cleaned and prepared Brother Andrew's body, the air around them thickened with panic, every other breath laced with the unceasing cries of their leader.

Father Preston had paced in front of the door. Some of the others watched him, doing nothing themselves. It was unnatural, this idleness. This thing, this plague, was eroding their sense of duty, their good work. Father Preston was certain it was evil. Brother Matthew refused to believe it was anything but a disease.

He'd passed the door of Brother Andrew's room, where a few men were scrubbing the floor. One of them looked up.

"Someone has to say the funeral mass," the man said.

Father Preston stared blankly at him. "But the Abbot—" he started, and fell silent.

The monk shrugged. "Maybe it can wait," he turned back to the dark stains.

The electric bells clanged for morning prayer. Everyone looked up. Father Preston started walking toward the church. He glanced back. A few of the brothers rose to follow him, but many sat still where they were, or went back to cleaning. He felt his lip curl back in a sneer, but he didn't waste his breath chiding them. Each man must discipline himself or fall apart. It was not for him to force them into piety.

He tried to clear his mind as he entered the dark, clean room. There were only a handful of brothers. They all looked at him as he crossed to the podium. The Abbot reserved the reading of the morning prayer for himself. But the Abbot was a raving devil, his breath still stinking of flesh and damnation. Father Preston cleared his throat and read the prayer. The Abbot's shrieks were a distant wail through the stone walls, but he still found himself clutching his book so tightly that he left fingernail marks in the covers each time he heard the sound.

When he emerged from the church, the Abbot had screamed himself to sleep, and falling snow made a hushing echo over the grounds. The illusion of calm was broken by a pair of brothers dressed in travel clothing walking through the monastery's front gate. Father Preston hurried down the stairs, followed by the few brothers who had been with him.

"Has the doctor finally come?" he called.

Brother Matthew was standing at the gate watching the others go. He looked up at Father Preston and shook his head.

"The police?"

No again.

"Have we received direction from the bishop?"

Brother Matthew looked sadly at the two men trudging toward the gate. They kept their heads down and refused to meet Father Preston's eye. He felt his face begin to warm with anger. "You're leaving? When your brothers need you the most you decide to walk away?"

"We have family out there too," murmured one of them.

"You think it's better out there?" cried Father Preston. "If the Abbot can succumb, how will we avoid it? Whether it's disease or judgment, you can't escape it." He jogged to the gate and stood in front of them, blocking the path. "If you leave you can never return. You know that."

Brother Matthew cleared his throat. "They can if they have permission to go."

"The Abbot is— is unwell. He cannot give

permission," stammered Father Preston.

Matthew placed a hand on Father Preston's shoulder and pulled him gently out of the way. "I have given it in his stead," he said.

"What? You? You cannot—"

"I am the prior, Brother Michael. Let them go. They will see that their loved ones are protected and they will return once the sickness here has passed. I have extended the license to all that are uninfected and wish to go. You as well, if you like."

The two men brushed past Father Preston. "The Revered Father wouldn't approve. Something terrible has happened, yes, but that is not a reason to abandon the faith—"

Brother Matthew shook his head. "They aren't abandoning it. I know they will keep their devotions, wherever they may go."

Father Preston stared out the open gate.

"I cannot keep them here," Brother Matthew said.

"The Abbot would," snapped Father Preston. "He'd tell us to be steadfast under this trial, that we ought to shoulder our sufferings gladly, that we are blessed—" the words withered in his throat as he saw the horrified look that Matthew bore.

"What has happened to our brothers is no blessing," whispered Brother Michael. "I'm sustained by the hope that they will be cured. May they remember nothing of their illness."

"Who will care for them? Who will recall our Reverend Father to himself if you allow them all to leave?"

"How can I make them stay, knowing they might be in danger of the same fate if I do? How can I sentence them to madness? To— to violence and rage?"

Father Preston sneered. "Are you leaving also? Will I alone remain his faithful attendant?"

"I am not leaving Brother Michael. But you may be the only attendant before long. Of the ten that remain, five are already ill. I too, have started having symptoms." He watched Father Preston for a reaction, but the priest stared into the blank white road beyond the open gates. The hand that Matthew had placed on his shoulder was shaking and finally he asked, his voice cracking and hoarse with fear, "What are we to do Brother Michael?"

Father Preston turned a cool, dry eye to his brother. "We pray," he said mercilessly. He swung the wooden gates closed and picked up a heavy snow shovel that lay nearby. He slid it through the gate handle. "Now no one can enter but God," he said and turned back toward the church.

Brother Matthew shivered, murmuring, "And hopefully no one can escape except those that are still sane."

The steady snow choked the road outside the monastery. There were no passing cars, not even ambulances, to disturb the quiet. The remaining brothers spent their day in devotions, stopping only for meals and to take turns caring for their Abbot. Except for the deterioration of the man he had both admired and loved, Father Preston would have found the quiet and the ceaseless prayer blissful.

The relative peace held until just before the Christmas holiday and Father Preston thought they'd turned a corner, that those who had begun to show symptoms must surely begin to recover. He half expected a series of hollow knocks on the gate from postman coming to deliver the holiday letters for the monastery. But no one came. Brother Matthew's words had become so slurred in the days before, that Father Preston took over the readings. The sanctuary glowed with lamps, the power had gone out a week before, but that made little impact inside the sanctuary. The brothers clustered in the front, almost huddled together in the empty church.

Father Preston loved the way words rolled across the long room, like a warm wave. He remembered the Abbot's voice curling and pulling at him in every reading. There was a sharp pinch in his chest when he thought of the man's shrieks that morning. Desperate and raw, with nothing human left in them at all. Father Preston shook himself, realizing he was staring silently at the Reverend Father's chair. The others were looking at him, waiting for him to continue.

"Peace be with you," he said and accepted the murmuring response as he turned to prepare the host. There was a shuffle and whispers behind him as the brothers turned to embrace each other.

A rumbling squeak erupted as one of the heavy oak pews was pushed out of place and then a few grunts and one of the brothers shouted, "Brother Matthew, stop!"

Father Preston whirled around to see Brother Matthew hugging another brother tightly. The man sagged with a muffled groan. Two of the others grabbed at Matthew's arms and tried to pull them open. Brother Matthew clenched tighter and a deep growl billowed from him and echoed down the chamber. Father Preston hurried down the steps toward the pew. Brother Matthew let the man he was holding go. He fell with a thud into the pew. The others lifted him while Brother Matthew turned toward the man who had yelled. Father Preston watched pink drool drip from Matthew's jaw and his limbs bend into a half crouch as if in preparation to spring. Father Preston reached him before he could attack.

"Brother Matthew," he cried, holding his prior firmly by the shoulders, "recall where you are. Can't you recognize us? Think, man! We've shared all of our days, all of our deepest prayers! Remember whose commands you live by, remember what you are!"

There was a breath of silence. Everyone waited and Brother Matthew stared at Father Preston.

Let this be my miracle, Father Preston had time to think, *let me be the hand of the divine.*

And then Matthew's chest rumbled and he stretched his jaw open as far as it could. Father Preston felt the wet heat of Matthew's breath and smelled the metallic tinge of fresh blood as Matthew lunged for him. This time the others were ready and held Matthew back before he could bite. Father Preston was shaken. He sat down carefully in the crooked pew. He gazed up at the carved crucifix. It had been restored only the year before, its paint brightened, its details sharpened by hand with fine sandpaper. It had been a source of pride when visitors exclaimed how lifelike it seemed, how much closer it made them feel to God. But as Father Preston looked up at it, his eyes seemed to play a trick. The thin threads of red that trailed from the figure's sharp crown now elongated, clustered on the corners of the mouth, to stain the thin wooden cheeks. It must be a trick of the shadows. He passed a hand over his eyes. One of the younger monks bent down near him.

"Brother Michael, what should we do?"

Father Preston shook himself and saw that they were all waiting for him. Brother Matthew strained and wriggled but was unable to harm anyone. The brother he had so fiercely embraced, however, bled freely from a wound in his neck and lay upon another pew.

"Put Brother Matthew in his room. Block the door, just as we've done for the Abbot. With time and prayer, he will hopefully recover. Brother Aaron's wounds should be tended to as best we can. I believe the first aid kit is in the kitchen." He sank back into the pew as the others hastened to either help or take themselves out of harm's way. A few of them stumbled over the threshold and Father Preston made a mental note to repair the flagstone, though he didn't remember any unevenness.

He tried to return to prayer. Though he knew the Abbot would have gently chided him for it, Father Preston was partial to Christmas Eve. It had formerly been his favorite night of the year, the most sacred in his mind. Not this year. The courtyard echoed with Brother Matthew's roar and the Abbot, hearing the commotion, joined in, multiplying the chaos. He looked around him. The pews were crooked from the sudden violence and there was a shallow pool of darkness where the injured monk had lain. Father Preston sighed and tried to concentrate on a short prayer before rising to clean. He bowed his head and looked down. There was blood on his stole from Brother Matthew's dripping mouth. Instead of praying, he felt hot tears streak down his face and catch at the corner of his mouth. The Abbot was mad, his brothers were sickening around him, and God had denied him. He leaned forward onto the pew in front of him and wept for sheer loneliness.

A clatter of wood on stone and the sudden chime of bursting glass woke him. Father Preston had cried himself to sleep on the hard wooden bench. He looked up, his eyes still blurry and crusted with salt. The church doors stood open and a table had tipped and its oil lamp crashed to the floor. Most of the others had gone out and the room was very dark. A dim glow came from the open door, whether from the moons reflection on the snow or the approaching sun rise, Father Preston did not know. A darker shadow of a man blocked some of the door and he squinted for a better view of who it was.

"Mile? Bru'er Mile?" the figure slurred and swayed as if he were drunk.

"I'm here," Father Preston called.

The man careened up the aisle and tripped on the edge of the crooked pew. Father Preston reached out and caught him before he could fall.

"Brother Joseph, What is it?" he asked, thinking the monk wanted to confess to breaking into the wine cellar. But Joseph's breathing was ragged and shallow, as if he had been running, not slow and sleepy with drink.

There was a terrified scream from the

courtyard. The monk glanced toward the doors and pulled on Father Preston's arm. "Bro'er George is sick, and Bro'er Matthew got free."

"Free?"

Brother Joseph nodded and another cry crawled along the stone walls. The monk lurched back toward the doors and pulled Father Preston behind him. "We have to go," Joseph muttered.

"And leave our brothers? They need our help, they aren't themselves."

Joseph tripped on the fallen table and Father Preston helped him up. "They'll kill ush. Look." He pointed out of the open door into the silver-blue snow of the courtyard. A man lay motionless and dark against the pale ground. Another man crouched over him. Brother Joseph went back into the sanctuary and emerged with a large flashlight. Its broad beam flickered and then arced over the ground and onto the two men. The one that was crouching spun around to look at them, squinting in the bright light. It wasn't Brother Matthew or Brother George, but another, also sick. He stood up slowly and Father Preston could see his clothes were rent and trailing and a clump of hair was missing from the side of his head.

"It's okay," said Brother Joseph and stumbled again as he descended the steps. The flashlight dropped and rolled and he went sprawling. The sick man wasted no time but sprinted toward Joseph. Father Preston stepped forward to protect him, but Joseph had risen and he pushed Father Preston out of the way. The two men grappled and fell into the snow. Father

Preston tried to pull them apart, but neither one paid any attention. Brother Joseph's face twisted into a snarl as he fought, and Father Preston heard a sickening, crunching snap as Joseph's arm was twisted too far, but the monk didn't even slow down. Joseph was able to twist himself over the other man and lunged in to bite. Father Preston realized Brother Joseph had succumbed to the Plague and it broke his motionless daze.

He backed up into the stairs, fell onto his back and turned to scrabble up them. He made it into the church and slammed the door. He pulled the back pew foot by foot until it stood in front of the door and refilled one of the remaining lamps with shaking hands. He turned it up high and lit the tall wax candles that sat at the end of each row to chase away the dark. He was relieved to see that he was alone in the building, though the flickering candles made him keep glancing doubtfully at the massive crucifix, his eyes tricking him into thinking the half starved figure was moving, reaching for him with thin, clawed hands and dull, ripping wooden teeth.

He crouched near the door, trying to peer out of the frosty windows at what was happening. But there were no more sounds from the courtyard. At last, the adrenaline wore off. Exhausted, he drifted off, his forehead resting against the cold glass.

When he woke again, a pale light sliced through the windows and the church was bright with morning. His stomach rumbled as he walked around the church extinguishing the candles. He pushed the pews back into place, except the one that blocked the door. He gently folded his vestments and placed them next to the podium. He found himself much calmer and knelt for his morning devotions. Halfway through, a creaking shudder came from behind him and he sprang up. Someone was trying to open the door. Father Preston walked quickly and quietly to the door. There was a soft, insistent rap.

"H-hello? Is somebody left in there? Please let me in. I'm not sick. I need to come in before one of those— one of those *things* finds me!"

Father Preston hesitated. The monk pressed his face to the small crack in the wooden door, trying to see in. "Please," he begged, "I've brought food from the kitchen. You'll need it too. We can share. Just let me in before they get me."

Father Preston pulled the pew away from the door, just enough for the young monk to slide his narrow body through. "Brother John, are you all that's left?" he asked.

"All that's sane," the monk replied and helped Father Preston shove the pew back against the door.

"Did you— did you kill anyone?" Brother John said into the echoing room.

That's not right, that's not what he said. Father Preston shook his head, trying to clear the memory. He was sitting in the hot hospital kitchen eight years after the chilly monastery. He didn't even remember walking here, though he'd intended too.

"I'm sorry, what did you say Juliana?" he played with the cup of water. She sat across from him, the harsh summer light making her look bleached, wrinkled, as if her skin were a size too large.

"I said, don't Christians say you 'ought not to judge, lest you be judged?' I don't think anyone who is still alive can claim innocence. You have no right to perform these executions. And you have no right to harm Ruth either. The people who asked her for help, they only did what they had to do to survive. And she only did what she thought was *right.* In all the time that you were sick, can you honestly say you never harmed anyone? Do you even remember? Didn't you ever have to kill anyone when you were ill, to defend yourself or to get— to get what you needed?"

"Ruth doesn't kill because she needs to—" he began shouting.

"That wasn't my question," said Juliana evenly.

But Father Preston didn't want to remember the Plague. He shouldn't have to justify himself. He was the hand of the divine. His cure was proof of a miracle, that he was *meant* to carry on his work, that he was *meant* to lead the people out of this silent Sodom. He burst up angrily from the table. "I am not on trial here. I don't kill little children because their parents tire of them or are greedy for their belongings. Think well, Juliana, who you are letting into this place. Your charges rely on you for protection. And if they cannot rely upon you, then I will make sure they may rely upon me. Ruth will never get her hands around their throats. I will not allow it! God will not allow it!" He left the kitchen and strode off into the overgrown field. He found Gray and reversed his earlier decision, instructing his Congregation to begin construction of another post. He'd shown enough forbearance. If kindness couldn't convince her, then righteous action must.

CHAPTER 25

The dog's sharp yelp woke Bernard. He sat up too quickly, forgetting his injury. He was instantly woozy and eased himself back down onto the restaurant floor. He tried to calm the dog with his good hand, but it continued to bark. When the world stopped spinning, Bernard inched his way up to the plate glass window. It was dark now, no one would be able to see in, but the dog's bark would alert anyone in the area. A streak of bright light smeared over the glass and then bounced away. Bernard squinted. It was an electric light. Rare these days.

He wondered if it were solar, like Ruth's little pocket charger. She had been excited to trade for that. They weren't just lying around for the taking. She'd said she was sending help. But what if it was Gray instead? Bernard stuck to the corner of the glass and kept trying to hush the dog. The light flickered on the glass again and swung away. Bernard could see it coming from the water this time. A boat. His muscles tensed. Was it his boat? Did they take it? He looked around, but the flat canoe still lay on the floor of the restaurant where he had dragged it. Who had a boat? Why? He leaned into the glass, excited. The boat was only a few dozen yards from the docks; farther out, he saw the hulking shadow of a bigger boat, a sailboat. Bernard forgot to be scared. It was someone else. Someone new, someone else was out there, out beyond the rotting concrete, someone was still alive. He hadn't seen someone from *out there* since before he became Bernard. What little he remembered of his life as Joe Mackey he tried to forget, not quite believing his own memory of a southern city, or soldiers, or cures.

He stood up slowly. The boat people were going to die if nobody helped them. They'd hit the rocks and sink or they'd fall into a subway station and drown. Or Ruth's plan would kill them. They'd be overrun by the Infected from the hospital before they even realized what was happening. He had to warn them, somehow. He snapped his fingers to call the dog and walked out of the restaurant and down toward the beach, waving to show he was unarmed.

The beam of light fixed on him. He walked down the beach to the shallow sand where he and Ruth had launched the canoe that morning. The boat followed him and slid in safely with a hiss.

"Hello?" A woman's voice came from the boat. Bernard waved as a tall figure unfolded itself and stepped out. It stepped forward and shook his hand before Bernard realized it was another man. "Are there other people here?" asked the woman in the boat as Bernard helped the man pull the small craft safely up the beach. The woman stepped out and helped push.

Bernard nodded and pointed toward the center of the city.

"Good," began the man, a smile crinkling a dark scar on his cheek, "We were beginning to think there was nobody left. I'm Frank Courtlen." He stuck out a hand to Bernard. Bernard shook it with enthusiasm, trying to pour as much friendliness into the gesture as he could. Frank and the woman looked at him expectantly. After a few seconds the woman stuck out her hand, "I'm Nella," she said, "Can I ask your name?"

Bernard hesitated. He hadn't been asked to explain why he couldn't speak since Ruth had found him beaten in the road years before. He shrugged and opened his mouth wide for them to see.

"Oh," said Nella, "I'm sorry, I didn't realize you were Cured."

"He can't be Cured," said Frank softly, "Nobody has come this far with it."

Bernard grabbed a stick of driftwood. "Cure?" he scrawled into the sand.

"Yes," said Nella, "There's a cure for the Plague. Do you have an Infected friend? Someone you are caring for?"

He pointed toward the city's interior. All Nella could see was a dull orange glow from some distant bonfire. Bernard waved at them frantically.

"Just a minute, friend," said Frank, holding up a hand, "we don't know anything about you. Why don't you tell us a little about where we're going and then we'll see. We don't know the city, we wouldn't want to get lost— or anything." He glanced at Nella and reached for her hand.

Bernard scrubbed his face with his good hand. There wasn't time. Ruth said to be ready for early morning. If she let the Infected go overnight, he'd never find them all. They'd scatter before they could get the cure. He tapped the stick on his shoe. He wasn't ever a big reader and his spelling wasn't great even before Gray had scrambled his brain with heavy fists.

But Frank and Nella weren't going anywhere until he tried. He couldn't blame them.

Bernard knelt on the damp sand and began the best he could. "Old crazy house. Lots sick. We help them." He pointed up toward the hospital. Nella sat down beside him and propped up the light so she could read. "No time. Bad people take them away, still sick. You have cure?"

Nella glanced up at Frank. "We've got it," she said.

Frank folded his arms. "Tell us about the bad people first."

Bernard brushed the sand smooth and started writing as quickly as he could.

CHAPTER 26

Ruth slung the last of the plastic bags into the rubble of the abandoned wing. It made a puff of dust but no noise. Even so, she glanced back toward the small guard fire to be sure that Father Preston's people hadn't noticed. She wasn't sure if they hadn't discovered her escape route yet, or if she were walking into an elaborate trap. They must know she'd left the hospital; Bernard's escape would have told them that. That they were still here told her they were waiting for her return— or Juliana's death. Ruth shuddered.

She went back to the road to hide the cart in the bracken. It didn't really matter if it was a trap, she decided. The odds of anyone surviving more than a few hours past dawn, herself included, were as thin as rice paper. Which was why her last errand had felt so pointless. But Juliana had insisted. Ruth crept back to the end of the abandoned wing and struggled to get the first large sack to the entrance door.

She'd managed to visit almost fifty different families scattered over half of the large city. They'd all been skeptical at first, and why not? She wasn't Juliana, and the families didn't know her. A strange woman coming to the door with an offer of free food and warnings about maddened zealots was enough to make anyone suspicious. But hunger won out every time. Each time they'd traded old clothes and shoes for a chance at Bernard's stash. Some had been related to the Infected in the hospital and some not. She'd wanted to warn anyone she could.

They'd agreed to meet and storm the garden

together. That part, at least, gave Ruth some comfort. It would make Bernard's pain worth something when all those people survived the winter. *And in three hours,* Ruth thought, *that coordinated attack will be providing a distraction for Gray and Father Preston.*

She grunted softly as she pulled the second bag to the door. She had received a lot but still, not quite enough. Shoes were in very short supply. Ruth was convinced they were just dressing the Infected in their burial clothes anyway. She was far more worried about the poppy shortage. They were roughly a dozen doses short. There was nothing to be done now, though: all the poppies were ash in the blackened greenhouse. She pulled the third bag up and carefully peered through the door. The entryway was empty and the bar lay across the front doors, just as she had left it.

"Now or never," she told herself and pushed the bags inside. The entryway was quiet and the thick, starchy smell of boiled beans hung in the air. Ruth crept quietly down the hall, careful to avoid brushing the walls or doors. The kitchen was silent but well lit. She risked peeking in. The gas lights made the room a pale, sickly gold. Juliana sat at the large, scarred table. She was dozing and her head drooped slightly. There was nobody else there.

Ruth let out a shaky breath, but she only traded the worry of immediate capture to a longer-term worry about Juliana as she watched the sleeping woman. The skin on Juliana's face was drawn too tight, thin and yellow, like old vellum. Ruth tried to pretend it was the awful dim light, but she knew it was more. Her friend looked exhausted even as she slept. She was thin, dry, a bleached, desiccated reed. Ruth wondered how she'd missed seeing it for so long. She had to end this whole thing. She'd take Juliana south, where it stayed warm. She knew there was no escape from the cancer, but Ruth knew there were still places out there that would make dying easier. She could make Juliana's last weeks peaceful. Quiet.

There was a metallic rattle of chains and some shouting from outside as another pole went up in the field. The Infected heard and groans began building in the hallway. Quiet. That's what they both wanted. Soon it would be quiet. She walked reluctantly over to Juliana and shook her gently by the shoulder.

Juliana smiled sleepily up at her. "I'm glad you're back, I was getting worried."

Ruth slumped into the chair across from her. "They were going to kill Bernard. I had to get him away first."

Juliana's smile faltered and Ruth patted the back of her hand.

"It's okay, he's safe. No more poppies though. We have to do this a little short."

Juliana sighed. "I wish there were some other way," she said.

Doubt bubbled up in Ruth's chest. She almost mentioned the cure, almost told her everything that had happened, but she shook her head. What good would it do now? They had no way to reach it, and no time. Father Preston was itching to just throw open the doors and take everything. His Congregation wouldn't stand idle much longer. It could only cause Juliana more anguish.

"I'm sorry," Ruth said, "but if you want to give the Infected a chance, this is the only way."

Someone outside began screaming and the Infected joined in. Juliana put her hands over her ears and started to cry. "I can't do this any more," she said.

Ruth stood up and held out a hand to Juliana. "We're ready to stop it. Let's start getting them dressed." They walked to the entryway and pulled a few sets of clothes from the plastic bags.

"How long do we have?" asked Juliana.

"The dose should last about six hours," said Ruth grimly. "We'll have to get them dressed first and then dose them or we'll run out of time before it wears off. I'll move them a few at a time when they are sleeping. I had hoped Bernard would be here, but we can do it. We have to wait for the Congregation to leave and the guards to fall asleep anyway."

The screaming outside stopped. The screaming inside did not. Ruth opened the first door. The woman inside was already frenzied. "This is going to be rough," she told Juliana. She grabbed the woman's thrashing arms and pushed them into her chest as Ruth backed the woman into the wall. Juliana began sliding baggy clothes onto the woman's wiry frame.

CHAPTER 27

The kitchen was slick with steam. Bowl after bowl of hot sweetened oatmeal sat on the tables. The smell made even Ruth dizzy. She had sent Juliana up to her room to rest after they had dressed the inmates. Ruth thought about saving one dose aside for Juliana. She didn't want her friend to have to see the Infected die on her own lawn. But they were going to have to move fast when it was over and she wouldn't be able to outrun the Infected if she were carrying a drugged Juliana. Besides, they were still short.

She slunk over to the window and pulled the curtain carefully away from the glass. The sun was too low to see, the baking horizon a hazy slate gray the melted into the ruined steel skyline. The field seemed empty apart from the growing line of posts, the bodies still hanging from them, like a gruesome version of forgotten tetherballs. She couldn't see anyone else moving around. It was only temporary, though. The Congregation would be hunting for their next victim or gathering together to finally assault the hospital. The garden raid would begin in twenty minutes and then she could be sure the attention of the Congregation was elsewhere. Just enough time for the light to fade. Ruth was running out of time. They all were. She piled the cart with plastic bowls and began pushing the drugged food down the hallway.

By the time she had emptied the cart, the hospital was quite dark and the field was in deep shadow. She didn't bother lighting any lamps. Better that no one saw her moving through the windows. She returned to the first room. After unrolling a large tarp onto the floor, she opened the door. The woman inside was asleep, tangled in her oversized clothes, her bowl empty beside her. Ruth untied the restraints and dragged the woman as gently as she could onto the tarp. The woman was heavily sedated and didn't react as Ruth slid the tarp slowly across the kitchen floor and out the door. She lifted the woman's head so that it wouldn't bang against the few steps down.

Ruth glanced around. Still no sign of the Congregation. Any glimpse of the garden was blocked by the dense cliff of shadow from the abandoned wing. Ruth decided to take advantage of the quiet and dragged the woman as far as possible through the long grass to the opposite end of the field. The weeds and brush were tall enough that, until she woke enough to stand up, the woman would be invisible to any healthy people in the field and to the other Infected around her. Ruth rolled her off of the tarp and hurried back to repeat the process. Aside from a constant rustle as she dragged each sleeping body through the grass, she made no noise. The light evening breeze and the creak of stretching rope on the steel beams covered what little sound she did make.

Her arms ached and wobbled. Body after body. Her throat was parched and she was dripping with sweat. But she couldn't afford to stop. Father Preston could return at any moment or the sedative could wear off. She had guessed on the dosage, unable to measure a homemade drug as precisely as she wished. A few of the Infected had paid for it already. She had found three stiffening in their own vomit. She had closed their cell doors again, so Juliana wouldn't see.

She was halfway through the second floor patients, her back screaming in agony as she slid a man down the stairs on the back of a metal cell door, when she saw the first flare of a torch. She cursed under her breath and slid the door the rest of the way down. She'd been using the front door to cover this side of the field. Now she'd have to use the abandoned wing. She couldn't just dump them in a group; they'd kill each other before they ever even noticed Father Preston's group.

It had to be close to midnight. A huge bank of clouds had moved in. The only light was from the occasional stutter of far off heat lightning and the flames of the torches that were winding their way into the field. Ruth stumbled a few times but she was quiet while the members of the Congregation talked freely, unafraid. They never even noticed her. She tried to hurry, but after hours of dragging and lifting, her body protested and began to betray her.

A loud chorus of shouts and the hissing snap of a riding crop startled her. She looked up from the body she was rolling into the grass. It was the half-police car that Bernard had been in. The bank of lights hung partway off the car, the torchlight gleaming through them like dull gems of red and blue. The yoked Infected snarled in their football helmets and pulled it forward, chasing the man jogging in front of them. Gray walked beside the car snapping the crop at the fingers sticking out of the cage. The people inside sobbed and screamed for mercy. Ruth couldn't see how many they had crammed in; she guessed it was five or six. A few faces pressed against the side windows but it was too dark to see them. Father Preston was standing on the front steps, his followers banging on the front door. A new row of beams was being erected behind the first, slightly offset so that a person inside the hospital would be forced to see every single body.

Ruth crouched in the grass beside the sleeping man she had just placed and rolled up the tarp. They were too close to the entrance, the people would see her if she tried to go into the abandoned wing. She'd have to wait until they moved away from the steps.

"Juliana!" roared Father Preston, "Juliana! I have proof that Ruth is not what she appears." He waited a moment, the snarling of the Infected men pulling the car and the screams of those inside cutting through. They were distant though, like a football game in a far off field or a television in a neighbor's house. Less important. Like something that had already happened.

"Juliana, she never intended to keep the hospital for you. She's stealing food out of the very mouths of your wards," he called again. Ruth saw a light flicker in the upstairs bedroom. Father Preston was too far from her to see his face, but she could imagine the triumphant smile.

She had to finish this, and fast, before something happened to the people in the car or Juliana ran out of bluffs. Ruth slunk around the edge of the field, skirting the edges of the torchlight. She watched the lantern descend the stairs of the hospital and knew Juliana was coming to the door. If she held the attention of Father

Preston's people, Ruth might be able to sneak into the kitchen side. But there were still five more Infected neatly laid out on the ground floor waiting for their turn on the tarp. She had to close the circle behind Preston or the Congregation would simply escape and massacre the Infected that followed them.

Juliana opened the front door and stood blocking the entrance. She swayed a little as a breeze passed by her. Even at a distance Ruth could see how pale she was. Her voice was strong and unwavering though. "Father Preston," she said, "you've worked to destroy my friendship with Ruth for as long as I've known you. I've listened to every crime you've placed at her feet, I've even taken your counsel on occasion and avoided or opposed her when I should have listened to her. While you lectured, she worked. She's given these people the best medical care she could, she's cleaned them, changed their bandages, even slipped donations of medicine and food I didn't think existed anymore onto the doorstep thinking I didn't know who it came from. What have you done beside lecture me about how bad she is?"

"I— *We've* ministered to their *souls*. We've let them know they aren't forgotten, that someone defends them in their helplessness— far more important than mere *housekeeping*," spat Father Preston. "As I am trying to minister to yours before you are beyond my aid. I know you are weary, Juliana, ready to hand over your good works to another. But do not let her deceive you, Ruth does not intend to help the Infected. She sent a mob to plunder your garden—"

"You mean after your thugs tortured Bernard as he was guarding it? After they burned the greenhouses to the ground? What was left to plunder?"

Ruth had made it inside. She was rolling another slumbering Infected onto the tarp. She froze as she heard Father Preston's tone change.

"She's here, isn't she?" he gasped. "Is she in there right now? Come out Ruth! We caught your minions ripping up the floorboards of the caretaker's cottage to get to the hoard of food underneath. They've admitted you sent them to do it. You and that gardener have been stealing food for months, haven't you?"

She could hear him climb a few of the front steps and Ruth's face flushed with anger. She reached for the gun that wasn't on her hip. Ashamed, she put her hand down and shouldered the tarp, beginning to drag the Infected back out the far door.

Juliana stopped him. "Bernard wouldn't do that. He was hiding the food from the men you sent to loot it."

"We are not thieves!" shrieked Father Preston.

Juliana's voice was calm but it vibrated through the whole field. "Yes. You are. You may not have meant to become a thief, maybe none of you did. Once you were good people. But now, now you steal food from those who can't lift a finger to stop you. You steal from me, who would have freely given you food, if you had asked. You aren't just thieves, but arsonists and torturers. *Murderers*."

A throaty, growling murmur passed through

the crowd. Ruth tried to speed up as adrenaline began pulsing through her.

"Oh yes, murderers," continued Juliana, "look around you. You kill men and women in the most brutal way possible because someone you don't like has a photograph of their loved one? You don't know the agreement between them and Ruth. And you don't even have the decency to bury them. You leave them to rot and disturb the Afflicted. We can smell them in here. We can hear them. You disturb our peace, these people you pretend to want to care for so badly."

"It was not murder, but justice," cried a woman behind Ruth.

"I know Father Preston has convinced you of that. That you believe these people are murderers. Even if I could agree, it doesn't explain Bernard. How do you justify what's been done to him? He's done no harm to anyone. He's only ever protected the garden and helped feed us. But he has been beaten, his hand and arm broken. Your own people burned down the greenhouses that held our medicinal plants. Medicine that could be used to help anyone. All gone, all wasted. What good did that serve? Father Preston, can you explain that?"

Ruth closed the circle a little more, rolling the Infected off the tarp and creeping back toward the kitchen. *Just a few more*, she told herself.

"Perhaps some of the men have been a little overzealous, but we will have plenty of food where we are headed, you don't need to worry about—" began Father Preston.

"I'm not worried about *you*," said Juliana sharply. "I'm worried about the people you are leaving behind. They've never done anything to you, but you destroyed what was left for them to live on. And when I send families of the Afflicted to retrieve the food Bernard protected, you throw them into this— this cart to be hurt or killed. And you enslave two Afflicted to pull it-"

"*You* sent them?" snapped Father Preston, "No, Ruth sent them. They are thieves. The Afflicted aren't enslaved. They are doing God's work."

Ruth was almost back to the kitchen. She watched as Juliana snatched the riding crop out of Gray's hand. "Then you don't need this," she said. "Let them go. Let all of them go and leave us in peace. This is the last time I will ask. Go now. You've committed the worst crimes that are left in a world as broken as this one is. What will happen when you're the ones who are judged?"

"Nothing will happen," spat Father Preston, "our motives are pure. We are not leaving without Ruth. We know these people are in league with her and we cannot let thieves run rampant in our midst. Stealing food is just a longer version of murder these days. Unless Ruth answers for their crimes, they will join the monsters already hanging in this field. You have until dawn to say your goodbyes and produce her. Then they will hang and we will retrieve the Afflicted you hold hostage ourselves. I cannot guarantee your safety if that should happen Juliana. We are *not* leaving. And we are done talking." He stormed down the steps. Ruth was already halfway toward the next empty spot. She crouched in the tall grass, ready to be discovered as the crowd milled around and Juliana shut the door. But the crowd was too restless and outraged to look around them, too confident in themselves to fear any outside interference. They posted guards at the doors and went back to their preparations, each expecting the others to spot any escape attempts.

Ruth went on with her solitary work, easily skirting the lazy guards who half dozed near the kitchen.

CHAPTER 28

"Why are we waiting for morning?" hissed Gray, "If you've made the decision we can take the hospital now. Don't give them time to prepare." He trailed the priest by only half a step. Father Preston whirled around.

"You really are an idiot, aren't you?" asked Father Preston. Gray flushed a deep red and puffed out his chest. "I've given you far too much leeway. Don't forget who's in charge here," continued Father Preston, "To you this is all just a sham, just a show. You think I'm either a doddering fool for upholding my faith, or I'm using it as a cloak to trick these people." His hand shot out and clutched Gray's collar closed. He lifted Gray up off of his feet and let him choke on the tightened cloth for a few seconds. "My faith is my strength. Don't forget it again," he growled. "The men told me you had a history with the gardener. In the end it will be *you* and not me who answers for his mistreatment. But I will not allow you to harm Juliana. Not while I am here to stop you. I will not have that stain, at least, upon me." He let go with a shove and Gray fell into the grass. Father Preston bent over him. "If that's too otherworldly for you, then consider this: If we began storming the hospital now, Ruth would begin killing the Afflicted, thinking there is nothing left to lose. The Afflicted we manage to save will be wild and dangerous in the commotion. If I tell them they have until morning then Juliana will persuade her to wait. In an hour or two I will send in a small team through the broken wing to begin quietly securing the building. They will catch Ruth unaware. The Afflicted will be asleep and

Juliana will remain unharmed. *You* however, will not be part of that team. You can guard the cart with its prisoners instead. Care for the Afflicted you have harnessed to it. Show me you have their interest at heart and maybe I won't throw you off as soon as we leave town." Gray glared at him and rubbed his neck. Father Preston just straightened up and strode off to comfort his angry Congregation.

Father Preston sat in a folding chair at a table while the others milled around him setting up camp, eating, poking at the criminals in the caged car. He had meant to sit down and make a list of a handful of trusted people to send into the hospital, but something about the yoked Afflicted made him stop and stare, his thoughts drifting like leaves in a greasy puddle. Juliana's voice kept echoing the word "murderer." She'd asked him who he'd killed. She'd asked him if he remembered. His gaze traced the deep lines of rage and want that had carved themselves into the snarling Afflicted's face. Did they remember?

No, they couldn't. Father Preston was special. He was chosen. Remembering had been the cost of his miraculous cure, surely. Remembering had led him to minister to the others, knowing the darkness they were caught in. It didn't mean that they would ever remember. He closed his eyes for a moment. What he'd done, what he was doing— it was all to a greater purpose, wasn't it? The Plague had been another flood. The world was not broken, despite what Juliana believed; it was *cleansed.* He alone had risen from the floodwater. He alone had to live with not just what he had done, but what they all had done to survive.

He was in the abbey again. The morning sun at last glowing through the tinted windows, the monastery silent. Brother John sat up in a nearby pew as he woke. Father Preston was exhausted. He hadn't been able to sleep under the gaze of the painted wooden figure, terrified it would climb down from its place and scratch at him, bite him in the dark.

"Brother Michael, what should we do?" asked John.

"Do?" asked Father Preston hazily.

"The Abbot is locked in his room. We have to feed him. There were a few monks still out there, sick, when I came in. They are prowling the monastery. Maybe harming each other. We have to lock them up until someone finds a cure."

"This is no disease. I told Brother Matthew that this was the devil. Possession. He was headstrong, wouldn't listen."

"We still have to do something."

Father Preston stood up and began pulling candles from their iron spikes. He hefted the naked candle holder, its sharp prongs thrusting out before him. "You'll need a weapon," he said.

"A— a weapon, Brother Michael?" stammered the young monk. "But these are our family— we cannot hurt them."

"They are not our brothers any longer," growled Father Preston, "only demons who wear their flesh. I will protect the ones that I can, but we must protect ourselves first. Find a weapon or stay here." His heart was pitiless. He had no time for cowardice. Brother John trembled but began hunting for a weapon, more frightened of staying alone in the church than of committing violence.

The pew squealed as they pulled it away from the large doors. Father Preston opened them and stared down into the courtyard. The remains of two bodies sprawled in dark coronas of blood. The monastery gates were still closed, held there by the shovel Father Preston had placed himself. He stumbled as he descended the stone steps and Brother John caught him. The smell of frozen blood was strong and coppery as they passed the bodies. Father Preston's stomach rumbled disturbingly.

"We'll see to them when the monastery is secure," he said nervously to cover the sound of his hunger. The wooden doors to the dormitory hung halfway off their hinges and the interior was a murky gray after the sunlit courtyard. They stopped to let their eyes adjust.

"Hello? Is anyone well in here?" called Father Preston.

"What are you doing?" whispered Brother John.

"It's what we're here for isn't it?" He gripped the candlestick harder and began rapping on doors. At the third cell there was a scrabbling noise. "Who is in there? Answer me so I know you are sane." There was a gurgling growl instead. "Well, one of them is in there anyway," said Father Preston and put his hand on the doorknob. Brother John shook his head and put his hand over Father Preston's.

"No, he'll leap out at us and— and eat us."

"We have to secure him and see if there is anyone else in there. Go get a sheet from another room. When I open the room, throw it over whatever is inside. We'll be able to tackle it without harming it."

Brother John scuttled back to the prior cell. Father Preston realized he was referring to one of his brothers, a man he had probably lived with, prayed with, worked with for years, as an "it." He shook his head to clear it.

Brother John returned. Father Preston turned the knob and yanked the door open. Brother John threw the sheet without even looking. The man beneath it howled and Father Preston leapt upon the writhing bundle. They lifted the man up and pulled him back to another room, tying him down to the narrow bed with more sheets. It was Joseph, the man who had tried to save Father Preston the night before. Father Preston said a quiet prayer for him as Joseph screamed and struggled. The sound attracted someone. Father Preston heard the sprinting footsteps of someone in the hallway. He spun around to face the door and pushed Brother John behind him. The man that sprung up in the doorway was barely recognizable. His face was smeared with mucus and blood, his eyes almost stuck closed with gore.

"Brother Matthew?" gasped Brother John. Father Preston hesitated. He had never been fond of Matthew, had found him weak and indulgent of the other monks, and deep down, Father Preston knew that Matthew had been the Abbot's favorite. But he was the prior, he'd been Father Preston's mentor as an initiate and for all his willingness to overlook the failings of others, Matthew's own conduct was unquestionable, even for Father Preston.

The twisted iron bar of the candlestick hovered between them for a second as Father Preston drew it back in doubt. Then Brother Matthew roared and leapt at him, his entire chest sinking onto the five sharp prongs. Father Preston cried out as if he were the one wounded, and dropped the candlestick. Brother Matthew rolled off of it, breath wheezing in a scarlet bubble out of his punctured chest. Brother John dropped beside him but Father Preston held him back. Even in his last suffocating seconds, Brother Matthew scrabbled and scratched trying to pull one of them in. Brother John sobbed. Father Preston hated him for it, even as he felt his own grief overwhelm him.

"Make sure Brother Joseph is secured," he snapped, "and then bring this body outside with the others. I'll find the rest."

He stalked off down the hall.

In the end, there were only two more, the Abbot and Brother Gregg, both sick. Father Preston helped Brother John secure the three living monks in their cells and they covered the bodies of the others in blankets, waiting for help to arrive.

Father Preston tried to pretend life was normal, continuing his prayers and cleaning the shattered monastery as if it were just another day. Brother John cared for the three sick monks but spent the rest of his days locked away in his cell, only begrudgingly coming to prayer when Father Preston commanded it. One morning, he entered the church on his own.

"We are running out of food," he said to Father Preston's back. Father Preston stood up from his kneeling position and turned around.

"We have to do something," continued Brother John.

"I *am* doing something," snapped Father Preston.

"We have to leave, find more. Maybe let the others go."

Father Preston shook his head. "No. We don't leave. The monastery is our home. God will provide."

"So you just want to sit here and starve to death?" Brother John became angry. "That may be fine for you, but we've got three people depending upon us. I can't watch them starve, too, instead of helping them. Or at least letting them go."

"Let them go? They'll kill each other. Or you. If they starve, at least they will be innocent—"

"I'll find a way to let them go that won't hurt anyone else," interrupted Brother John. "If I do that, will you help me?"

Father Preston thought for a moment. "Yes. If you find a way, I will help you," he said. He slammed his prayer book shut and walked out of the church, stumbling and weaving across the courtyard. He told himself he was just dizzy from standing so quickly. Brother John didn't even notice.

A few mornings later he heard the light chimes of bells in the hallway as he was rising from bed. He opened the door and Brother John was leading the Abbot down the hall. The older monk was still bound, a brass hand bell tied to a string around his neck.

"What are you doing?" asked Father Preston.

"I'm letting him go. I'll let Brother Joseph go tomorrow and Brother Gregg the next day."

"And the bell?"

"I read about lepers using them. It will give others some warning."

"That's degrading. I won't allow it. The Abbot int 'illy." Father Preston stopped speaking, snapping his mouth shut in horror.

"What?" Brother John struggled to hold the Abbot while looking at him.

Father Preston spoke more slowly, concentrating on each word. "I can't let you do that. The Abbot is a holy man."

Brother John shrugged. "It's the only way."

A flash of rage seared the nerves behind Father Preston's eyes. "He 'atha 'tarf," he shouted. Brother John stared at him and backed slowly away, pulling the Abbot with him.

"Come ba'ere!" screamed Father Preston. Brother John began to run. So did Father Preston. Brother John slammed the dormitory door closed behind him.

"You are not yourself," he called to Father Preston. The sound of the bell retreated and Father Preston could hear the front gate creak open. He took a deep breath. The rage subsided and shame took its place. He walked quietly back to his cell and shut the door. He was immersed in desperate prayer when the next bell rang the next morning and sobbed loudly as the third passed by that evening.

He believed he was alone. In the darkest part of the night, he crept past the motionless forms of his brothers in the snowy courtyard and into the church. He could see the massive gray gap of the open monastery gate but turned away from it. Let them all flee. He would keep his word. It was too dark to see the carved statue but he knew it was laughing, gibbering at him. It rang a bell, mocking him. He began to curse it aloud, shrieking for the bell to stop, but it just got louder. Something cold clapped against his throat and tightened.

"I'm sorry Brother Michael," said a voice, "but I can't let you out without it. May you think better of me when you wake."

Father Preston blacked out from the pressure of the cord. He was being dragged out of the gate, thrown out of his monastery like a pile of snow covered garbage when he woke up a minute later. He snarled and the man dragging him jumped. He was little and fat and Father Preston was so hungry. His teeth hurt. The bell wouldn't stop ringing. He leapt up and shook the man.

"Please, Brother Michael, it's me!" cried Brother John. Father Preston bit the fat cheek as hard as he could, his lips suddenly splashed with salty heat, his teeth pressing the rubbery skin.

Someone shook his shoulder and Father Preston woke from the hell of the broken monastery into the torch filled field staring at the dark, hulking hospital. He could still feel the thick skin rolling between his front teeth. He swallowed against a rush of nausea, and forced himself back into the present.

"Father? Father, shall we begin setting up scaffolds," asked a heavily bearded man next to him.

Father Preston smiled and pressed the man's hands. "No, Daniel, I have a more important task for you now."

CHAPTER 29

Ruth slumped on the bottom stair watching the men finish welding new steel scaffolds as the sky began to lighten into a deep gray. She didn't think she could move any more. The circle was closed. The Congregation was surrounded. There were only the ten undrugged Infected in their rooms. They were sleeping naturally. As soon as she summoned the energy, Ruth would quietly open the doors to their cells and she and Juliana would lock themselves into the bedrooms.

She knew Father Preston was coming. It was only a matter of when. He wouldn't be able to hold onto Gray much longer. She could see the tension between them. If they didn't try to come in before the Infected started waking up, they definitely would by the time they were under attack. And Ruth planned to have a surprise waiting for them. She racked her brain for some way to save the people in the cop car, but she was exhausted. More than she'd ever been. Even her thoughts moved as if they were underwater. There was a creaking noise from Ruth's left in the dark, and a spike of adrenaline pinched her awake. They were already here, trying to come through the abandoned wing. She jumped up and ran up the stairs. On the second floor she began quietly opening cell doors and creeping away. She could hear the people below her shuffling and whispering. She reached the stairs just as the first Infected woke and shuffled into the hall. She raced up the next flight and flung herself into Juliana's bedroom. She tried to keep quiet as she pulled the heavy dresser in front of the door. Juliana woke, squinting at Ruth in the weak predawn light.

"Has it started?" she asked sleepily.

Ruth opened her mouth to answer, but a scream of agony from downstairs did it for her.

Father Preston snapped out of a light doze as a thin scream pierced the hospital walls. The people around him stopped what they were doing and looked around. He offered the Congregation a comforting smile. "The Afflicted are hungry. Don't worry, we shall be providing for them soon, and there will be no more distressing screams."

He rose from his seat and drew closer to the hospital. He thought he'd heard a word in the scream. His team should have just entered. Maybe it had been Ruth. The people in the cop car reached out to him and cried as he passed. It irritated him; he wanted to hear what was going on inside the hospital, not the whining of thieves.

The others went back to their work, the men finishing up the scaffolds, the women cooking a meal for the Congregation. Gray sat sharpening the fire ax with a rusty file he'd found. Father Preston ignored him.

The sun broke over the horizon and lit up the heavy mist in the field turning the crushed weeds a dull sepia, like they'd been splashed with a light rain of gore. Another shriek came from the hospital. Far off in a corner of tall grass near the road, an Infected woman sat up and blinked at the glaring white fog around her. She heard the shriek and stood up, unbound from a wall for the first time in years. Her legs were weak and shaky from disuse. She stumbled a few steps toward the sound, became confused and stopped for a moment. Her mouth hung open and she sniffed the air, turning her head from side to side. Somewhere in the nearby fog someone was humming. If she'd been well, she would have recognized it as an old spiritual her mother had been fond of. But her brain only connected the sound with the possibility of food. She shuffled toward it, then broke into a trot as the sound continued and grew closer.

An ancient crown of white braided hair separated from the mist and the Infected woman lunged at it. The humming stopped as the old woman snapped like a twig under the Infected. There was one high crooning whoop of triumph and fierce joy from the Infected before she bent over the old woman and tore into her throat.

The women cooking over the massive bonfire in the back of the camp stopped and looked at each other. "What was that?" asked one.

Another shrugged. "Was it Mildred?" asked another, "She was laying out rope for the— the judgments. Maybe she tripped in a rabbit hole. You know, her bones aren't what they used to be."

"I'll go check on her," said another who had been stirring a great pot of hot cereal. She tucked the long spoon into her tidy apron pocket and straightened her skirt.

"Mildred?" she called as she disappeared into the fog. Her voice woke three more Infected. They stirred and sat up. If the fog had been any thinner they would have seen each other. Instead they moved toward the voices and the crackle of the fire.

"Mildred, are you all right? We heard you

call and were afraid you had fall—" the woman's gasp swallowed her last word. She found herself only a foot or two from the scraggle of hair and limbs that crawled over Mildred's small body. Teeth snapped and the Infected woman's head jerked up, spraying tiny fans of blood droplets. They spattered the woman's white apron and the skin on her bare arms. She screamed and backed away, waking more of the Infected. She ran in the direction she thought she had come, but no gold warmth of the bonfire met her, only more cool swirls of fog, like clots of milk bunching around her. She kept screaming. The other women were calling her, but she couldn't hear them over the blaring thud of her heart and the shrill cries that tumbled out of her own throat.

A skinny hand shot out of the fog and grabbed her arm. It yanked her down onto the crushed grass and knocked the wind from her lungs. She lay there, limbs aching, gasping at the thick air. A ring of jagged yellow teeth opened over her face and descended. Clawing fingers scraped her skin and twisted into her hair. *It hurts!* Her brain screamed, *It hurts!* But she fainted before it really could.

Ruth sat on the bed staring at the dresser, willing it not to move. Juliana paced, her breath ragged and her eyes huge, listening to the struggle on the stairs outside. Neither dared to speak. Ruth checked and rechecked the small knife in her pocket. There was a distant scream from outside the hospital. The grunting outside the door paused for a second and then resumed. *They're waking up,* thought Ruth, *we just have to hold on a little longer*. The dresser jiggled as something banged into the door. Juliana jumped a little and then sat next to Ruth on the bed. Ruth grabbed her hand and held it tightly. The dresser squealed as it moved a half inch from the wall.

Commotion near the new scaffolds made Father Preston turn around, irritated that his attention was being divided. He was *so close* to defeating Ruth. *So close* to routing out the evil that had held sway over the hospital and Juliana for so long. And now, in the hour of his greatest triumph, he was being called away, for what? Someone would answer for this distraction. He stomped toward the rear of the camp. The fog was beginning to burn away around the campfire and he could see the shadow of figures moving very quickly as he drew closer to it. There were shouts and a few screams. The turned leg of an antique table stabbed out of the fog toward him, its end blazing. Father Preston dodged it, ducking sideways.

"F-Father, I'm sorry," stammered the man holding it, his arm was bleeding and his eyes darted wildly side to side. He grabbed Father Preston's arm and dragged him back toward the hospital. "You can't be back here, not safe. We have to get to the hospital, where it's safe."

"What is going on?" growled Father Preston.

"It's the Infected— dozens of them. The devils came in with the fog. Attacked the women. They are everywhere."

The man whirled around with the burning table leg. Figures struggled all around them, shrouded by the fog. There was a sudden shriek near Father Preston's left ear. He dropped to the ground, flattening himself against the rough weeds. An Infected sprang onto the other man's back, ripping at his shoulder with its teeth. The table leg fell into the grass and began to smolder. Father Preston leapt up to help, but the Infected turned on him with a snarl. He grappled with the wiry, bony thing, its face too criss crossed with scars and missing chunks to tell what gender it had been. The other man held his shoulder and stumbled backward into the fog, hollering for help.

Father Preston was furious. He recognized the bandage covering the Infected's missing eye. This was Ruth's work. *She let them go. She's used them against me. Against ME. How dare she? I'll kill that bitch myself!* His rage gave him as much strength as the Infected. He beat it down, stomping it to the ground. It flailed and twisted against the smoking grass, its hair and clothing catching almost immediately. Father Preston backed away, but it rose up and lurched toward him, a flaming pillar of teeth and claws and hate. Gray emerged from the fog, screaming at everyone to stop, not to harm the merchandise. Father Preston sneered at him and snatched the ax from his hand. One hearty swing and the momentum of the crazed Infected were all it took. It fell down, headless, starting small grass fires. Father Preston clutched the ax and shoved Gray aside. He plowed through small knots of people locked in death struggles and up the concrete steps of the hospital. He threw open the front door.

It was very quiet inside. The foyer was dark,

windows still untouched by the rising sun. He crept down the hallway. The cells gaped open, all empty. It felt like he was walking backward in time, for a moment his mind overlaid the monastery dormitory. As if he were still watching his brothers succumb to madness, as if he were still sick. Maybe he'd never really recovered.

The kitchen too, was empty. He opened the pantry door, expecting them to be hiding there, with their spoils. He was dumbfounded to find it barren. He'd never bothered to look when he was living there. There had always been enough. Juliana had always fed them all without blinking. He'd just assumed there was always more. Dust lay on most of the shelves. She'd been struggling for a while then. For a swift second, the thought of Gray burning the greenhouses and ripping up the garden, bubbled up inside him, enraged him. But it was shoved aside by the idea that Juliana had known the hospital was failing. She'd *known* the Afflicted wouldn't survive the winter; he had thought she was bluffing. She'd never have to face the consequences, though. She could play the saint and would be long dead by the time the suffering started.

That's why she'd chosen Ruth. That's why she wouldn't give the Afflicted to him. It would have exposed her even more than her speech. Everyone would know that she had failed, that it wasn't just a tactic. He felt a sour sickness begin in his gut. All this time he'd protected her. All this time they could have taken the Afflicted away. Moved south and started over. And he'd waited because he didn't want to disturb a dying woman.

He'd been weak. He'd let sympathy get in the way of duty. Now the Afflicted and his loyal flock would slaughter each other to pay for his wavering. He couldn't let Ruth get away with it. She'd put Juliana up to it, he was sure. She'd been the puppetmaster the whole time. She wouldn't leave this building without paying, in blood, drop by drop, for all the agony she'd caused him.

He stalked back down to the entryway, no longer hearing the carnage outside, no longer seeing the bodies of his brother monks in each empty cell.

"I'm still here Ruth," he roared, "You used your charges against me! You thought you'd trick me. Run me off, kill me. But I'm still here. And I'm coming for you, Juliana or no." He brandished the ax and began pounding up the stairs, bouncing a little with each step to create a more intimidating stomp. There was a scrabbling sound, like a hundred large rats scraping a wall at once.

Father Preston stopped, peering up at the gloomy attic. A handful of figures stood at the top of the stairs, breathing heavy, heads turned toward him. Father Preston had time to back down one step before the Infected reached him. He fell, his head hitting the stairs even as the heat of their breath made him scream in fear. A jaw snapped shut on his outstretched leg. He realized he had wet his pants as the ax flew away behind him and needles of pain dug into his soft belly. His head was lifted by squeezing hands and then dropped again as one of the Infected shoved another back. His head hit the tiled floor again, and this time he blacked out. He didn't even have time to call upon his God for help.

CHAPTER 30

"I'm no sharpshooter Frank," said Nella with a sigh. They stood on the edge of the field, trying to peer into the fog that was rising gradually in thick strands as the sun arced higher above the horizon.

"Maybe they're distracted enough that we can just stab them with the darts. I mean, listen to that."

The shrieks and grunts floating through the field overwhelmed almost everything else. Nella glanced at her husband.

"It takes about ten minutes to work, remember?"

Frank shook his head. "If we wait for the fog to burn off, everyone might be dead. There's no other way. How many darts do we have?"

Bernard hovered anxiously nearby, his good hand holding the dog. Nella pulled two large boxes from the pack. "Well, they were manufactured with the idea of encountering massive hordes. I think each case has five hundred darts, but we only have two cases with us."

Frank looked over his shoulder at Bernard. "There's no way they were able to take care of a thousand Infected. He said it was just him and his friend." He sighed and rubbed his head. "There's no way we're going to be able to tell who's Infected. And if we leave the Immunes awake, they'll just continue killing the others to be safe. We'll have to dart every person. That way no one will be able to kill someone while they are vulnerable and sleeping."

"And if they turn on us?"

"Bernard, if we run straight from this point

we'll hit the hospital?"

Bernard nodded.

"And your friends will let us in if we need help?"

Bernard hesitated. He untied the sling Ruth had made him and handed it to Frank. Frank looked at it for a moment and nodded.

"Okay, you stay here. Be ready to run when we get back, if your friends are in bad shape, we'll need help," Frank turned to Nella. "Don't leave me in there," he said quietly, "I know you'll be all right, you've taken care of yourself a long time before I came around. But I don't know if I'm ready to see—to see *us* in a large group."

Nella brushed her thumb over the raised scar in the palm of his hand. "They are no more to blame than you were, and in a few days, they are going to feel as terribly as you have. They'll need to know there are others like them in the world."

He scanned the field, his face drawn with worry. She pressed several cool plastic darts into his hand. "I'll be right here, the whole time," she said when he looked back at her. "Aim for a limb, you'll be more likely to hit a vein. Don't pull the dart out, it takes a few seconds to release the full dose."

He pocketed a handful of darts and grabbed more from the box. Nella stuffed her own pockets as well. "We'll have to stay low until the fog clears," she said, "We can see underneath it that way, and we'll be less likely to run into someone's weapon or teeth." She put a handful of darts in Bernard's hand too. "Just in case anyone wanders out. But don't try to fight them. Just hide. It takes a few minutes, not like the movies used to show." Bernard nodded.

She knelt next to Frank. "Ready?"

He took a deep breath and then nodded. Crouching, they ran forward into the fog. The grass swished around them, the sweet smell of it crushed underfoot and mixed with wood smoke from a nearby campfire. The thuds and groans of people fighting drew closer and Nella dragged Frank toward an opening in the grass. She pulled a dart from her pocket and held it point out in her fist. A man knelt over another form, the butt end of a welding torch descending onto the unconscious face of his opponent. He saw Nella and Frank as the mist evaporated between them and hesitated.

"I— I didn't mean to, what could I do? He jumped me. Would've eaten me or the Father. All of us I guess. I know we're supposed to forgive them, that we need them but—" he continued to babble as Nella stood up and put a calming hand on his arm. Frank stabbed the dart into the other man's arm.

"What's that?" asked the man with the torch.

"We're here to help," said Nella, "Just medicine." She poked her dart into the back of his neck. He reeled back trying to reach it, his eyes wide and his mouth opened in a surprised "o." "Leave it there," said Nella in a soothing voice, "When you wake up it'll all be over. All of it, you are safe now."

The man set the unlit torch on the grass. "You from the government?"

Nella could feel Frank staring at her, but didn't dare return the glance. "That's right," she said.

"Well, what— what should I do now?"

"Just take a seat, let the medicine work. We'll explain everything when you wake up."

The man sat down in the grass next to the Infected. Nella gave him a reassuring pat on the arm, then grabbed Frank's hand and pulled him toward the next screaming knot of people.

"They aren't all going to be that easy," said Frank.

"No. He just wanted to be told what to do. Wanted someone in charge again. Maybe most of them do, but someone's going to fight us before we finish."

But the next group of five was too locked in grappling to even realize they'd been injected. Nella couldn't even tell which were the Infected. Maybe they all were.

They reached the campfire and the fog burned away only to be replaced by thick, greasy smoke. A burning body lay in the grass, spreading the fire in a large patch. Naked steel beams stuck out of the earth to either side of the fire and a few dozen people were broken into pairs battling or moaning as they crawled along the grass or totally still and dangerously close to the flame.

"If they are sedated and the fire keeps spreading—" began Frank.

Nella nodded. "We have to stop the grass fire first." She looked around. "None of these people are going to help us." She began dragging a wounded woman away from the flames, stopping to inject her with the Cure and each of the other bodies she passed, not even checking to see whether they were alive.

Frank spotted a few large pots sitting on the edge of the bonfire and an old, dirty cooler beside it. He tossed the lid of the cooler aside and found it full of filthy water. He picked it up and heaved it over the flaming body and the blackening grass that surrounded it. The water sizzled and put out about half of the flames. Frank ran back to the fire and opened one of the pots, burning his hand. A thick sludge of oatmeal. He looked around him but there was nothing to help him pull it out of the fire. He slid out of his shirt and bunched it between his hands. He picked up the pot with the flimsy t-shirt and walked quickly to the remnants of the fire. Dumping the oatmeal, he threw the pot aside as it burned through the shirt. The old string of bite marks on his arm shone an angry red in the heat and the scars on his face and chest darkened. He stomped out the last few patches of grass fire.

Nella looked up and saw a man racing toward Frank. "Look out!" she cried, but it was too late. The man threw himself onto Frank's back, making him stumble sideways. Nella dropped the man she was dragging and sprinted toward them. The man had his hands around Frank's throat.

"That's right," he was saying, "Don't want to damage you, just go to sleep."

Frank tried to pull the hands away but he was off balance and panicked. Disoriented, he kept walking, trying to find something to shake the man off. They disappeared into the far edge of the fog.

"Frank!" Nella cried, still running after them. They couldn't have gone far, but she didn't see them. "He's not Infected!" she yelled. "Let him go, he won't hurt you, he's not Infected!" She turned around straining her eyes to see into the fog around her. She wasn't sure which way the campfire was or which way Frank had gone. She didn't have time to guess so she just began running in one direction. "Frank!" she called, but there was no answer. Someone reached out and grabbed her. She stabbed the hand with a dart without stopping. It flinched and drew back into the gray blank. She heard a dog barking and tried to head for it, thinking it must be Bernard.

Nella almost smacked into a tall steel beam before she saw it. It was like the others but this one had a bundle drooping from its cross section. She kept running, only registering the foul smell as she passed underneath the dark bundle. The fog cleared again near a smaller campfire. She found Bernard's dog jumping around it, frenzied and growling at the dark rear lights of a police car. Screams came from inside and she could hear thumping and grunts nearby. She pulled a bunch of darts from her pocket and ran up to the car. Frank was lying stretched out beside it. The man who had grabbed him was swinging his fist at Bernard. Nella darted forward and grabbed his arm. The man was caught off guard and flailed but wasn't able to pull free. She aimed carefully and jabbed the dart's slim needle into the bulging vein at his elbow and let go before he could react. He turned toward her just as Bernard's fist came down on his cheek. He fell next to Frank and Bernard straddled him to hold him down.

Nella ignored them and hovered over Frank. He was breathing. In a few seconds he opened his eyes.

"Are you okay?" Nella asked

He grimaced. "Headache. Otherwise I'm fine."

"Take a few deep breaths to get rid of the headache," she said, helping him sit up.

Bernard was struggling with the man,while the dog circled and barked. Nella helped hold him until the drug kicked in and he slowed down and then stopped.

"He thought I was Infected. He wanted to tie me to the cart with the others," rasped Frank through his sore throat.

Nella stood up. "The others?" she asked and approached the front of the car. It wasn't there. Instead the yoked Infected tried desperately to turn themselves toward her. She injected them, but she could see they were far too thin. They'd die before the sedative wore off. There were more inside the car.

"Help us!" cried a young man, threading his fingers through the wire cage.

"You aren't Infected? Are you with this Father Preston?"

"No, no! We just wanted some food. Ruth sent us to get food from the garden. She said nobody wanted it, that Father Preston was burning it. But they caught us anyway."

The fog around the car lifted as a breeze swirled around them. Nella was fumbling with the door when the foul odor hit her again.

"What happened here?" gasped Frank. Nella got the door open and people started tumbling out, more than she thought could fit in the small space.

"Where are you from?" snorted an older

woman. "Father Preston's been hanging people up if they did business with Ruth. We thought most of em had taken care of themselves years ago, but he always finds someone. This should put an end to it though," the woman cackled but the others looked unnerved.

"Why? What did this Ruth do?" asked Frank, but Nella cut him off.

"We don't have time. Go with Bernard, get out of here. We have lots more to do—"

A loud chorus of howls punctuated by a short, shrill scream erupted a few dozen feet from them.

"Must have reached the hospital," said the woman, "Look, we're grateful to be free, but we have to move before anyone finds us."

Bernard nodded and motioned for the others to follow. Nella touched the dark ring around Frank's neck. "Go with him, you're hurt."

Frank shook his head. "No way. That sounded like too many, even for you, Nella. We'll go together."

The fog was clearing quickly and a line of beams spread out to either side. "My God. What did this Ruth woman do to cause all this?" asked Nella, "What if we're helping the wrong people?"

Frank shook his head. "We're curing people that have been waiting all this time. How can that be wrong? I don't care who this Ruth is or Father Preston. The Infected aren't meant to be used this way." He pulled the helmet from the yoked Infected who were now sleeping in their harnesses. Nella helped him untie the straps and lift the yoke away from their sitting forms. Then they turned toward the large building that was gradually solidifying through the fog against the warm sun.

CHAPTER 31

The dresser wiggled again. Juliana pressed herself against the headboard of the bed. Ruth stood in front of the dresser, debating whether to press it back to the wall or keep silent. Whoever was out there wasn't friendly. If it was Father Preston's people they wouldn't be stopped by a dresser. But an Infected might give up. She slid around the edge of the dresser and peered through the crack in the door, careful to stay in the corner's shadow. She couldn't make much out, just a lot of movement. It seemed as though there were several people outside, all struggling with each other, none of them realizing she and Juliana were inside the room. She crept over to the window, thankful again to be on the third floor. She eased it open and looked out. The sun was hitting the back of the building now, dispersing most of the fog.

"How are you feeling today?" she whispered to Juliana. Juliana crawled carefully over the bed toward her.

"You want to go out that way?"

Ruth shrugged. She didn't see an obvious way down. "Maybe we can wait them out."

"We're going to die here aren't we?"

Ruth sagged onto the bed. There was a bang on the wall outside the room. "I'm sorry," she said, "It was a shitty plan to begin with. I thought I'd have time to fix it. I thought I'd get us out."

Juliana hugged her. "It's okay. The Afflicted will escape, some of them. I just wanted to give them a chance. The fog will help them get away. I hope someone else finds them and helps them."

Ruth began to cry and she shook her head.

"No Juliana, there's nobody else out there in the world like you. Maybe there's nobody else out there at all. But they won't have to suffer for too long."

"You can't think that way. There's a reason we're still here. All of us. Maybe we don't get to see the happy ending, maybe we're just the midpoint of the story, the what did you call it? The krìsis. But the story goes on after it passes us by. The happy ending is out there. It must be."

There was another bang and the dresser teetered on its two front legs before settling back down. "Why? Why does there have to be a happy ending? Where is that the rule?" cried Ruth, her voice shaking between sobs.

"Because you are still sitting here with me. Because after eight years, this place was still going. The helpless, the useless, were still cared for and fed until *everyone* was starving. Nobody had to care for them. They didn't add to anyone's chances of survival. But they *were* cared for, by more than just you and me. Evil never lasts, not even the Plague. But love does. Even after threats and violence and betrayal, it sticks around. Someday, these people will be cured. I know it in my bones. And even if they can't remember us, they'll know that someone watched over them for a long, long time. They'll know they were loved even after the world ended. And how can that be anything but a happy thought?"

The dresser crashed onto its face in front of the bed and the door swung open. Ruth curled herself around Juliana in a hug, trying to shield her as long as she could. But as the first drooling Infected snapped its teeth and stepped onto the back of the dresser, Father Preston's voice came charging up the staircase at them and everyone stopped. The Infected pivoted, their heads swiveling in the same smooth motion toward the door. Ruth stared as they began scrambling over each other, boiling down the hallway toward the roaring priest. Ruth leapt up and shut the door as quietly as she could. She lifted the dresser slowly and pushed it back into place in front of the doorframe. Juliana stood up.

"We can't leave him," she said.

Ruth turned to stare at her. "What are you talking about? He was coming to kill us. To drag us out into that field and— and *crucify* us."

"They'll eat him alive. It's what, half a dozen to one?"

"Wasn't that the point?"

Juliana shook her head. "No Ruth, the Infected were supposed to buy us time. To make a distraction. But I thought everyone would flee. I thought we'd all escape."

Ruth's lips tightened into a hard line.

"If we let him die because of the Infected, we'll be just as guilty of using them as he was planning to. If you won't do it for Father Preston, think of how the Infected would feel knowing we allowed them to devour someone."

Ruth pushed aside the dresser. "How are we supposed to stop them?" she asked as she opened the door.

"Maybe we can get them to chase us out the door. The confusion in front should distract them after that and we can double back— or leave."

Ruth raced down the steps shouting and

waving her hands. Father Preston was already on the floor, two of the Infected snapping at each other like wild dogs over their kill. The other three were already gnawing on him. None of them paid attention to Ruth. She leapt from the stairs and smashed into one of them, using her full weight to bowl him over. They fell and tangled in with a third. Growling, they made a weak attempt to catch her as she sprang up, but almost immediately fell back to Father Preston as easier prey. Ruth pulled the knife from her waistband.

"No!" cried Juliana.

"There's no other way," said Ruth, holding her hands out toward the vicious splatter of the Infected. "He's dying. Do you want me to save him or not? No other choice Juliana."

Juliana hesitated, then nodded. Ruth yanked the head of the closest Infected backward by his hair. She pressed the knife against the rough, stubbly skin of his neck. His throat was already sticky with Father Preston's blood. The front door swung open, and the foyer was bathed in bright morning light. Two figures stood in the frame. One of them leapt at Ruth. "Stop," cried the other, "Stop, we have the Cure!"

The knife was pulled from her hand and slid, skittering across the floor. The man who had leapt at her pulled the Infected man away from her. He stabbed the man's neck with a shining glass tube and backed down the hallway, dragging the man with him.

"These doors lock?" he yelled.

Ruth was in too much shock to answer. "Yes," answered Juliana shakily, "just close the door."

"Help me," commanded the woman in the door frame. She ran forward and pressed a handful of glass tubes into Ruth's hand.

"Wha— where do I?" stammered Ruth, the cool weight of the glass slowly dissolving her disbelief.

"Anywhere," said the woman, "the closer to a vein the faster it works."

Ruth stabbed it into a nearby arm, not even certain whose it was. She grasped and pulled. Juliana helped her drag the Infected off the priest and down the hallway. The woman took the last one biting Father Preston, leaving only the two who were still squabbling over him.

Ruth slammed the cell door. Juliana bent over, breathing heavy. "How is this possible?" asked Ruth.

"Later," gasped Juliana. They went back for the last of the Infected, but the two strangers had already subdued them. Juliana pulled the hospital door shut. Ruth looked down at Father Preston. He was mangled, needed stitches probably. But he'd live. Ruth looked at the dart in her hand.

"Is there a sedative?" she asked the man. He nodded, trying to catch his breath. "How long?"

"Roughly three days. It takes the Cure that long to work."

"Will it hurt healthy people?"

He shook his head.

Ruth knelt near Father Preston. "This is more than you deserve," she muttered and injected it into his arm.

"Are you Ruth and Juliana?" asked the man.

Juliana nodded.

"I'm Frank, this is Nella," he said, pulling the woman close to him. "Bernard sent us. We need to get you out of here."

"Okay," Juliana started but Ruth cut her off.

"No. We aren't going anywhere." Juliana stared at her. "Those people we injected? We fed them for eight years. Listened to them scream for eight years. Changed their diapers, cured their wounds, lost sleep, lost food, lost friends for them. Well, except this one," she nudged Father Preston with a toe, "and you burst in talking about a Cure after all this time. There's almost a hundred of them out in that field. Been waiting just like us, all this time. If it's really a cure, we aren't leaving until we track down every last one of them. And before we go anywhere with you, I want to know where you came from. Where have you been? How long have you had it?"

Nella glanced at Frank. She pulled a few handfuls of darts from her pocket. Frank handed Bernard's sling to Ruth.

"It really is a cure," said Frank quietly. "I'm living proof."

"*You* were infected?" asked Juliana, "Ruth, what if he's like Father Preston?"

Ruth shook her head. "The odds are almost impossible."

"You have a Cured person here?" asked Nella.

"We have a survivor. His body cured itself after a massive bout of pneumonia," answered Ruth. She took a few of the vials and rolled them in her palm, the glass glittering as her eyes filled with years of unshed tears. "How long?" she asked again. Juliana put a hand on her shoulder.

"Later."

Ruth wiped her nose on the back of her sleeve. She opened the door. The fog had mostly burned away and the field was a matted wound, the trampled grass clotted with ash and dust. Some groups still struggled but the ground was littered with the unconscious and the wounded and dying.

"Maybe you should go get your kit," said Juliana, already bending over Father Preston's wounds. Ruth nodded and ducked back into the interior. She picked up her knife where it had landed. The steel beams were already hot to the touch, but she went from one to the next, cutting the ropes and slowly lowering the bodies down as she passed. If only she could have taken it back. It all seemed so pointless now. She wandered from one injured person to the next, injecting them, bandaging them, dragging them into the cool shade of the hospital. She didn't really notice anyone. She just went on. It wasn't connected to her. She was lost somewhere between Charlie's death and that morning, still lost in that neverending loop of shrieks and hunger and cruel, hard survival.

She'd never be free.

The sun was setting as she pulled the last body inside. It was Gray. She thought about leaving him outside with the corpses of his victims, but they had been her friends. If anyone were to blame for their deaths, it was her. She didn't want to leave him near the sleeping Infected; it was like leaving a wolf among sheep. She left him inside with Father Preston and the Infected who had attacked the priest. Let them sort out what to do with the two of them once the Infected woke up and found out what they had intended. Ruth wanted nothing else to do with either one.

Juliana collapsed on the front step of the hospital. Her eyes were puffy and red, but she smiled at Ruth. "They are almost all here. I checked."

Ruth nodded. "Good." She stared for a moment at Juliana, as if she had suddenly lost her place. She shook her head. "You should rest. You shouldn't have done as much as you did."

Juliana laughed and brushed sweat stuck hair from the edge of her face. "Ruth, I'm dying. I'll have plenty of time to rest soon enough. This morning I thought most of the last decade would be wasted. That everything I'd done, everyone I'd cared for would be gone by this afternoon. And then, at the last second, I found myself doing the very thing I've dreamed about for eight years. We cured people Ruth, we ended this awful disease! This is one of the happiest hours of my life. How can you think I'd rather be lying in my bed?"

Ruth sank down beside her. She was silent, but her thoughts raged. She knew she ought to feel happy for the Infected, for Juliana. Instead she was crushed with guilt and terrible sadness. Frank and Nella emerged from the hospital.

"Your friend, Bernard, will be worried," said Nella gently.

Ruth glanced at Juliana. "I don't know if we can go as far as the docks tonight," she said, "besides, what happens when everyone wakes up?"

"That won't be for a few days."

"There are bedrooms on the third floor. We'll go in the morning."

"We don't have to stay any more Ruth. We can go where we want," said Juliana.

"These people will be confused when they wake up, they've lost eight years of their lives, they aren't going to understand what's happened."

Juliana exchanged a long glance with Nella. She patted Ruth's hand. "Come on, I'm up for it. And Bernard's bandage probably needs changing. Besides, I'm sure he's worried sick." She stood up and walked down the front steps. She looked back once at the silent hospital, its edges turning lavender as the sun sank away. Frank and Nella followed. Ruth pulled herself up and plodded along behind them, all the fear and fire of the past few days drained out of her, like a hard-wrung rag.

CHAPTER 32

Ruth sat on the rotting pier in the dark. Bernard and the others were behind her in the restaurant, sleeping deeply. She liked it here, on the edge of the city. It was almost separate, almost free of the baking concrete and slumping steel of the crowded buildings. She should have visited the docks sooner. She should have done a lot of things sooner. The pier shifted and creaked. Ruth turned around. Frank walked up to the edge and sat down beside her, his long legs folding until his feet dunked into the cool water.

"You're a doctor?" he asked.

"I *was*. A pediatrician."

"Nella's a psychologist." He was quiet for a moment. "It wasn't in time."

"What do you mean?"

"The Cure. It wasn't in time for your son. Not in time for a lot of people. Juliana said that's the question that would keep you up. It wasn't discovered before your son died."

"When was it found?"

He looked up at the pale, moonlit clouds. "Six years ago. By the same people that made the disease in the first place. There was no way you could have found it. Nobody could. Just them."

"Six years? Do you have any idea how many people I killed in the past six years? And all those people, waiting, for what? Where have you been?"

Frank shook his head. "I don't know. Before a few months ago I assumed our governor had sent out people. I thought the Cure was winging its way over the whole country. But your city is the first place we've found anyone alive. The capitol is gone, the coast is empty. Maybe the people in charge just thought our home was all that was left."

Why couldn't you have waited one more week? Why couldn't you have missed us? I need never have known, she thought, but she knew it was selfish and brushed the thought away.

"I'm a murderer," was what she said out loud, her tone flat and dead.

"We all are," said Frank, "be grateful you had a choice about it. Not all of us did."

"But if I'd just waited— if I'd just listened to Juliana—"

"Did you do it for yourself? I mean, to get things? Or did it give you a kind of thrill? Did you enjoy it?"

"No, never."

"Then why?"

"Because when my husband asked me to kill my son, I couldn't. Not even knowing what he was going through. I couldn't do it. So my husband did it for me. But no parent should have to do that. Since I couldn't do it for mine, I did it for others. So they wouldn't have to."

"The man that recovered, did he ever tell you what it was like? What it was like to be Infected?"

Ruth shook her head. "I don't think he remembers."

Frank cleared his throat. "He remembers. He remembers everything. And when those people wake up, they'll remember everything too. Everything they've done, everything others did to them. Do you want to hear the truth? Do you really want to know what you've done?"

Ruth stared at him for a moment and then

nodded, swallowing the lump in her throat.

Frank sighed, rocking back slightly on the splintering board. "For some reason, the people who were immune always seem to think it's like being forced to watch as someone or something else takes control of your body. Most of the time, it's kinder to let them go on thinking that way. But it isn't true. I knew what I was doing. I even, sometimes, knew it was wrong. But I didn't care. People get the wrong idea when I say I was 'compelled' to hurt someone, to eat them. They think it means I had no control. Did you ever have the Chicken Pox? Or poison ivy when you were a kid?"

"Sure," said Ruth.

"Imagine that urge to itch enhanced by a power of one hundred. Or— or a pregnancy craving, that's more the feeling, but stronger, so much stronger that you felt yourself going mad the longer you held out against it. And once you give in that first time, it's impossible to go back. It's worse. But it was still *me* that killed my wife, not some alien that had possession of me. It was still your son inside. It was torture not to be able to find— to find meat. It was torture not to be ripping or chewing or fighting. My teeth ached for it. My arms and legs bristled with adrenaline and no way to run it off. Every second that I wasn't doing those things, I *hurt*. I *ached*. So did everyone else. All those people in the hospital. All those people you killed. They all hurt for every second of every day."

Ruth felt her chest contract as she listened. She wanted to cry, but she found she couldn't.

"The thing is," continued Frank, "as much as

being Infected hurt, being Cured hurt worse for a while. While I was sick, I knew what I was doing. I thought that I had to do what I did. But I didn't care. I was caught up in this passion, this rage. Even though the civilized part of my mind knew, deep down, that what I was doing was terribly, unforgivably wrong, I didn't care about the consequences. I didn't care what would happen in the next year or tomorrow or even the next hour as long as I could get what I wanted. But waking up after the Cure— it all hit me. It was like my conscience was dead for a year and suddenly revived, way too late. I killed my wife while she was trying to help me. I ate the body of a little boy. I destroyed everything I loved. *I* did that. No one else. And the worst part is, every day I think, if I'd just summoned a little more willpower, if I'd just been less weak, I could have stopped myself. We all could have. Managed it somehow."

Ruth shook her head. "I don't believe that. If it were that easy, someone would have resisted. Someone would have stopped themselves."

"Don't you understand?" asked Frank gently, "it doesn't matter how much you or the other Immune people protest that we weren't in control, that it wasn't our fault. In our hearts, we feel— we *know* that we were. We have to carry that around for the rest of our lives. I was lucky, compared to some. Locked away in a bunker, I got sick late and cured early. I didn't have a chance to hurt too many people. Most of the Cured around us were only sick for a few years, two or three. Nella used to work distributing the Cure and helping people come to terms with themselves and the new world. Even with hundreds of people supporting them, many, many of the Cured killed themselves. They *still* kill themselves six years later. I can't imagine enduring a moment longer than I did, but the people in this city have been ill or cared for the Infected for six more years." He shook his head. "I don't think what you did was murder. It was mercy, Ruth. For the Infected, and for their families."

"But if I had waited, I would have my son. If I had waited, all those people would have their loved ones back—"

"No. No one will get their loved one back. You wouldn't know your son. He'd be a stranger to you. You've had separate worlds. If everything started up again tomorrow, if all the lights turned back on and the traffic started up and everybody went back to work, you wouldn't be the person you were before the Plague. Neither would your son. No one can go through what we've been through without changing. You might think you'd have a sweet little boy again, but your son would be an angry young man. He would remember being tied up for years. He would remember hurting you or your husband. He would remember how badly he wanted it all to stop, and that you, even though you would have done it out of love, you withheld relief. You'll see. The day after tomorrow, when those people start waking up, they'll find remaining relatives maybe, but they won't know them. Even if they were old enough to understand what Juliana has done, to appreciate what you all have sacrificed, they cannot be the people that you expect. They aren't just going to pick themselves up and carry on."

"Why did you come then? Why did you bring the cure after all these years? Why not just let them die?" Ruth tried to hide the anger in her voice but it leaked through.

"Because if it were me, I wouldn't want to spend another day as a monster. No matter how badly I felt after the Cure. Even if I were to kill myself, I'd still rather die sane than raging and wandering." Frank paused for a moment and flicked a speck of rotten wood into the water. "And because we knew someone had to be waiting for it. For us. If we hadn't brought it, and you found out later that we had it— what would you think?"

Ruth was silent for a long time.

There were quick shuffling steps in the sand behind them. Ruth looked back toward the beach. Bernard sprinted toward them. Frank stood up and helped Ruth to her feet. Bernard pointed wildly toward the restaurant.

"Is it Father Preston? Or Gray?" asked Ruth beginning to run down the dock. Bernard shook his head. "What's wrong?" she asked, then stopped at the edge of the sand. "It's Juliana isn't it?" Bernard nodded slowly. She was close enough to hear his panicked breath and see the tears streaming down his face.

Frank squeezed the big man's shoulder. "It's okay, Nella knows what to do until we get there," he said.

"Is it too late?" asked Ruth.

Bernard shrugged and sobbed. Ruth held his good hand and they walked quickly toward the restaurant.

CHAPTER 33

Ruth sat next to the table where Juliana lay sleeping on a pile of tablecloths. She watched Bernard and the dog as they paddled the canoe out behind Frank and Nella's rowboat. They were carrying fresh water to the ship, withdrawing from the empty restaurant so Ruth could be alone. She didn't expect Juliana to wake up again though, the last seizure had been too severe. There was nothing to do but wait.

All this time, she'd wanted to be free. To leave the city, to leave the Infection behind. She was free now. Her only friend lay on a dusty table, unable to wake. The Infected were Cured. They didn't need her or Juliana anymore. The choices Ruth had thought she'd had to make were gone. Despite what Frank had said, she was convinced she'd been making the wrong one all these years. She'd survived the death of her son, the suicide of her husband. She'd outlasted looters and cannibalistic Infected, the fiery clutch of Father Preston's unyielding zeal.

She thought about tomorrow. Juliana would be gone. Nella might help, but the Infected didn't know her. Ruth was going to have to walk back to the hospital and explain the world to those waking up. Alone. Or she could let Father Preston do it. She could sail with Bernard somewhere else. And do what? Become a witch doctor? A healer with herbs they grew? Watch the few people left succumb to tetanus or childbirth or the flu?

Ruth had survived a long time. But she'd had Juliana to keep her moral compass sharp. She didn't know if she'd survive tomorrow without her.

She didn't know if she wanted to bother any more.

"Oh, don't look like that," said Juliana sleepily. Ruth turned toward her. "Isn't this what you wanted? What we both wanted? No more hospital, the Infected are cured, no more arguing about what's best for them. No more worrying, they can care for themselves. Nothing tying you here. Free to get out of this baking city. No more Father Preston and no more screamed sermons."

"I'm sure there are more Father Prestons out there," said Ruth dryly.

"Then you must go and be the Ruth to battle them all," laughed Juliana lightly.

"I'm not sorry that I battled him. But I'm sorry I fought you. I'm sorry I kept making the wrong choice about the Infected."

"There was no right choice, Ruth. We both acted out of compassion. I hope Father Preston did too. But we were all wrong sometimes. Who is going to judge us? Who are you apologizing to? Me? I kept people alive in agony for years because I believed in some mythical cure. I risked pneumonia and dysentery, starvation even. Because I couldn't let go. Are you sorry for the families that begged you to relieve their loved ones? If Nick were here, he'd tell you he couldn't have gone on a single day more. That Emma couldn't have endured another day. That he's as grateful to you today, knowing there is a cure, as he was a week ago. They reached their end. It was their time."

"But they could have been cured six years ago. They wouldn't have had to endure all that they did."

"They *weren't* cured six years ago, Ruth, and

that has nothing to do with any of us. We can't go back and undo all the harm that's been done, no matter how much we want to. You have to stop trying. You have to start going forward, you have to start putting things back together, get out of this terrible rut of guilt and sorrow you've had on repeat since Charlie died. You have to stop doing penance for something that never was your fault."

"I don't know what to do now. I don't know who I am without Charlie, without the Infected. Without you."

"*Then find out.* There's a whole world waiting out there. You are one of the most valuable people left alive: a real, trained doctor. You will be welcome wherever you want to go. There are a lot of people waiting for someone like you. Even more Infected maybe, if that's really what you want."

They were quiet for a while. Juliana dozed but kept her hand in Ruth's. The small market boat was beginning to float back toward the shore when Juliana spoke again. "I wanted to see them wake up. I wanted to know they were going to be okay."

"Frank was okay, after his cure," offered Ruth.

Juliana sighed. "I know, but it's not the same. Nobody wants to quit the story just before the happy ending." Her eyes fluttered and then closed again.

"I'm glad you caught me stealing agrimony, Juliana," she whispered. "Thank you for making me stick around this long after I lost Charlie and Bill. I'm glad you're my friend, even if it took the Plague for us to meet."

The sun was warm on the large windows,

and the waves in the bay melted into the soft breathing of her friend. Ruth hadn't slept well in days. She dozed off with her warm hand wrapped around Juliana's cooling one.

CHAPTER 34

Frank helped Bernard into the small boat and watched him paddle slowly back toward the restaurant with his one good arm. Nella was pushing bottles of water around trying to make them fit back into their cubbies. They both turned when the radio crackled below.

"It's not the normal time." Nella frowned slightly.

"Maybe it isn't home," said Frank with a grin. "Maybe it's someone new."

They headed down into the cabin. The voice was tinny, worn thin by distance, patchy, but it was Christine's voice nonetheless.

"Nella? Frank? Are you there?" Her voice wavered but Nella couldn't tell if it were stress or bad reception. Frank sat at the small table while Nella fiddled with the tuner.

"Please be there. I need you," said Christine, amid the pops and crackles of the radio.

Frank sat up. "Don't lose the signal," he said, his brow wrinkling.

Nella picked up the microphone. "I'm here Christine."

"Thank you, thank you," the voice sobbed, "you have no idea how much I needed to hear you."

"What's wrong? Where's Sevita?"

"Are you coming home?" asked Christine. "I should tell you not to come home, but I have no one else to help me. There's this kid here too—"

"The baby?" asked Nella.

"No, no, a teenager. She needed help. I can't help her. I can't help anyone. Nobody can."

Nella glanced at her husband. He frowned in

confusion. "Slow down, Christine. Take a deep breath. Start from the beginning."

The radio was silent for a long moment. Nella itched to delicately nudge the tuner, thinking she'd lost reception, but she waited.

"It was that goldsmith. The one Frank and I went to see."

Frank stood up with a jolt. "The one that was making the special pens for Dr. Pazzo?" asked Nella.

"Yes. Frank asked him about the ink, I swear he asked him. I kept him busy for ten minutes while Frank went over and over those pens. How were we to know? We couldn't have forced him to tell us—"

Frank began pacing the small cabin, rubbing the sides of his head frantically.

"I remember," said Nella, "it was just a trick. Something to distract us while he infected himself with the incurable version of the bacteria."

"No, Nella," said Christine, her voice sinking into a dull whisper, "it wasn't a trick. The goldsmith lied. Or else he didn't understand what we were asking. He delivered the pen to the jail a week after you left. He delivered it to Dr. Carton. The goldsmith and the nurse were the first to turn —" Christine dissolved into weeping again.

"Turn?" asked Nella faintly.

"Please come home," begged Christine, "Sevita— Sevita is infected. Most of the city is infected."

"No," boomed Frank and shook his head. Nella was silent, watching him.

"Please, Nella! You're the only one who can

stop this." Christine's voice became more urgent, demanding.

"Me?" Nella said into the mic, "there's no cure, Christine. I'm not a physician anyway. I wouldn't even know where to start."

"Start with Ann. Ann Connelly knows. She was there. You have to make her talk. You have to get it out of her."

"I can't— there's no— even if I could figure out how to repair the damage in her brain enough to find out what she knows, there's no cure. Dr. Carton told us. There's nothing, Christine."

There was a long moment of silence. "I'm sorry," said Nella into the microphone.

"Please, Nella. She's your best friend. She's the love of my life. She sits outside the bunker door every afternoon and talks into the intercom. Tells me she loves me, in case it's her last chance. She's getting slower Nella. She sounds drunk. She loses her train of thought. Every day, she still comes. Tells me not to open the door for anyone, even her. The City is falling apart around her. Yesterday she had blood on her shirt. But she still comes every day. You have to try."

The radio fell silent again. Nella looked at Frank. "No," he said. "No, not even for Sevita." His eyes were red. He passed a shaky hand over his head, clutching at his own skin.

"Please," Christine's voice came shakily through one last time.

Nella pressed the microphone button. She let it go. She looked at her husband who shook his head in silence this time. She pressed the button again. "I'm coming, Christine. Hold on. I'm coming home."

The radio whined and blared static. Nella turned it off, not certain Christine had heard her. She laid the microphone gently in its cradle as Frank sank on the edge of the bed.

"Why? Why are you going back? You know there's no cure. Sevita knows there's no cure. And if she isn't immune, you might not be either. Or me."

She slid her arms around him. "Because Christine is in trouble. Because my friend asked for help."

He shook his head. "You can't help her. There is *no cure.* All you can do is die with her. Or become— become like me."

"We have to try. We have to find Ann. Find their notes."

"We were at the lab. There's nothing. She was an *intern.* An intern, Nella. Even if they had a cure, she wouldn't know where it was. She took care of the animals, washed the glassware, took down observations. They didn't design it to have a cure anyway."

"She was Pazzo's lover. If there was a cure, if there were even the hope of a cure, she knew about it. He took care of her for almost two years after he found out about the other strain. She was the only person he had to talk to, even if she couldn't understand him at the time. He tried to save her. We both know that. If he thought of anything he would have told her. And if I can make her remember— it's worth a try. Not just for Christine. For all those people. There's no place left like the City, Frank. Nowhere. If anyone can be convinced of that, it ought to be us. We've seen it first-hand."

"You don't understand what you're asking. I can't let you do this."

Nella pulled back a little. "I know what I'm asking. But it's not permission. I know how frightened you are of reverting to the time you were Infected. I understand. We'll be careful— we'll find the safest way. We'll find suits before we get close. Ann isn't in the City anymore. She's out at a Nursing Home a few miles beyond the Barrier. They are self sufficient, probably no one there was even close to the City during the infectious period. Christine said she is in a bunker. We'll find out where— she knows all the shortcuts from when she drove the ambulance. I'll be in and out in no time. I won't make you come."

"I can't let you," he said.

"You can't stop me."

"You think I'm scared of the Infected? I'm not scared of them. The Immunes either. They're all just the neighbors we left two months ago. Or that I'm scared of getting infected again? Sure, Nella, that frightens me." He stopped to pull her closer. "But I'd go anywhere for you, even into the hell you are asking of me. Not because I love you. Because I know you wouldn't ask me to do it unless there was no other choice. But I can't let you go. When we were in quarantine, my biggest fear was that I would turn in front of you. That I'd hurt you. I thought that was the worst thing that could happen. I was wrong. If *you* got infected, if I had to watch you turn into a monster—"

Nella started to protest but Frank shook his head.

"If I had to watch you turn into one of— of us, that would be worse. Knowing the pain you would be in, knowing the rage you had while you were sick and the agonizing guilt you would have if you ever got well— that would be worse Nella. I can't do it. You can't ask me to do this. There's no cure. The Plague will burn itself out when the City is empty."

"It won't, Frank. The Infected don't die until someone kills them or cures them. They'll wander for years, infecting other people they run across."

"Then let's leave. Let's find an island far away. Or stay here. They'll die out before they reach us."

"Christine and Sevita and the people in that City are the only family I have left. She *begged* me to help. She's got no one else."

"*I'm* your family. I'm begging you to stay away. Stay safe, with me."

Nella was quiet for a long time. He watched her face as she struggled.

"Okay," she said at last, "you win."

Frank was too relieved to feel stung at her choice of words.

The evening had already set in, the restaurant shone with a few lights on the shore, but the rest of the large city was mostly dark. No more fires lit the old hospital, no large clusters of lamps showed a Congregation of the living. The Infected and Father Preston's group still slept in the field, unaware of the world around them. Frank remembered the bright glittering chains of light that his own city had cast upon the water as they sailed away. He had friends there too. *There's nothing you can do,* he told himself, *There's no cure. There's no enemy to fight. People die. It just happens. Let it burn out.*

"It won't, Frank," Nella's words echoed in his mind, "They'll wander for years, infecting other people."

And the whole world will look like this, he thought, *or what little is left of the world anyway.* People would have heard about his City by now. The people they had cured yesterday would spread the rumor of the City at the edge of the world. The new Eden that had the Cure. People would come. And what would they find? Who would they find? Desolation. Like the capitol. Death and madness. Worse than hopeless. And it would be Frank's fault. *Nonsense,* he told himself, *you can't save the world. What exactly are you supposed to do?* But the idea of Ann kept rattling around. The idea that Dr. Pazzo had tried to save her in those fourteen months of solitude. But he hadn't found it, had he? *Someone's got to stop it, Frank. Someone's got to end it. Cure or no cure,* he thought. If they couldn't fix it, they had to wipe it off the map. Make it a place to dread instead of an oasis.

There was the group that had left, the Cured who had walked out of the City. They'd start over. Be the new government. Be the haven for the uninfected. But only if they weren't threatened by the Plague. Only if he and Nella stopped it.

Frank walked into the cabin where his wife was sleeping. He brushed the hair from her face and shook her gently.

"What is it?" she asked, "What's happened?"

"I'm sorry," he said as she sat up, "you were

right. We have to try."

CHAPTER 35

"You can come with us," said Nella, "we can always use more doctors and I heard the head gardener left the city a few weeks ago."

Bernard shook his head. He tamped down the last of the loose dirt and waved an arm out at the hill.

"Bernard belongs here, rebuilding the garden. There are still lots of people here, people that will need help and food," said Ruth, "And Juliana is buried here. He wants to watch over it. Make sure people know what she did here."

"I wish we could stay," said Nella, "but the people at home need us now." She didn't mention how shocked she'd been to hear Christine crying over the radio, or how she and Frank had spent the night agonizing and arguing about what to do. .

"I understand," said Ruth.

"What will you do?" asked Frank.

"I can't come with you," said Ruth. "Not when there are other people out there waiting for the Cure. Or for rescue. Every day that passes they get more desperate. Father Preston— his Congregation wasn't really evil. They just wanted the world, the Plague, to make sense. There are people like him all over the world. And there are people like Gray who would take advantage. Or people like me. Lots of people like me. I have to stop them, before they destroy themselves."

Nella shook her head. "I'm not so certain we should be stopping people like you. Juliana may have had her happy ending, but the people we cured... six years ago, the suicide rate for the Cured was roughly thirty percent. It's gone up the longer people have been Infected. Maybe these folks will be different. Maybe because you and your friend cared for them, they have less to regret. I hope so." She handed Ruth a heavy pack.

"What's this?"

"Another three cases of the Cure, all that was left on the ship. A map to the City, in case you change your mind or you need more darts. A few medical supplies that we could spare."

"That's very generous of you."

Nella shrugged. "They are only useful when someone has the skills to do it properly. I don't like hoarding when so many need help so badly."

Ruth turned to Frank. "The Infected— the people we cured, they'll remember right? Who they are, what's happened?"

"All but the last couple of days, those will be fuzzy because of the medication. They will still be confused. It would be better if they woke up to a friendly face."

Ruth shook her head. "Not mine. I can only represent death to them. But Bernard is here. And Father Preston will wake up with them. He has to have some shred of fellow feeling for them. He's been through the same process. It's probably best he lead them."

Bernard shook his head. Frank frowned. "They need you," said Nella gently, "even if it's only to tell them the straight story. They should be waking up soon. Talk to them, just once. Let them choose who to believe."

"Father Preston's people are in there. They'll still want to kill me."

"Juliana would want you to *try,*" Frank said,

and Nella squeezed his hand. Ruth nodded.

"I'll try." She looked over the long row of graves, her gaze lingering on Nick's and then Juliana's. Bernard hugged her. The dog thumped its tail.

"I'll be back before winter," Ruth said. "Don't overuse your hand, Bernard. I'll send help. Food, if I can." He just nodded into her shoulder. She turned away from them and walked down the hill and out of the park. Though she was dreading it, it didn't take long to reach the hospital. They had been back to move the sleeping bodies into the shade and cool them with water from the kitchen handpump. They'd removed the corpses and buried them with Juliana, so seeing it wasn't as much of a shock as it might have been. Still, Ruth felt a pang as she walked up to the broken walls. It should be Juliana here, not her. She looked up to the third floor hallway windows, half expecting to see Juliana's shadow on the staircase. But of course, nothing inside moved.

A long line of people lay against the gray brick walls out of the sun. Ruth stopped at the post they had hung Nick from. She sat down in front of it, her back against the warm metal, and waited. She watched the people shift and stir one by one or a few at a time and sit up, still woozy from the sedative. Some of them saw her and glared. She hoped they belonged to Father Preston, but secretly she was frightened that they'd all hate her. That she was sitting where she'd die.

After a long while a woman got up. Her cuffs were rolled up and she held her pants up with one hand. *She must be an Infected,* Ruth thought, *her clothes don't fit.* The woman shuffled slowly over to Ruth and stood for a long moment looking down at her. Then her face burst into a smile and she squatted down. "I remember you," she said, "You fixed my broken arm when I first came here. Thank you." She held out her free hand and shook Ruth's.

"You're welcome," said Ruth, not knowing what to say. The woman sat down in front of Ruth and waited. A man walked up and shook Ruth's hand as well. He sat next to the woman. A few more came. Then a dozen. Soon Ruth was surrounded by people. A few waited on the wall, their faces scowling or turned away from her. She saw a flutter in the downstairs windows of the hospital, but nobody came out. It was a relief. She knew Father Preston and Gray were inside. She didn't want to fight. That's not what she was here for. Ruth stood up and cleared her throat.

"Frank says you remember. That everything up to three days ago will gradually come back. I'm sorry. I'm sorry for what we did. And for what we didn't do. I'm sorry you were in pain for so long. I'm sorry for the things that you did or were done to you before you came here. I'm sorry that you are waking up in a broken world. If I could fix it—" she trailed off. She looked at the sea of shaved heads that turned up to face her, like disciples. "We didn't know about the cure. We had nothing left to feed you with. Juliana did her best to help you. It should be her here, not me. She wanted to be here when you woke up. She thought this was your happy ending. But she is gone. And this is only the beginning for you. I didn't believe you'd ever wake up. Some of you hate me for what I've done. For what I meant to do to you. I know some of you even intend to kill me. But we tried to do the right thing — no, we tried always to do the *kindest* thing for you. And if we'd given you to Father Preston— you would have been slaves. I thought that you would suffer more. So what happens next?" she fell silent, but no one answered her. She shifted uncomfortably. Someone coughed. Ruth sighed.

"I'm sure you are thirsty and hungry after three days of sleep," she began again, "There is some food left in the pantry of the hospital, and a hand pump with clean water. You'll need to share. This world isn't so great about sharing. But you had the best model there was. If you wish to honor the woman who cared for you all these years, the best you can do is to share with each other. Some of you have families still in the city. They don't know yet that you are cured. They did what they thought was kindest too. Please forgive them if you can."

"And the rest of us?" someone called.

Ruth shrugged. "It's a big world. The people who brought the Cure came from another city, somewhere south, past the capitol. You could head there. Or you could help Bernard build the garden into a farm and stay here."

"What about you?" asked the woman in front, "what are you going to do now?"

"There's a whole country waiting for the Cure. People just like you maybe, who've been waiting for years and years. Someone has to find them. If you want to help, I'll be heading west." She stopped and pulled a dart from her pack and held it up. "If you're coming to kill me, I'm still heading west. But make sure to take the doses if you do.

There are several thousand doses. There's more in that southern city. Whatever you think of me, of what I've done, I would hate to think of them all going to waste when I'm gone." The people around her looked troubled. She didn't know what else to say. She took a long look at the dark hospital. "Goodbye," she said, and turned to walk back out of the field.

The sun was starting its slide down as she passed onto the baking pavement. She didn't look back. The buildings fell away behind her, the smoking steam of the subway stations screened them. She climbed onto the exit ramp of the freeway, her little shadow a cool flutter passing over the four wide lanes as they tumbled away west. Behind her a dozen other shadows trudged along the warm road, never letting her quite out of sight.

CHAPTER 36

His stomach was an itchy flame. His arms pulsed with pain and the little light that leaked through his closed eyelids pierced his head like needles. He didn't want to open his eyes and risk more pain, but the itch on his belly convinced him that he'd better, before something worse happened. A few badly mangled faces hovered over him, meeting his gaze.

"He's alive," said one looking up at someone he couldn't see.

"That's a relief anyway," said a voice.

"Do you know who you are?" asked the other face.

"Brother Mi— *Father* Michael Preston."

"I remember you here. You used to yell things through the door. Were you sick too? The only wounds you have are from— well, we're awfully sorry about that."

"Sick? You mean Afflicted? Once, a long time ago. I was blessed to recover though. Who are you?"

"Me? Well my name is Diane if that's what you mean. I lived here. My family brought me years ago."

Father Preston sat up slowly.

"Careful," said Diane, "The stitches might come out."

"Stitches?" He looked down at the scratchy skin on his stomach. A line of tiny black crosses crossed it in a jagged line. *"Ruth,"* he spat. "Where is she?"

Diane shrugged. "There were lots of people here. All over the building. They've all been asleep, but they woke up yesterday. Like Sleeping Beauty's castle." Diane smiled. "Most of them are gone now. Except us. We couldn't leave you like this. Not knowing what we'd done."

"What happened?" asked Father Preston, confused.

"It's a little fuzzy. I remember the door to my cell being open and I was hungry. So hungry. I heard noise as some men came in to the hospital and I— I raced to them thinking they must have food. I wasn't the only one. We chased them upstairs. We were so hungry. You were sick once, you understand."

Father Preston nodded, not really wanting to hear the rest.

"There wasn't enough to go around. So we started fighting with each other. Someone was in the upstairs bedroom near us, we could hear them whispering. We finally got through the door and I leapt onto a box, but then someone— *you*, yelled from the staircase. We found you. We bit you. I'm sorry. We don't remember anything after that."

Father Preston looked around at the half dozen creatures who were trying to remember how to be human. "None of you remember after that?"

They shook their heads.

"It was like a spell, or, or a miracle," exclaimed Diane, "it was as if as soon as we bit into your flesh we began waking up, began remembering who we were. But that's hardly possible is it?"

Father Preston's pulse began to speed up.

A man nearby said slowly, "Well, he did say he was sick and recovered. What if whatever cured him is still inside him? What if *he* cured us, because we ate his blood?"

Ruth's voice echoed in Father Preston's head. *That's not how it works,* she'd said. *You aren't special*, is what she'd meant. But God had proved otherwise, *this* was his miracle.

He noticed a man sitting on a bench in a corner. The man leaned forward into the sunlight and picked up a slim tube from the floor. He rolled it between his fingers and looked up at Father Preston, waiting to see what he would say. It was Gray.

Gray stood up and pocketed the tube before anyone but Father Preston noticed it. "We owe this man our lives, our sanity," he said in a slow, thunderous voice, "He was saved from Affliction by God, and now he heals others through his own flesh."

The others helped Father Preston gently up. He felt light, strong, unwavering. Holy. He smiled at Gray. Gray made a low bow and smiled his greasy grin back. But Father Preston had no room for doubt in his miracle and the sly wink of the other man went unnoticed.

"What should we do, Father Preston?" asked Diane, trembling slightly with awe.

"There are other Afflicted out there," said Father Preston, "We can leave them to suffer no longer."

"But where do we start?" asked another.

"South," said Gray with a slight smile.

"Yes," said Father Preston, "We must first find the Congregation."

It was a few weeks before Father Preston heard rumors of another city, one where a medical cure had been found. But now the city was in crisis, gripped by a resurgence of the plague. Only a miracle could cure it now. *Only I can cure it,* he thought. He wandered toward it with his band of miracle Cured and his faithful flock. They came to a large settlement on a warm morning in mid July. The people were building walls and planting crops far too late. A lanky man with an unlit cigarette hanging from the side of his mouth stopped them on the road.

"Whoa," he said, spitting tiny bits of stale tobacco onto the road. "We already have too many. Look, we don't like turning anyone away, but unless you brought your own tools and seeds—"

"We're here to help," said Father Preston.

The man snorted. "That's what you all say. We needed help a year ago. We needed the cure, but nobody ventured out of the City to help us then."

"These people were just cured themselves, a few weeks ago."

The man squinted at Father Preston in the shadowy burlap cowl he wore to cover his scars. "We were the last ones, the governor said."

"We've come a long way," said Father Preston, "A long way to help."

The man tapped his cigarette against his palm as if he could tamp the loose remains of tobacco tighter. "You better go see Henry then," he said at last. "But just one of you. The rest can wait here until there's a decision."

"I'll take care of them Father," said Gray, "and maybe make some trades with—"

"Rickey," the man offered. "What have you

got?"

Gray grinned. Rickey pointed Father Preston up the road to a large barn. He heard two men talking as he approached the door.

"Did you hear about the Plague?"

"Yes, Melissa told me this morning." The man's voice sounded familiar to Father Preston. Sort of exotic. As if it had been many places. Sad, as if it had seen too many things.

"Are you in favor of closing our gates too?" asked the first man. Father Preston opened the door and slid inside, unnoticed.

"What choice do we have? If we don't protect the people that are already here, there will be no safe place for anyone." The speaker was grayer than Father Preston remembered. A little stooped.

"Marnie is out there somewhere."

The older man put a hand on his comrade's shoulder. "And you did what you said that you would for her. You went back as you promised her mother you'd do. You offered her shelter and help as you promised you would do. And you didn't follow her as you promised not to do. You've made other promises, Henry. To the people here. To your friends. These people trust you to do what's right for them."

"Isn't there some other way?"

"I believe there is," said Father Preston. Both men turned to look at him. Father Preston recognized the other priest. He waited at the end of the barn to be recognized. The morning light filled with dust motes and floated around him like a halo.

"I'm sorry," said Henry, "I don't believe we've met. I'm Henry. Who are you?"

"The savior," Father Preston replied. The priest stepped forward, side by side with Henry.

"What is it you want?" asked Henry.

"To give you another way."

"And what way is that?" asked the priest, his hand closing over the shovel that leaned against a nearby barn beam.

"Why, Brother Vincent, Transubstantiation of course." Father Preston pushed the cowl from his scarred face and Brother Vincent gasped and dropped the shovel.

JUST A NOTE

Dear Reader,

Whether you picked up Krìsis without ever hearing about After the Cure or this is the third time you are experiencing the world, thank you for reading! I hope that it has entertained you, made you think, or just moved you in some way. I hope that you loved it, but maybe you'd rather throw the kindle at me instead. But I'd recommend against it, those things are pricey! Instead, drop me a line and tell me how you feel, I'd love to hear from you, whether you are railing against me or just want to know what the weather in Maine is at the moment. You can always find me at dk.gould@live.com while I can't promise to answer *any* question you ask (wouldn't want to spoil the ending after all!) I will do my best to answer what I can or just say hello and make a new friend in zombie- er, *Infected* and post apocalyptic appreciation. Or you can pop in to the After the Cure facebook page to see how the series is progressing (or to find out about other awesome science fiction and horror books that I've run across and want to share): https://www.facebook.com/Afterthecurenovel

Of course, I always appreciate sharing how you feel with the rest of the reading world too, and if you felt sad, angry, happy, satisfied, frustrated or excited for more, I hope you'll leave a review for this, and *any* book you read. Finding out someone loved or loathed a book is usually how I find my next read!

Thank you for traveling through this dark novel with me, and I hope you are looking forward to reading the next few books in the series as much as I am truly looking forward to writing them!

2/4/2015
Deirdre Gould

OTHER TITLES

In the After the Cure Series:
After the Cure (Book 1)
http://www.amazon.com/After-Cure-Deirdre-Gould-ebook/dp/B00ERVTFCM
The Cured (Book 2)
http://www.amazon.com/The-Cured-After-Cure-Book-ebook/dp/B00J2EJAOM
Coming Spring 2015: "Igor" in The Z Chronicles
https://www.facebook.com/groups/futurechronicles/

Sans Zombie:
The Robot Chronicles
http://www.amazon.com/Robot-Chronicles-Future-Book-ebook/dp/B00M3GIBUK
The Jade Seed
http://www.amazon.com/Jade-Seed-Deirdre-Gould-ebook/dp/B00BNIIEBK
The Moon Polisher's Apprentice
http://www.amazon.com/Moon-Polishers-Apprentice-Part-Queen-ebook/dp/B00J8U6WB4

Made in the USA
San Bernardino, CA
13 October 2016